PRIVATE SECTOR

PRIVATE SECTOR

Jeff Millar

The Dial Press   New York

Published by
The Dial Press
1 Dag Hammarskjold Plaza
New York, New York 10017

Manufactured in the United States of America
First printing

Design by Mary Brown

Library of Congress Cataloging in Publication Data

Millar, Jeff, 1942–
Private sector.

I. Title.
PZ4.M64455Pr   [PS3563.I3723]   813'.5'4   79-17493
ISBN: 0-8037-6965-2

For everybody who said *yes*
when it would have been
just as easy to say *no*.

PRIVATE SECTOR

1

IT WAS A TEXACO GASOLINE DELIVERY TRUCK, THE KIND THE LOCAL
distributors used to fill the buried storage tanks of gas stations,
and it was rolling downgrade insanely fast over the icy
highway.

The driver took his eyes off the dizzying tunnel his headlights
pushed through the dark and snow and he looked into the outside rearview mirror. The headlights were there still, no further
away and no closer than they had been the last fifteen miles of
vertiginous West Virginia switchbacks.

In all that distance the driver had not seen a side road, nor a
driveway, not even a turnout at the side of the crumbling, narrow, two-lane blacktop: no place to evade the pursuing headlights except straight ahead, into the night.

In the second he'd taken to look in the rearview mirror, the
blacktop switched back again. The man sitting in the rider's
side made a strangled sound and pushed at the dashboard with
both his hands as if the force would repel the rotting wall of
railroad ties that spiraled toward them. The railroad ties, which
held back a hundred-foot-high dam of tailings from a played-
out coal mine, instantly filled his field of vision. The truck was
skiing over ice; the driver realized he had no idea what to

do. He couldn't think. He only knew it didn't make any difference, because there was no time.

So he did nothing, and it kept him alive. A component of the truck's velocity skewed it parallel to the shoring. It caromed off ties and tracked a course, sideways, along the lip of the switchback. The driver, his hands wrenched completely off the wheel, saw his headlights slice through the black vacuum ahead. Then, as if the maneuver were routine, the truck's wheels touched unfrozen pavement, found purchase, and ended up traveling parallel to the phosphorescent center stripe.

The wind was inside now, swirling snow and pellets of crumbled safety glass into the driver's face. Suddenly, he was screaming with laughter at the banality of their salvation. He looked for an instant at his companion, who seemed to sense the joke. In profile, he was smiling.

When the passenger turned toward him, away from profile, the smile grew. And grew on past his right ear, where the right side of his face was bunched in red folds, and a foot-long sliver of creosoted railroad tie protruded from his neck.

The village of Copper Creek was as big as the West Virginia mountains would let it be. It was the only place within ten miles where land was level enough to live on. A gas station was jammed along the north valley wall, against the state highway, and the scummy stream, stinking with the oxides leached from the mine-tailings dam that squatted at the east end of the town. Across the highway were Wycheck's grocery store, the Laundromat, and ten wooden houses whose yards sloped upward, almost from the bottom of their back steps, and quickly turned into hard, vertical rock.

It was snowing—snowing frighteningly, as it had been everywhere for endless months—as if winter wanted to prove that all the coal the miners worked twenty-four hours a day to bring up from the inside of West Virginia could not lift its arrogant, aching chill.

After his wife divorced him, Junior had signed up for grave-yards at the mine—it paid four dollars more a shift—and started doing his laundry at five in the morning after he got off work. He could always get a machine at that hour and he didn't have to talk to anybody. He put the first load into the washers the owner had designated for work clothes, black with anthracite dust, and then started it with a quarter and a dime.

He didn't want to read the copy of *Oui* he had found in a toilet at the mine, and he didn't want to read yesterday's paper. And the only station you could get in the valley that played country-and-western music didn't come on the air until sunup.

So Junior watched the snow, which fell black or blue, de-pending on how the crystals refracted light from the two mercury-vapor poles planted at the points where the highway descended into and then ascended out of town. He saw the headlights first. They came down around the tailings dam. He knew from the way they jittered that the vehicle was big and stiffly sprung, like a truck.

"Booger's going some," said Junior. His breath fogged the window glass. He watched as the headlights disappeared be-hind a rock cut just before town. When it came out from behind the cut, Junior saw that, upon sighting level ground ahead, the driver had speeded up.

"God damn, buddy," said Junior. "You better—"

It was a truck. He could see it now—a Texaco gas truck, just entering the pool of mercury-vapor light. No way it would make the curve at the edge of town. He fell silent and stood quite still in solemn attendance of death. He knew that he should be frightened, or repelled, but he felt important. He did not want to turn his head away to keep from seeing.

The Texaco truck rose slightly on its outboard wheels as it left the turn. Its pitch smoothly increased until it went effort-lessly onto its cylindrical side and slowly began rolling on its axis as it slid across the gravel in front of Wycheck's store.

As the tank section smashed into the abandoned gas-pump island in front of the store, Junior thought about fire. The concrete island changed the truck's trajectory and started it spinning. Junior stopped thinking and started diving behind a row of washing machines.

Like a fugitive blade from a lawn mower, the truck scythed through the front of the grocery store, sucking from it fishing tackle, clothes, hardware, cans of beer. With its northwest corner torn away, the old building folded in on itself. The truck rolled on across the narrow gravel road and rammed its nose through the front of the Laundromat.

Junior, wedged up to his waist between the washing machines, hugged his head more tightly, as if it were the noise, not mass and inertia, that was trying to kill him. He felt arrowheads of glass in his legs. He waited for the two washing machines to crush him, but they only crabbed sideways around him. He felt a liquid—gasoline—and remembered helping bring up the bodies after the fire in the Flat Hill #2. Then the noise stopped, except for a final sprinkle of glass as it relinquished its hold on the window molding. A washing machine was chugging.

Junior had screwed his eyes so tightly shut that his cheeks fluttered with tiny muscle spasms as he pulled them open. He was panting from fear as he rolled over on his side to extricate himself from his Westinghouse fortification, and he cried out as a sliver of glass rammed further into his thigh. His fingers slipped twice on his blood as he picked it out. The inside of his nose suddenly stung, and he sneezed. He brushed instinctively at the sides of his face, and his hands came away white.

Soap, he smelled soap. And water. Instead of gasoline, he was lying in a puddle of steaming water and his wet clothes. The washing machine had been knocked over on its side, and although its work had been dumped out, it still dutifully chugged. *The truck's tank hasn't broke open*, Junior thought, *but that don't mean it won't.*

He was suddenly chilled by the wind. The supine cab of the Texaco truck filled all but a foot of the storefront. Junior got up, slipped, got up again. He felt he was wrapped in insulation;

it kept him from reacting to what was going on around him. As he staggered closer to the cab, he could hear the radiator crackling as it cooled.

"Now you just wait up, ace," said Junior to the truck. "You wait about thirty seconds while ol' Junior get his self across the road there, and you can blow up all you want."

As Junior pushed himself up between the canted grille of the truck and the wall of the Laundromat, he could see blood on the inside of the shattered windshield where it was wedged against the floor. And a matted spray of hair, stuck to what was left of the glass.

"Just twenty more seconds, ace," said Junior, to the truck, convinced that if he touched it in the slightest way, even brushed it with his pants leg, it would explode. "You *promise* you'll let me by—"

Junior edged around the cab and broke into a limping run across the littered gravel. But his vision was narrowing to a dim tube in front of him, and his breath was like boiling water in his lungs. He had to stop.

Bent forward, hands on knees, he saw something swim into focus among the litter around his feet. It was a piece of the tank. Junior could see the TE of TEXACO written on it. A surge of blackness washed over him, and he took a stumbling half-step, onto the fragment. It shattered beneath his feet.

Wrong. Junior made the word appear among the phosphenes and eddies of ink that were filling his brain. Pieces of metal tank shouldn't break. For a moment the luminous snakes stopped crawling in front of Junior's eyes, and he could see that the tank shell was made of fiberglass.

He looked for the first time at the bed of the truck. Chunks of the camouflage fiberglass were yet in place, still trying to conceal a smaller container of rounder shape and obviously more secure design. It was made of seamless, burnished steel. Into it opened one hatch two feet wide, closely riveted for strength and closed by the kind of wheel-thrown bolts used to secure against great pressure differences. Junior thought, as his vision dimmed again, of the airlocks they put in mine tunnels that were subject to sumping with poison gas.

The wind was suddenly furious. He could barely stand. It blew the air away before his lungs could claim it. It was roaring now. It seemed to come from everywhere, but principally from straight overhead, down upon his shoulders. He clapped his hands over his ears against the roar. The gravel rose up and sliced into him. He saw each piece in clear, definite, impossibly brilliant light, coming from the same direction as the wind. It was all he could do to push his head back, so he could look up for the light.

A helicopter was hovering twenty feet above him.

As the helicopter gently turned about, Junior blindly pirouetted with it, spindled by the hypnotic light. When he turned around and dropped his eyes, he saw, in the swirl of gravel and snow, eight men who stood around him in a semi-circle. They wore identical phosphorescent-orange quilted jackets with hoods. In the intense light from above, their faces were empty holes, defined only by the white plastic curve of a microphone mouthpiece. Behind them, Junior made out a large gray van sitting in the middle of the highway, its lights still on. The men were all pointing automatic weapons at him.

As Junior looked about him in bewilderment, one of the men walked up to him. Junior tried to say something—anything—as the man in the orange parka raised something to Junior's eye level. Junior recognized it as a small aerosol can, just as the man pushed the plunger and sent a fine mist directly into Junior's face.

Consciousness was stripped from Junior like sheets off a bed. As he fell, he thought that he would have liked to see their faces.

The squad leader's head suddenly jerked away from the anes-thetized man, in the direction of the wrecked truck. The driver had pulled himself halfway out the upward door and hung there gasping, his hand slowly losing grip from the blood sluicing down his arm. He brought the men in the orange jackets into focus and smiled at them. Then he fell back. Two of the men in the luminous parkas took a step toward the truck, but the squad leader cupped his hand over his microphone. The men instantly stopped and held their positions. It was just beginning to get light.

Inside the smashed cab, the driver, with his one arm that still worked, pulled at the corpse of the other man. What he wanted was in the right pocket of his coat, the side now wedged between the seat and the floor of the Laundromat. He had worked very efficiently, he thought, all things considered; somehow he convinced himself that the three screams of pain it cost him to get what he wanted had come from someone else.

It had started as a walkie-talkie, off the shelf from Radio Shack. Its modifications were crude but functional. The instructions—EXTEND ANTENNA . . . PULL OUT A . . . THEN B—were applied on the side with labelmaker tape.

The arming procedure required two hands and conscious effort. To do it with conscious effort meant that the two arming pins had to be pulled out, being very careful not to let one's finger slip off the red button.

He got one out, and then he started giggling. "Kid," he said to the corpse beside him, "I gotta look like fucking John Wayne, right? Holding . . . holding off those . . . Japs down to the last grenade." He vomited blood. Then he pulled the second pin.

The squad leader saw the modified walkie-talkie first. The driver of the truck stuck his arm out so that it preceded him out of the truck. The button under his finger was a blinking red light.

The blinking light was superfluous, thought the squad leader. He knew the device functioned as a remote dead-man switch even without the cliché effect. The person who manufactured it was probably a traditionalist. He cupped his hand over the microphone again. Instantly the helicopter rose and left the area.

The driver was unable this time to lift himself out of the upward door of the truck, so he pushed through what was left of the windshield. There didn't seem to be any point worrying about slicing open your face when you were vomiting blood. He lay on the gravel and panted, then pulled himself up to a sitting position, propped up against the underside of the truck. After a moment, he grinned at the squad leader and gestured him forward.

The squad leader walked very slowly, talking into his microphone. When he was about fifteen feet from the truck, the driver waved him to a stop.

"Buddy," said the driver, "you . . . ought to know better . . . than to tailgate people . . . like that . . ." He vomited more blood. "Well. Time just flies by when you're having fun." The squad leader stood exactly still. The driver held up the walkie-talkie. "This thing is . . . simplicity itself to disarm." He held it up so the squad leader could see it. "You push B, then you push A." The driver looked up into the sky. He closed his eyes, then stuck out his tongue until a snowflake lit upon it. He closed his eyes and smiled. He looked at the squad leader.

"Okay, Clint Eastwood," he said. "Let's see those nerves of steel." With an immense payment in pain, he flung the device as hard as he could into the air. His movement produced conditioned reflexes in three of the seven orange-parkaed men, who opened fire. The driver was cut apart before his hand had reached full apogee.

The Radio Shack walkie-talkie arched slowly into the air, the silly red light still blinking. It blinked as the squad leader dropped his weapon and took three steps to get under it. It blinked as it settled down and he cradled it in his arms. It blinked as he snatched it out from the soft crook of his parka's arm and oriented it antenna upward. It blinked as he pushed button B.

Before he pushed button A, it had stopped blinking.

It wasn't more than a medium-loud pop. It didn't take much to fire the explosive bolts in the hinges. The five atmospheres of pressure inside the cylinder were more than enough to blow out the hatch, which rolled on the gravel briefly like a large coin. The contents of the cylinder sighed out asthmatically.

Within moments, billowy steam filled the bottom of the Copper Creek valley.

No one moved for an instant. Then three of the men in the orange parkas dropped their weapons and ran for the gray van. After a few yards they slowed and stopped, for the steam was going to envelop them no matter how quickly they moved. The steam turned into a thick fog. After a few moments, the men quietly returned to the squad and picked up their weapons. Everything was very still. The squad leader cupped his hands over his microphone.

They had heard the truck crash, of course, and the helicopter. But then when they went to their windows and saw the men with the guns in front of Wycheck's store, the seventeen people who were in Copper Creek that night turned off their lights and watched from the dark.

But because the men in the orange parkas who came out of the fog to knock on all their doors smiled and produced convincing documents and said the right things, they willingly grabbed their coats and gathered in front of the Laundromat, especially after they were told that the truck was full of chemicals, and they might need to be evacuated for a while. There were eight men, seven women, an eleven-year-old girl, and a baby. It was lighter now, and snowing very hard.

They stood in a frightened clot, shivering and stamping their feet. Junior was among them, back on his feet, still unsteady from the effect of the stunning chemical and still confused.

The men in the orange parkas were moving very slowly toward the van. Two trotted up to join them, having made a last reconnoiter of Copper Creek. They said things into their microphones, and the squad leader nodded.

The eleven-year-old said she wasn't going to go without her Big Bird doll, and she ran back toward her house to get it. The squad leader said something into his microphone. When she got a few yards away, one of the men in the orange parkas shot her through the head.

───────── 11 ─────────

Then the men started firing into the clot of people, working in from the outside, making sure to put down first the ones who tried to run. It took about four seconds to kill everyone.

What was supposed to happen now was supposed to happen very fast. They had all been told in training that the faster the response to this contingency was begun, the more likely it was to go right. All the members of the squad were to lay down their weapons. They would each toss into the leader's cap a small vial they carried at all times. They would each draw a vial, inside of which was a compressed-air-charged styrette. At the count of five (a count of five seemed to work the best, for some reason), the squad members would discharge the styrettes into their forearms, and they would all be effortlessly dead within seven seconds.

The psychological evaluators—considering the kind of men who had been recruited for the cadre, and the degree to which they'd been motivated, trained, and cautioned over the last eighteen months—estimated a ninety-four percent probability that all the men in the squad would discharge the styrettes simultaneously.

That six-percent failure possibility, of course, was entirely unacceptable; so, as he'd been instructed to do in a special seminar, the squad leader killed his men himself, opening fire the instant the last townsperson had fallen.

The squad leader watched the helicopter waiting, over the tailings—well away but in sight—as he took a few moments to warm the muzzle of his .45 in his palm. When he slid it into his mouth, it wasn't a bit cold.

There were almost certainly special seminars for helicopter pilots.

When the helicopter pilot saw his squad leader put the weapon in his mouth, he turned up the gain on his receiver. The shot was an explosion in his ear, the fall a clatter as the squad leader jerked backward, half-turned, and landed on his side. The microphone did not break. There were three or four liquid burbles of breathing. Then only a hiss of static. The pilot put the helicopter down, very carefully, on top of the tailings dam and listened again. There was no more breathing. He idled the rotors.

The pilot reached behind him for a satchel, zipped up his parka, got out, and opened the door. Three charges, a two-minute timer. He activated the timer. Two charges would probably do it, he thought, as he lit a last cigarette and slid the satchel down the dam face. You could give this halfass dam one good kick and it would probably be enough.

2

THERE WAS A RULE THAT NO ONE GOT INTO CBS NEWS AFTER five p.m. without his employee ID card with his photograph on it. That meant the president of CBS News, that meant Cronkite, that meant John Harland, even if he had only gone half a block for burgundy cherry ice cream.

Harland had fumbled the card out of his wallet and had it clenched between his teeth as he pushed through the lobby door, even though the face laminated in the plastic was so recognizable that Harland had signed two autographs in Baskin-Robbins, even though he and the guard at the lobby security desk had been on a first-name basis for three years. Harland brushed snow off his coat and held the card out for the guard to see. He wouldn't get into any trouble if he was passed upstairs without showing it, but the guard might.

As the guard noted Harland's arrival on his log, Harland noticed that he'd been watching WCBS on a tiny Sony. The headline segment the network sent out at half-hour station-break time, the one Harland had taped twenty minutes ago, was being broadcast.

Harland watched himself read—not too grimly, not too lightly, with what he thought was professional detachment—

that the death count in the West Virginia coal-country dam collapse could be anywhere between ten and fifty.

"That guy," said Harland, "does a terrific job, wouldn't you say?"

The guard shook his head and smiled. "I don't know why you don't send one of the messengers out after that ice cream."

"Can't trust 'em," said Harland as he poked the elevator button. "Somebody has to watch those bastards at Baskin-Robbins like hawks, or they'll short you on cherries."

Harland would often send the CBS News messengers down to research, or to the newsfilm library, or to the Xerox room; but he never felt comfortable sending them on personal errands, even though food runs were clearly within the services available from the messengers, and lesser lights than Harland used them generously. Harland supposed it had something to do with his father, who had always told him to do for himself. To Harland it was never strange that Jimmy Carter carried his own garment bag off airplanes, even though many people, like the guard, considered it phony egalitarianism.

Riding up, Harland allowed himself one of his little downtime success fantasies. He wondered if, in a few years, after he had been made the anchor, people would think it was phony if he walked down to the Baskin-Robbins to buy his own ice cream.

Harland had the top off the one-pound, eight-ounce-size carton and was spooning up the burgundy cherry as he walked through the newsroom. Jerry Lee, who would write most of the script Harland would read on the newscast, looked up and shook his head. "The coldest winter in a hundred and seven years, and the guy walks two blocks through it to eat ice cream."

"If you grew up where it was eighty-three degrees and ninety percent humidity at midnight and you didn't have air conditioning and you lay there in the bed and sweated and felt the mildew growing in your armpits, you'd *like* being cold too." Harland stopped himself from looking over Lee's shoulder at what he was typing: what CBS's share of the six-thirty audience would

---
15
---

hear Harland tell them an hour and twenty minutes from then. Harland almost always wrote his own news copy, but he had been working on a *CBS Reports* and the air date was rushing toward him. He never felt comfortable anchoring *Evening News* without hands-on participation in making judgments, working with the editors of newstape and newsfilm and mini-cam tape, watching the broadcast take form as airtime approached. But the memos had come from the executive floors of Black Rock, the CBS headquarters on Sixth Avenue: He was to be groomed for the number one chair. Harland was to be anchor, someday.

Harland would stop work on the *CBS Reports* to look over the script just long enough to be able to mouth Jerry Lee's journalism on the air and make it look like his own. He felt a little guilty about it. There was some lower-middle-class boy left in Harland. His father would have told him that the true labor of this work was writing it; reading it was not a day's work deserving a day's pay.

Sometimes Harland would look in wonder at the entries in his bank statement where his salary checks from CBS had been credited to his account. What was it about this work that made it that much more valuable than the work for which his father had been paid three dollars and three cents an hour at the refinery? He also remembered transcribing Cronkite in order to write the lead-ins for the local anchor to read over the CBS station where he'd had his first job. He'd promised himself that if he took a permanent anchor job he would always write his own copy. Harland told himself that if a broadcast newsman wrote his own copy, he was a journalist. If he only read his copy, he was in show business.

"Not to worry, golden throat," said Jerry Lee. "It'll make you sound just as earnest, calm, sincere, and trustworthy as *TV Guide* says you are." After Harland had been brought up to the network from the CBS affiliate in Dallas, he'd worked for almost a year to convince CBS News to hire Lee, then a reporter for the *Times Herald*.

"Is Len still going to lead with West Virginia?" said Harland.

"Depends. He's looking at tape now. But those 'feared dead' had better start turning into real stiffs if Len's gonna think top-of-the-show. Mr. and Mrs. America will not look up from their Swanson's long enough to get led into the laxative commercial unless we come up with a real ball-breaker of a body count."

"Asshole print-medium cynic," said Harland, spooning out a couple of bites of burgundy cherry into Jerry's empty coffee cup. Harland went on back to the editing room, where he met Len Meyer, the producer, coming out. "Good stuff from West Virginia," he said. "We'll lead with it, then go into the weather, then probably to Carol at the White House to see if the President is still thinking national state of emergency on energy. We got Moore on the FAA inquiry, then into the 747 crashes and a file from Schaftner on the class-action suit against offshore drilling in Massachusetts."

"I'll come out early," said Harland, pushing through the door. "I want to run this cut once more." Harland walked down the corridor between the editing cubicles. Most of them held the electronic gear used to edit the three-quarter-inch videotape used in the miniature video cameras. There was one cutting room left for the occasional story covered with a film camera. The video minicams were cheaper and faster to edit, and had become standard in the industry. But Harland insisted on using film camera to shoot formal one-on-one interviews.

Along with the fact that he was handsome but not too handsome—the research people said that television viewers did not find very handsome news personalities entirely trustworthy—Harland's one-on-ones were the basis of his success, and he didn't want to change in any way how he did them. Back in Corpus Christi, Harland had worked out with his cameramen a surreptitious system of signals. Upon his gesture, they were to turn the camera conspicuously off, open it up, and change the film whether it was running or not. Harland would relax. After his subject did too, Harland would ask a question in a tone that implied they were speaking privately. Since the camera was obviously immobilized, the subject would usually reply in kind. But the audio recorder, which was kept in a corner of the room, was left on. Harland would later ask the subject to take a brief stroll outside, so the cameraman could shoot them from behind. Later, in editing, Harland would splice in the revealing quotes there.

The editor had gone, leaving their day's work threaded up on the KEM editing table for Harland to review. Harland turned the machine on. The Academy leader counted down and the bleep of the sync mark went past on the voice track. Harland had written every word of his own narration on this one. And, he thought, it wasn't bad.

The camera was panning toward and zooming in on Harland across an immense building, which, Harland thought, could not really exist outside a coffee-table book on visionary architecture. Even in the dim, grainy screen of the KEM table, behind the scratches of the battered work print, the building still stunned Harland. It was the most beautiful building in the most beautiful location he had ever seen.

Harland's voice came over the KEM table's speaker. "This is the headquarters of the Sandstone Foundation, which is built next to, and in some places into, a slope of the Rocky Mountains forty miles north of Denver. It took three years to build. Even before it was finished, Martin Vandellen moved in, and since then he has never left. This is where Martin Vandellen, in his fifty-second year, has decided to anchor his life . . . where, after almost thirty years of being one of the country's most public persons, he has gone on to become one of its most private."

The picture went black then, and only the audio continued. Later, the editor would put together a clip of still photographs and footage from file newsfilm to counterpoint Harland's narration.

"Martin Vandellen once joked that if some people are born with silver spoons in their mouths, then he was born with a formal setting for twelve. The Vandellen fortune, based mostly on oil, is one of the oldest in the United States. But whoever was blessing Martin Vandellen was just warming up. Sole heir to the country's largest fortune, he would grow up to have the kind of rugged good looks that could have earned him another fortune as a movie star. And then, to make sure there was nothing Martin Vandellen couldn't do, or couldn't have, it was arranged that he be born a genius.

"At age eighteen, as soon as he was legally able, he put all his interests in the Vandellen companies in blind trusts, and to this day has never had the slightest hand in running them. Instead, as soon as he graduated from MIT, he started a series of high-technology businesses. He made design and development breakthroughs that enabled his new ventures to dominate the industry. Soon he sold them, as his curiosity shifted to something else: From computer technology to aerospace. From aerospace to nuclear engineering. Then into genetics and health care. From health care into urban planning. And suddenly, into politics.

"A two-term governor. Then, almost without opposition, United States senator. Twice he was nearly to get his party's nomination for the presidency of the United States, missing the second time by only a handful of votes. Vandellen resigned from the Senate and all but dropped out of sight on his Colorado ranch for two years. When he appeared at all, it was as an oracle of science and technology. He returned to them again . . . returning like a backslider to his old church . . . turning away entirely from politics to science, as if it were civilization's last real hope. Finally—Sandstone."

The picture returned, showing shots of the facilities inside the Sandstone complex.

"No one knows how much it costs. No one knows how much it costs to operate. Not that it's a secret. Vandellen says he doesn't know the figures because no one's ever bothered to add them up. The operating budget of Sandstone—the largest non-governmental research facility in the world—is so immense that even the Vandellen fortune can't support it. Ninety-three of the country's largest technology-oriented corporations fund Sandstone's research."

The camera moved down a hall in the apartment building where visiting Sandstone scientists lived. "Vandellen calls it a place to think. It is basically a support facility for pure research, conducted by some of the finest minds of this century. The scientists invited to Sandstone—they range from sociologists to plasma physicists—may pursue the most esoteric and impractical theories for as long as they like, with no pressure to justify their work in terms of useful application. If any patentable idea or procedure is developed here, Martin Vandellen requires the inventor to assign the patent to Sandstone, which makes the development free to anyone who wants to use it. Sandstone, according to Martin Vandellen, is manufacturing knowledge."

Another cut, this time to a structure Harland—despite his own best rational arguments to the contrary—thought of as ominous. "Twenty miles from Sandstone, thirty from Denver, Colorado—as close as a nervous government would allow it to be built—is Green Falls. It's the Sandstone-designed, Sandstone-built nuclear generating plant. It represents the largest concentration of fissionable materials outside of military hands, and it's capable of generating fifteen million kilowatts. Fission power is another of Martin Vandellen's visions for America. Green Falls represents what he thinks the state of the nuclear art could and should be. But the federal government has not allowed him to build another one."

The picture cut to a shot of Vandellen and Harland walking through the foothills, with Sandstone and the Rockies in the background. Harland realized all over again that yes, that was John Harland of Angleton, Texas, walking and talking with Martin Vandellen. It was the first interview Vandellen had granted to anyone in more than four years, and he had agreed only if Harland would do it. Harland had learned that Vandellen had been watching Harland since he was with CBS's Houston bureau, covering NASA. Vandellen thought Harland was good at what he did, and if he was going to be interviewed, he wanted to talk with somebody who could ask him questions that would interest him enough to answer.

"Senator . . ."

This was recorded on audio at the very beginning of the session, while the lights and other items were still being set up.

"Try Martin, or 'hey, you.' I haven't been a senator for seven years, Mr. Harland."

"I'd be more comfortable with 'Mr. Vandellen.' "

"I'd be more comfortable with Martin. But you go ahead."

On the video portion he and his host were still strolling the grounds. Harland liked the change in Vandellen's smile. It was said that smile had cost him the presidency—not that it wasn't big enough, or brilliant enough, but voters perhaps sensed that Vandellen resented having to smile when he didn't feel like it.

The picture cut to the wing of Sandstone where Vandellen lived. The residence was natural stone and glass, fashioned at impossible expense to look austere. The camera panned across Vandellen's immense art collection, consolidated from other places where he had maintained homes. Harland remembered that the cameraman had missed a couple of the more celebrated pieces. He made a note: When they went back to Sandstone in two weeks to finish the interview, he would ask Vandellen to pose with several.

The camera had been rolling from here on, and Vandellen was aware of it.

"Are you a bitter man?"

Vandellen smiled one of his diminished smiles.

"You withdrew from public life so suddenly after you lost the California primary, that—"

"I guess it did look like a pout, Mr. Harland, and I guess there was some pride involved. I am still full of an urgent need to be of service to this country. I knew when I entered politics that I would never be able to work at full efficiency as a politician at a level less than the presidency. The second California primary made it very clear that I would never become president, and that my time in public office was over. I saw no point in filling for two more years a chair in the Senate that someone else could use."

"Do you think you would have made a good president?"

"Of course. Otherwise, I would not have offered myself."

"Do you still think about being president?"

"Honestly, Mr. Harland, I just don't think about it."

"Not even what you could have done differently that might—"

"Been born poor, perhaps. I am not bitter, that's too extreme, but I was disappointed that the basic issue in my two primary campaigns was never 'Will Martin Vandellen make a good president?' It was only 'Can the richest man in America buy the presidency?' But I have come to realize that it was important for the American people to prove to themselves that no, he can't. If my not being president puts to rest any . . . fears, then I am content."

"You no longer want to be president."

"I don't think I need to be, no."

"Then you feel that as chairman of the Sandstone Foundation, you can be as useful to the country as the president."

"As the American presidency, no. As this American President, certainly."

No smile.

Just as the red light atop camera two came on, indicating they were on the air, but before he got the hand cue from the floor manager for him to say "Good evening . . . ," Harland always made it a point to pick up his script and give it a couple of tamps on the desk top. He had evened out the pages before the light went on, of course, but he wanted the folks to see that he had a script there in front of him.

The script was virtually a prop. Harland read almost all the news off a device that refracted typescript through a pane of plate glass in front of the camera lens. Reading off the PrompTer was more efficient than shifting one's eyes between the lens and a hand-held script; but the research boys were convinced that viewers were unconsciously suspicious of the appearance of *not* reading something obviously intended *to be* read. And the networks, more than anything, wanted people to trust their anchormen.

He kept his eyes on the script and shifted his weight very slightly in his chair while the announcer said: "From New York City, this is the *CBS Evening News*, with John Harland substituting for Walter Cronkite, who is on vacation . . ."

He had to take an unnecessary look at the second page of his script to pad out the announcer's extra sentence. The idea was that his eyes should meet the lens of camera two just as the floor manager dropped his cue. *Ah*, thought Harland. *Show business*.

"Good evening," said Harland to CBS's seventeen share of the early evening audience. "At least thirty people are missing in West Virginia after a dam made of tailings from a coal mine collapsed early this morning and buried the village of Copper Creek. Fires from coal left in the tailings, which had been smoldering inside the dam for years, reignited, and officials say it may be years before any bodies can be recovered . . ."

Harland had already finished making the guacamole and had put it in the refrigerator. The enchiladas would go into the microwave oven thirty minutes before they were to be served. He'd made a salad and set the table. He'd done his share of dinner. He leaned on the kitchen doorjamb with his beer and watched Molly at the kitchen counter. He was trying very hard not to laugh.

"Will you give me a break?" she snarled. "Will you give me a fucking *break*?" She slammed both fists into the lump of phlegmy pie dough with which she was pleading. She snatched the kitchen phone off the wall and Harland saw her, again, stab the area code for Little Rock. A bit of dough, which had migrated to the phone from her hands during the last call, now affixed itself to Molly's hair. "Mother, *now* it is sticking to the goddamn *rolling pin*," she said without preamble. ". . . I put five *pounds* of flour on the goddamn rolling pin."

Harland had to duck back into the dining room and muffle his mouth. It was not the time to let Molly see he was laughing.

"Start *over?*" she said. "Thanks a *lot*, Mother. You billed this an idiot-proof recipe . . . Mommie, it has to be more than simple if you expect *me* to do it. It has to be see-Spot-run. This little number is Pillsbury Bakeoff time, Mother . . . It's absolutely the worst day of my life. It's thirty minutes until the people get here, the cat is stuck to the refrigerator, Harland is laughing at me . . . I don't *give* a shit anymore, Mother, I am using the frozen pie crust." She hung up the phone, gathered up the pie dough in the waxed paper, and threw the whole thing into the garbage, where it sent up a soft white cloud of flour.

"I'll tell Julia Child," said Harland.

"Asshole," said Molly, flicking the dough still clinging to her fingernails at him. "Look, this fun-filled regional-heritage food festival is *your* swell idea. I think *you* ought to fix the stinking old-family-recipe peach cobbler." She snatched open the door of the freezer, then slammed it. "I've got an even better idea. You just trot on down to the House of Pies and *buy* two deep-dish peaches, and we'll just *tell* everybody that I made them. Does that sound fair? If you do that, I won't blow the whistle on the enchiladas."

Since there was no way to improve upon the enchiladas made in the roadside stand beside the bend of the Brazos River in Richmond, Texas, Harland had had the entree for tonight's dinner party taken to Houston, and then air-freighted to New York, at a total cost of about three dollars per enchilada. Harland was intending to take credit for cooking them himself.

He was unable to go another moment without holding her. She smiled and slid into his arms as he moved to her. She kissed him on the neck, hugged him with her elbows. "Let me wash my hands."

"Did I ever tell you that one of my strongest adolescent fantasies was doing it standing up with a woman who was completely covered in pie dough?"

"Seriously, folks."

"You think I'm not serious?" Harland rubbed against her.

Molly pushed her hips against the pressure. "How do I know that's not just a roll of Tums in your pocket?"

"Jesus, lady. Tums?"

"*Tums*," she said, crumbling his fragile ego. "Covered with pie dough, huh. Completely?"

"No. I made it up. I've only had one fantasy. Doing it with Molly Rice, on our bed, no pie dough, missionary position, forty minutes before our guests arrive."

"It's your lucky day, kid." Molly sucked in her stomach so Harland could undo the buttons on her jeans.

They had invited Peter Harz, who worked with Molly, and his wife Dell; Jerry Lee; and Nona, whom Molly had known from college at the University of Missouri and who now was an actress in a soap.

Harland blithely accepted credit for the enchiladas and Molly for the pie, which they served with Irish coffee. Harz exchanged a smile with his wife and Jerry Lee. From his briefcase he produced a large envelope. "One of the advantages of being connected—and I mean connected at the very highest levels— is that you get the very best tables at the Burger King *and*"— he opened the envelope—"the very earliest advance copies of next week's *People* magazine."

"Oh *shit*," said Molly, who slumped back in her chair and threw her napkin over her face.

"My God, it's the *cover*," said Nona as Harz took the magazine from the envelope.

"How bad is it, Harland?" said Molly. She put her hands over the napkin on her face.

"Oh, that's a dynamite picture, Molly," said Nona. "It really is. The way John has his arm around you. You look like Mr. and Mrs. Warmth."

" 'CBS News's John Harland and Molly Rice of the *Times*,' " Harz read from the cover blurb. And then, savoring it: " 'America's Clout Couple.' "

"Oh Jesus. Oh Jesus," moaned Molly.

Harland winced. "Clout Couple?"

"And on page twenty-six, where the story appears in the 'Couples' section . . ."

Molly whipped off the napkin and reached out to snatch the magazine. "It doesn't *really* say 'Clout Couple,' does it?"

"Not a chance," said Harz, protecting it. "It *cries* to be read aloud. Nona?" He handed it across the table to her.

" 'Clout Couple' is pretty bad," said Harland.

"Why did we do it?" cried Molly. "I can understand *you* doing it, Harland. You're in show business. I can't understand why *I* did it. I'm a real journalist. I used to have credibility, before this."

Harland knew that Molly knew exactly what to expect when she'd agreed to do the interview with *People*. They had pretended they'd done it for laughs. They'd both done it for ego; he was prepared to admit it, but Molly wasn't.

Nona read with a Rona Barrett accent. " 'Does Macy's tell Gimbels? Maybe, but in the world of big-time journalism, everyone wants to know if Harland and Rice tell each other.' "

Dell Harz beat her fists upon the table. "Can you *stand* it?"

"The *Times* is going to kill me," wailed Molly.

" 'John, CBS News's clean-up hitter and heir apparent, and Molly, rising star of the powerful *New York Times*'s national affairs desk who got a governor impeached, started tongues wagging last summer when they began chasing each other as hard as they chase down news.' "

Molly made little mewling noises and threw the napkin over her face again.

"I like 'clean-up hitter,' John," said Jerry.

" 'Molly and John now share a cheerfully chaotic East Side apartment—his. Those two extra bedrooms they—obviously—don't need, have been converted into his-and-hers studies that are strictly no-person's-land to each other. CBS and the *Times* have no need to worry: These are lovers who have *plenty* of secrets from each other. "We work for competing news organizations," says John, "and recognize that we each know things that the other, as a reporter, shouldn't. We respect journalism and each other too much to ask the other for help we ought not to give." ' "

"It's exactly what I deserve," said Molly, "for living with a man who has an agent."

" ' "Anyway," said Molly, "we don't see each other long enough at a time to say more than 'Your turn to do the laundry.' " ' "

"You bitch," said Molly, waving her fist in the direction of the Time-Life Building. "I didn't say that, *he* said that."

"It's too soon after dinner for the paragraph about how they fell into each other's arms on assignment in Plains," said Harz. "Jump down to the next quote."

"You mean," said Nona, "after 'Is marriage on John and Molly's list of approved subjects to talk about?'

" ' "I've been married once and I'm not too wild about it," said Molly. "But I think John wants me to make an honest man of him." ' "

"My God, Molly," said Dell Harz. "Did you really say that?"

"Everything's a blank," said Molly.

"Ready for the big finish?" said Nona. " ' "It depends on our schedules," said John. "I'm old-fashioned. I'm not going to get married unless I can have a honeymoon." ' "

"What can we say, folks, after we say we're sorry?" said Harland.

"I think it's sweet," said Nona. "My God, kids, don't knock it, it's the *cover* of *People* magazine."

Harland and Molly gave their dinner parties on Wednesday nights; the cleaning woman came Thursdays, and she would clean up. After the guests had left, Harland saw Molly looking at the copy of *People*.

"It is dumb," said Harland.

Molly nodded. "Dumb."

"It should be on the street tomorrow. How many copies should I get for you?"

"Twenty should be enough," she said. They laughed and held each other. "Cover for me on the laundry, huh? I have to go out of town tomorrow." Molly had been out of town forty-five days of the last sixty.

Harland never asked where she had gone.

3

HARLAND HAD BEEN DEPRESSED AT THE THOUGHT OF GOING TO
LaGuardia and trying to fight aboard one of the shrinking numbers of Washington shuttles still flying. The Federal Energy
Administration had cut the aviation-fuel allocation by eighty
percent the month before. The thought of going to Washington
standing up in the smoking car of the Metroliner got him even
more depressed, so he called CBS Transportation on the very
long chance that one of the corporate airplanes might be heading that way.

Miraculously, one was. A Gulfstream, not quite full of CBS
division heads on their way to Miami for a sales meeting. He
had ridden out to Teterboro Airport in a limo with two of
them. Harland balanced four film cans of Martin Vandellen
interview on his lap. The others balanced thin suede attaché
cases. Harland so often had seen such cases go past him on elevators to the upper floors of the CBS headquarters building that
he suspected the company issued them.

The division presidents, mostly sales and marketing types,
were pleased to have Harland along. They never got to meet the
CBS stars except at affiliates' conventions, and then it was

usually sitcom and cop-show actors. Harland was a class act. They enjoyed exhibiting their currency in world events and the quality of their strategic thinking. Harland was offered a couple of "hot" story ideas, exposés of how the advertising agencies, "those bastards," wanted CBS to rebate on time charges when brownouts kept the network from delivering audience.

From National Airport Harland rode downtown in the same limo that had brought the final CBS division president to occupy his seat in the Gulfstream continuing on to Miami. The limo had eased past the chaos of people trying to get into the diminishing number of cabs. Publicly the corporations said they were tightening their belts at the same ratio as everyone else who operated automobiles, but division presidents still did not ride public transportation to airports.

The limo dropped Harland off at CBS News's Washington bureau. Harland rearranged five days' unattended detritus on his Washington desk and made room for the cans of Vandellen film. Then he checked in with Peter Tolliver, producer of *Weekend News*, who was screening minicam newstape that would be used on that evening's show.

"Is it Little-Jimmy-Goes-to-the-Country time again?" said Harland. Harland liked doing the *Weekend News* in Washington, away from the immediate and nervous attention of the New York news executives. But Saturdays and Sundays were the slowest news days of the week. Not much happened, besides disasters, or a coup pulled off in some bush-league country. A measure of its underdevelopment: its revolutionaries didn't realize that to get adequate media play in the States, political unrest had to be exhibited on weekdays.

The show's opening story was so often a report on the President's All-American weekend leisure activities that a Washington bureau staffer had had phony story-rundown sheets printed with "Little-Jimmy-Goes-to-the-Country" as the perennial first story.

On the videotape monitor, the President and his wife were

displaying a modest string of sea bass caught off the Georgia coast.

"Stop the presses," said Harland, who shook his head at the picture.

"There's a rumor," said Tolliver, "that the Navy used three nuclear subs to herd those fish."

"Look at him. What's it down there today? Twenty-eight degrees? I guess it's a gesture to convince the country that it's not really cold outside. Where's the kid? I'll bet she's already jumped into the limo, where it's warm, right? I like the kid. She's got a terrific sense of what's bullshit."

"That's an angle," said Tolliver, making a note. "The symbol thing. That the country has to ignore the weather as best it can."

Harland rolled his eyes. "I'll read it," he said, walking away. "But I won't write it."

Harland's mail had come in two large packets: One, from the CBS mail room, contained standard-sized letter envelopes. Harland never opened the second packet without a small regretful shake of his head for the poor Republic. All large or thick envelopes addressed to news personalities came in a packet stamped: SCANNED FOR EXPLOSIVES AND SEALED BY U.S. POSTAL SERVICE.

Harland shuffled through the odd-sized envelopes and packages, looking for the style of address that his graphological instincts told him could be the work of a nutcase. Although Harland hated crank callers—mostly because the callers exploited Harland's instinctive urge to be courteous, and he felt like a sucker for surrendering the time it cost him—he loved his crank mail. His secretary had firm instructions to screen nothing and to collect the crank mail discarded by other CBS correspondents who were unamused by it. When Harland's huge laugh spilled from his office, his colleagues knew it was Harland reading hate mail, or tips on the Big Story, being offered exclusively. He loved letters that offered him tips on the international conspiracy to suppress some new invention—typically, a process that would convert anything, from cow pee to old Coke bottles, into gasoline. Sometimes Harland would go from desk to desk to share them with his colleagues, especially the obscene and grotesque death threats. The other on-air correspondents were made nervous by threats of violence, but Harland was genuinely amused by them. He knew that because his face appeared on television, often saying unpleasant, frustrating, and disturbing things, there were probably at this moment any number of people, heads full of eels, who would like to kill him. But the ones who'd really do it wouldn't write him about it.

This latest batch of letters didn't look too promising: the usual stack of magazines, sent by their editors in hopes Harland would pick up an item and credit the publication. A Jet-Pak padded mailing bag from Bantam Books. Harland was about to shove it aside when he noticed that the original mailing label had been peeled off, and the address handwritten. The writing was small, block-lettered. Secretive, Harland's sense of graphology told him. The New York cancellation was scratched over. No new return address, but the new cancellation was Rifle, Colorado.

The assurance of the U.S. Postal Service that the package would not explode was good enough for Harland, so he pulled the stapled opening apart and dumped out the contents.

It was a videocassette, the paperback-sized Betamax cassette that goes in Sony's home-use half-inch model. Harland grinned. He immediately called the studio control room and asked if there was anybody down there who could cue him up a Betamax tape. There was, and he headed for the control room expectantly. The last time he was sent a Betamax tape, the accompanying unsigned letter assured him that it was proof positive of the unsuitability of an important senator to hold his office. It had turned out to be a blurry silent porno whose male protagonist looked fleetingly like the accused senator. Harland and Molly would occasionally pull out the tape and play it for guests at home, at first solemnly telling their innocent guests that what they were about to see was eyes-only, and it was going to blow the lid off the Senate.

The technician's name was George. All he had to do to show the tape was shove the cassette into the machine and punch three buttons on a control board. Harland could do it perfectly well himself, but it was a task sacrosanctly within the jurisdiction of members of the National Association of Broadcast Engineers and Technicians. The monitor glitched and rolled over and a wall of static came from the speaker. A picture of a man, facing the cameras and talking, came blurrily onto the screen, oscillated briefly and then disappeared as the picture broke up, then swam back, the face smeared sideways across the screen.

"Geez, Johnny, when do we get to the good parts?" said George.

"This one doesn't look like it's going to be any fun at all," said Harland. "I suppose that glitching is on the tape and can't be straightened out?"

"Yeah," said George. "To begin with, it looks like it's about an eighth-generation dub. A copy of a copy of a copy. No resolution. And the machine had dirty recording heads. It'll keep breaking up like this the rest of the tape. Typical consumer electronics. Touchy." George said "consumer electronics" with a sneer, the one that all network techies affect in referring to any piece of equipment not capable of functioning nominally while being run over by a truck, and costing less than thirty thousand dollars. "I don't know what happened to the audio," he added, turning up the blank static.

"Well, at least I got a free Betamax tape," said Harland. "Even discount those sumbitches cost . . ."

For about four seconds, the picture had stabilized enough for Harland to recognize the man talking silently on the screen. It was Martin Vandellen.

". . . fifteen bucks apiece." Harland finished the sentence slowly.

"Seen enough?" said George.

The picture broke up again into eye gibberish.

"Yeah," said Harland. George ejected the tape, walked with

it to another machine. "Want me to put it on the bulk eraser? Makes it a lot cleaner to record over if it's degaussed."

Harland suddenly reached out for the tape, taking it back. "No . . . it . . . I'll play the rest of it sometime. There might be fuck-and-suck stuff at the end."

"If there is," said George, "I want a dub."

Back at his desk, Harland tried to analyze his almost reflexive reaction of yanking the tape back before the technician erased it. He decided to attribute it to dumbness. It was a blurry dupe videotape of Martin Vandellen making a speech. Martin Vandellen has made a million speeches. Why would a nutcase send him a blurry dupe videotape of it?

Because a nutcase is a nutcase.

He opened his desk drawer and put the videocassette inside. It's worth fifteen bucks, Harland told himself, and things have a way of walking away by themselves around here.

4

MOLLY SAW THAT THE MAN SITTING ACROSS THE TABLE FROM HER needed more time to decide if he should say what he wanted to say. He was taking three times longer to eat his cheesecake than a man who wasn't half-sick with worry about what the rest of his life might be like, beginning with this moment. Molly looked around the anonymous, anaerobic hotel restaurant designed for anaerobic, anonymous business lunches. Her lunch partner had taken—either by design or instinct—a table as far away from the sunny windows as he could. In the distance, through the snow swirls, she could see an intense greenness that might be Grosse Point. Fifty stories below, out of her line of sight, was inner-city Detroit, across which the cabdriver had transported her that morning to the Renaissance Center with windows up, doors locked, past the boarded-up department stores.

Renaissance Center had done little to rejuvenate inner Detroit, but it did make it comfortably easy for the comfortably off to enclave themselves in burnished office buildings and apartment towers, with thirty stories of cultural insulation between them and the streets.

The man sitting across from Molly was named Timmins. He was about fifty-three. He still had all his hair, but it was half gray. He wore a suit with a vest. From the way he ordered ginger ale, Molly understood that he wanted vodka, still after five years, after going down on his knees in front of his wife and boss and swearing that he'd never drink again. Timmins folded his napkin for the third time and talked without looking at her, smiling slightly. "I guess I'm getting what you'd call cold feet, Miss Rice," said Timmins. "I'm sure I sounded angry enough on the phone to spill my guts out all over this table, and I was. But I have since realized there are . . . considerations. I was fired, yes. I'm not deluding myself about that, but technically it's early retirement; and Federal Motors' pensions are generous, for someone at my income level. But I have no legal right to the pension. It's a perk. It's how the company insures the discretion of its aging executives. My chances of getting a job somewhere else aren't so hot."

He looked at her, took a sip of ginger ale. "I'm surprised you came out here in the first place. I'm sure you'd be inclined to discount half of what I say as bullshit. The fired employee lying to *The New York Times* to screw the company back, right?"

"Norm, look . . ." Molly was going to use first names if Timmins wasn't. When a source wanted to talk but felt he needed someone's permission, it never hurt to establish dominance.

"If you have to use my name, I can't talk with you."

"Norm, I won't have to use your name. But, obviously, the more sensitive information is, the smaller the circle who know it, and that means—"

"—that it's easier to figure out who talked. I realize that." He looked out the window for a moment. "Excuse me."

Timmins walked off in the direction of the restaurant foyer. After he'd been gone for ten minutes, Molly decided she'd lost him. He was heading back to the FedMo administration building now, Molly thought, to fill out the two months they gave him and to worry if anyone had seen him in the Renaissance Center with a reporter from *The New York Times*. Molly leaned down to look in her purse for the American Express card to lay on the lunch check. When she looked up, Timmins was sitting across from her. His eyes were rimmed with red, and he had to start his sentence three times.

"I . . . was with that company for thirty-one years. When they called me into that room on Thursday, I expected to be put on the board. And they sent me out like I was a piece of shit. Fuck 'em." He took a very deep breath and rubbed his eyes. "Miss Rice. The significance is not what I know, but what I don't know. At all levels above me, and at some below me, there has been . . . a lot of activity. I realize now that I have been very carefully excluded. . . . But. Anyway. Whatever is being discussed, or planned, or whatever, the meetings are not taking place in the administration building. I'll bet not even in Detroit. I know that terrific amounts of documentation have been copied at headquarters and flown out of town. For the past two months, so few top-level executives have been around here . . . well, office boys have been authorizing new-car lines. And the last time the chief executive officer left town, his chef went with him." Timmins smiled. Molly felt intensely sorry for him. "I realize that the CEO's chef being out of town sounds like a thing of very small significance. But when you've been with a company for thirty-one years, you get a feeling for the way the company lives, and you can sense changes without there being signs of changes. Something immense is happening. The company is holding its breath."

"You have no idea what it could mean?"

"None, and I'm no longer in a position to find out. I hope the *Times* can." Timmins smiled with pleasure for the first time since Molly had met him. "And I hope it's illegal."

Visitors needed a pass to go upstairs in the FedMo administration building, but Molly didn't need to go upstairs. She did need to stay an undetermined amount of time in the lobby, though, without getting run off. She laid on what remained of her Arkansas whine and told the large black man at the security desk:

"Sir, I have to go get the keys to my apartment from my roommate."

"Name?"

"Her name?"

The guard sighed. "*Your* name, honey."

"Well, it's Wanda Kuteck, but—"

The guard ran his finger through a sheaf of small slips of paper. "Did she send down a building pass?"

"No, see, she don't know I locked myself out on account of I haven't been able to get her on the phone at her desk, see, and I gotta take my prescription—"

He shook his head impatiently. "Can't let you up without a building pass signed by her department manager."

Molly keened her whine up half an octave. "Well, cain't you *call* her? On account of I have to take these pills for my—"

"Use the building phone," the guard said, nodding toward a bank of phones on the wall near the elevators.

"Oh, okay," whined Molly, folding her arms under her breasts. "*Durn.*"

Every now and then for the next hour, the guard would look Molly's way, and she would dial four numbers on the house phone and screw up her face and look frustrated. Finally, having decided that if the dumb girl was desperate enough to stand there and dial the phone all afternoon it wasn't his problem, he stopped noticing Molly at all.

At 11 a.m., the second pay phone from the end rang.

"Miss Rice?" Timmins's voice was breathy.

"Yeah, Norm."

"Kentwood is coming down the elevator now."

"He's a division president, right?"

"Finance. One of the biggest buddies of the CEO. He's got a blue suit, an overnight bag, and a briefcase. You better get on out and watch for him from your car, because he'll probably have a limousine and driver, and he'll get off the plant grounds in a hurry."

"Any idea where he's going?"

"No. I have to hang up." And he did.

"You giving up on those keys?" said the guard as Molly strode past toward the main entrance.

"Well, if I get pregnint tonight," Molly snapped, "it'll be *your fault*."

In front of the administration building there was a car—a black Cordelle—with a driver standing beside it. Molly walked past to where her rented Pinto sat in one of the spaces reserved for visitors. She unlocked the door as a man she recognized immediately to be Kentwood strode out the front door and within eight steps was inside the Cordelle.

Molly started the Pinto. "Okay, charlie," she said in the direction of Kentwood's limousine as it went past. "I hope you've never been followed before, because I've never done any following."

The guard at the entrance gate waved Kentwood's car onto the street. Molly surrendered the visitor's pass and the guard logged her license number out. Before she pulled out in the same direction as Kentwood, she allowed one car to go ahead of her. She had planned to keep one car between Kentwood and the Pinto if she could. She remembered that's what they seemed to do on the cop shows.

Miraculously, the car just behind Kentwood's made the first five turns Kentwood's car did. After the fourth, Molly began to wonder if the driver of the VW Rabbit was following Kentwood too. After the fifth, she began to wonder who it was. Had Timmins jobbed his story around? Was that somebody from *Newsweek* ahead of her? And from *60 Minutes* behind? Would Kentwood arrive at his destination leading a convoy of press?

But somewhere—Molly saw a street sign that said McNichols Road—the Cordelle turned and the Rabbit didn't. Molly didn't make the light. She didn't know for sure if one could turn right on red in Michigan, but she did anyway. More street signs went past: McNichols Road, Connor Avenue . . . Molly saw hangars, small airplanes tied down. The Cordelle turned off Connors Avenue at a sign:

DETROIT CITY AIRPORT

"Son of a *bitch*," said Molly, beating her palm on the seat beside her. Kentwood, as befit his corporate position, was going to leave Detroit on a company airplane, and Molly would find it difficult to tail him in a Pinto. The Cordelle headed toward a complex of three hangars with the firm's logo painted on each of them. It stopped at a gate in the ten-foot-high chain-link fence that encircled the area. A guard in a FedMo uniform looked briefly inside the car and waved it through.

The Cordelle headed between the hangars where, on a ramp on the runway side of the hangars, Molly could see a twin-engine waiting, a six-seater, its passenger-side door open. When the pilot saw the Cordelle approach, he started to turn over the left engine. Molly had forgotten how incredibly free of hassle it was to fly in a private airplane. Kentwood would probably be in the air within three minutes.

Molly pulled the car to the curb and stared into her lap and thought intensely. If there was any way she could get past the guard, maybe get into the FedMo flight operations office, she might . . .

Kentwood got out of the Cordelle and stepped up into the plane. The door closed behind him. The right propeller started to turn over.

Molly opened her purse, dug through it. Then suddenly reached into the backseat, where she'd tossed the copy of the FedMo report to stockholders Timmins had given her; it contained pictures of all the FedMo top managers. He had put it in a FedMo interoffice envelope. Molly quickly scribbled "Mr. Kentwood" on the envelope, tossed it aside, and yanked the Pinto back in gear. She pulled into the guard station and braked impatiently when the guard didn't lift the electric gate.

"I'm Mr. Kentwood's secretary," said Molly. She waved the envelope. "He's *got* to have this. I mean, literally, *got* to have this. I forgot to give it to him, and it's going to be my *ass*."

"I'm sure he's got to have them, but lady, you're too late." The plane was moving out of sight behind the hangar, the registration numbers just—

The numbers. The edge of the hangar was swallowing them up as Molly realized that she had to remember them.

N . . .

She was terrible with numbers. It took her months to memorize a new home phone number . . .

6 . . .

She felt around for her pencil on the seat, knowing she couldn't afford to take her eyes off the plane to find something to write on . . .

2 . . .

6 . . .

Same as the first number . . .

5 . . .

Or was the first number . . . ?

R . . .

Six. Two. Four—no, *Five.*

"Honey," said the guard, "could you back out of here? I need—"

"Shit!" said Molly. "Do you know where he's going?" And immediately knew she shouldn't have said that.

"Honey, I don't know where all these planes are going. I don't even think they'd tell you at operations, unless . . . Look, why don't you call his office? His secretary . . ." The guard stopped, looked at Molly intently. He looked back at the phone in the guard station. "Just a second, I'll—"

"You got a pencil, ace?" Molly plucked one from the guard's shirt pocket, wrote "N6265R" on Mr. Kentwood's package, dropped the Pinto into reverse, and squealed back into traffic.

She pulled off at the first hangar that had AIRCRAFT RENTALS

AND FLIGHT INSTRUCTION written on it. She heard a rumble behind her, turned to see the twin starting its take-off run.

The woman sitting at the desk was on the phone, so Molly pantomimed holding a phone to her ear. The woman nodded and pointed off to a small room. There was a blackboard, charts on the wall, and a phone. Molly saw what she needed—it was written with labeling tape and stuck to the handset of the phone. There was no indication as to what the phone number was, but Molly punched an unlighted circuit on the phone and dialed it. Molly picked up an eraser, worried it at the blackboard.

It rang. Five times. Ten. Twenty-five. "*Shit!*" Molly threw the eraser across the room. A snarl overhead was probably Kentwood's plane. She hung up, dialed again. It rang five more times. *Please, God,* she thought, *let a man answer.* Fifteen times. The government was putting more and more women into these jobs. *Hooray and all that* . . . Twenty times. *But this time, please let it be a man.* She'd never be able to bullshit a woman.

"Flight Service Station." It was a man. *Thank you, Jesus.*

"Are you . . . are you the people with the government who . . . uh, keeps track of the airplanes?" Molly was thinking of a girl she'd gone to high school with in Fort Smith, Jo Beth, helpless Jo Beth, and how her every sentence was an interrogatory.

"Yes, ma'am," Molly heard the condescending smile already spreading in the man's voice, and began to hope she'd drawn a winner.

"Well, my boyfriend, he's a pilot for FedMo. And I'm always afraid he's going to crash? So he told me that whenever he flies anywhere, he always tells the FAA where he's going, and if he doesn't get there, the people at this number will know?"

"Yes, ma'am."

"Well, he's almost two hours late, and I'm so worried I don't know what to do."

"Ma'am, have you checked with FedMo?"

"Well, my boyfriend told me not never to call FedMo because . . . well, because we're not exactly married? Well, he's married, but not to me?"

"Ma'am, we haven't had any reports of any aircraft overdue. It could be he's landed, and just hasn't told you." The man was all but sniggering.

"I just *know* he's crashed, couldn't you look it up? His name is Bobby, and . . ."

"Ma'am, see, all the flight plans are filed on audio tape, and to find out his name, we'd have to play them all back, and normally, we keep records of flight plans according to the aircraft numbers, and—"

"Oh, he wrote it down," said Molly. "He wrote it down for me, so I . . . here it is, it's N Six. Two six. Five, Are?"

"Six-five-romeo? Oh now, honey . . ." said the man at flight service.

Oh go, *you condescending superior asshole. Put my dumb-little-broad fears to rest.*

"Look, we're not supposed to give this out, but six-five-romeo just took off five minutes ago. He opened his flight plan in the air, to Fourteenmile direct. Honey, if you're lonely tonight—"

Molly slammed down the receiver and wrote "Fourteenmile" on the blackboard. Then she went back into the office, fumbling around in her purse.

"Can I do something for you?" asked the girl at the desk.

"Yeah," said Molly. "You can rent me a Skyhawk." Molly held out her pilot's license.

The little single-engine Cessna bumped along at eight thousand five hundred feet, heading northwest toward the Ishpaming VOR, the radio navigation aid. The Michigan peninsula was an almost featureless white, but the VORs that dotted the country painted stripes in the sky leading to themselves, and all Molly had to do was keep the needle on her nav radio centered to stay on course. When she looked at the thermometer she was astounded again by the outside temperature. During the cursory check ride she had to pass before the FBO would rent her the Cessna, she had told an emergency lie about her winter flying experience. Only because it was clear and dry, and appeared to intend to stay that way for a couple of days, had she even considered flying in this climate. Early in her flight she tried to dredge up, from a flying-magazine article she'd read long ago, what one should do to survive in the cold, but she subsequently decided she simply would not have to make an emergency landing.

Molly had learned to fly after the *Times* had assigned her to the Atlanta bureau. She had quickly grown weary of the vast distances she had to drive, and the South's bestial roads. She thought of flying as another useful job-related skill, like touch typing, and developed no great affection for it. The experience of soloing for the first time failed to send her into Saint-Exupéry ecstasies. She had learned quickly. Her instructor said she had a natural ability. She got her license at fifty-five hours and piled up a hundred and sixty hours quickly. But after the *Times* had moved her to New York and the national desk, she worked the kind of stories where commercial-airline travel was more practical; she hardly flew left-seat anymore.

Molly looked down upon the almost totally white terrain and was pleased to notice that her next checkpoint, a highway intersection, was coming up five minutes ahead of schedule. She looked back down into her lap at the Green Bay sectional, the aviation chart of Northern Michigan. Her eye moved along the course line she'd drawn upon it from its margin to the magenta dot that represented the airport at Fourteenmile Point.

The private airfield at Fourteenmile Point on the Superior shore was shown to be unlighted, unpaved, four thousand feet long. It was twenty nautical miles away from the nearest town, and there were no roads leading to it. Fishing camp for rich people, Molly thought.

She had had no chance of catching the twin-engine Aztec, six-five-romeo, which not only had half an hour's head start on her but also cruised at least sixty knots faster than the Skyhawk.

It was only the sudden flatness ahead and below that told her the frozen land was meeting the frozen lake. Off to her left, a town: That must be Ontonagon, she thought. She'd drifted a little south. She came to a heading of zero-two-zero, reduced power, and eased off a few thousand feet of altitude. She tracked down the coastline and within five minutes saw a straight black line appear in the sea of white.

"What the *shit*?" said Molly, loud enough to startle herself. The sectional was wrong. The private airport at Fourteenmile Point was not unpaved, unlighted, and four thousand feet long. It was lighted. Paved. And at least eight thousand feet long. An airfield like that served a city the size of New London, not a fishing camp.

She overflew the airport at thirty-five hundred feet, banking a little to the left so she could see below her. There were four big hangars, and she could see several planes—all big twins— tied down in front of them. She saw four snowplows parked by the edge of the taxiways. A thin black line of a plowed road led away from the field, squeezed between the shoulder of a small hill and the shoreline, and went to what Molly at first thought must be a ski lodge. But none of the hills around were steep enough to ski.

Molly tuned in the airfield's ground-air communication frequency, heard nothing. From this altitude and angle, she couldn't tell if any of the planes on the ground were six-five-romeo. Which means, she told herself, I'm going to have to go lower.

She made three-quarters of a right-hand circle over the runway, losing altitude in the turn. About nine hundred feet above the ground, she partially extended the flaps, reducing her airspeed. The unicom crackled as someone keyed in on the frequency. "Cessna Skyhawk . . ."

Molly was down to five hundred feet. She leaned forward in the seat, looking at the planes lined up on the ramps, wishing she knew her twin aircraft better. Was that an Aztec? No, a Baron. One tied down at the end, that could be it.

"Cessna Skyhawk," said the voice on the unicom again, "this is a private airport. You do not have permission to land."

Two hundred feet. The registration numbers were easier to read now. Five-five-eight. Zero-two-hotel.

"You do *not* have permission to land."

Molly had anticipated this. She opened her mike. "Uh . . . I'm a student pilot on my first solo cross country . . . I think I'm lost, and uh . . . Am short on fuel . . . uh . . ."

"You can land at Ontonagon, Skyhawk," the voice said with increasing hostility. "Heading two-five-zero, twenty-five miles away."

And there was six-five-romeo.

"This is a private field, Skyhawk. Are you declaring an emergency?"

That ploy, thought Molly. Owners of a private airfield could not deny permission to land to an aircraft experiencing an emergency, but asking the pilot to declare one was to remind him that he would have to prove to the FAA later that it really *was* one. Molly was only about fifty feet above the runway.

"Uh . . . I don't . . . uh . . ." She released the microphone switch and said to herself: "Je-he-sus Christ . . ."

She was low enough to see inside the hangars. Pushed inside, packed as tightly as possible in a random, frantic jumble, were a squadron of corporate jets. Top-of-the-line models: Lears, Citations, Gulfstreams, four-million-dollar airplanes pushed together like hundred-horse trainers in a T-hangar.

To get them out of sight.

"Going to Ontonagon," said Molly slowly into the microphone. She pushed the throttle full in and retracted the flaps. The Skyhawk gained altitude. As Molly looked back, she could see the doors to the hangars start to roll closed.

There was a short paved strip at Ontonagon. It was not as immaculately plowed as Fourteenmile. Molly loped through the enervating cold into the portable-building field office and asked that the Skyhawk be tied down and its tanks topped off.

"Hey," Molly told the fixed-base operator who ran the airport single-handedly, "I came in here from the northeast, and—"

"You came across an airport that showed it has four-thousand-foot unpaved runways on the sectional, and it looks from the air like it must be a mile and a half long and definitely paved and you thought it had to be this airport so you tried to land there and some surly son of a bitch gets on the unicom and runs you off." The FBO didn't even look up from his paperwork.

"Yeah. It *does* show four thousand unpaved on the sectional, doesn't it?" She looked at the back of the chart to make sure it was current.

"It was until October, when they built a seven-thousand-five-hundred-foot runway over it. Put up three new hangars. Goddamn driving us crazy, son of a bitchin' FedMo jets all times of the night . . ."

"That's FedMo's airport?"

"They own just about everything from here to Beacon Hill. It's what they call your ex-ecutive re-treat. The bigshots from Detroit get to come up here and fish and walk around in the woods and get spiritually charged up or some kind of shit so they can go back and figure out ways to jack up the prices of cars. Gonna have to double it to pay for what it costs them to keep that place open in the winter."

"It's never been open in the winter before?"

"Jesus, no. Those candyasses from Detroit couldn't stand fifteen minutes outside in a peninsula winter." He cranked Molly's credit card through the imprinter. "My God, there's gotta be ten thousand of 'em. Run outa room at the lodge out at Fourteenmile, so some of 'em had to start staying nights in the motel here in town. Every morning, about two hundred cars pull up in front of the Holiday Inn and they takes 'em out to the lodge, and then takes 'em back at night. I don't know why they bother to start coming now. You fly over Fourteenmile Point, you never see anybody outside the lodge. Never ice fishing, never snowmobiling. I guess they just stay inside and . . ." The FBO noticed Molly's gender and decided to clean up his act. "Well, any day now, I expect some poor bastard's going to try to put his Comanche down there and those creeps is gonna shoot him down with a goddamn missile. How many nights you want to tie down?"

"I don't know. At least one." Now that she knew where Kentwood had gone, Molly realized that she had no clear idea of what she was going to do next. "How do I get into town?"

If Kentwood was sufficiently second-echelon to be assigned a prop job while others came to Fourteenmile in Lears and Citations, then he might be second-echelon enough to have been bumped into the motel with the hired help when the lodge filled up with his superiors. Molly had no idea where along FedMo's perimeter she could move in. She was going to have to reconnoiter.

The cab driver told her that only one motel besides the Holiday Inn stayed open during the winter, and a nice-looking lady like her wouldn't want to sleep in it. He skiied the car down the icy main street and deposited Molly beside the familiar star and arrow of the good ol' Holiday.

There were three or four ahead of her at the registration desk. As she pulled off her gloves and unbuttoned her sheepskin jacket, she sensed motion from the corner of her eye. Through the lobby doors she could see a convoy of uniform black Cordelles pull up under the portico. Two or three men got out of each of them, all of them carefully and expensively turned out in the L.L. Bean-gear look, most carrying briefcases. One man waved a goodbye to the man he'd ridden with, who was headed for the coffee shop, and walked toward the desk. The second he turned full-face to Molly, she knew it was Larry Amble. There was never any doubt of that, but what dizzied her for a second was the effort to reconcile the context. Larry Amble was not usually found dressed like a lumberjack in a snowed-in Michigan Holiday Inn. Amble was encountered after thirty-story elevator rides up into a Manhattan office building, smiling blandly from behind a chrome-and-teak desk, and at press conferences where he smoothly non-answered questions on behalf of his bosses as director of press relations for Encon America.

Molly recovered in time to realize that Amble—their eyes meeting as he closed on her—was having the same vertiginous moment. Neither was prepared to formulate lies for the other about why they were there. They acknowledged it to the other by simultaneously avoiding eye contact as Amble passed.

She sneaked a look in the direction he'd gone, and saw him standing by the elevator, staring at her. The look instantly frightened her. Clearly, blackly, he wished her gone.

5

Lieutenant R. W. Wesley of the Oklahoma City Police shivered pitifully and stared across the street at the corpse of the Drummer's Hotel—nine stories of boarded-up windows and pigeon droppings standing alone in a block-square slab of concrete foundations scraped clean by bulldozers. The abandoned hotel and Lieutenant Wesley were being pelted by wet snow.

Somewhere above the second floor, an undetermined number of people—they wouldn't say how many—held six men at gunpoint. That in itself didn't make Wesley uncomfortable; to encounter situations like that was precisely why Wesley loved being a police officer, and he had taken special training to be in command of hostage incidents for the OCPD. What made him uncomfortable was the police response. Wesley's instincts were to secure the area quickly and firmly. Seal off at least four blocks around the building and present a show of force to demonstrate to the perpetrators that they had no opportunity of escape. Roll up the motorhome that had been converted into a mobile police communications and command center; conspicuously deploy the SWAT team; send over the helicopters.

But the complete OCPD response consisted of six officers, four police-band hand communicators, and two pickup trucks, one of them Wesley's, the one with the camper top he took fishing to Lake Texoma.

Late in the summer, the chief of police had collected Wesley and his sergeant and taken them to the Federal Bureau of Investigation office in the Federal Building, where they had been briefed by a man whom the local FBI agent in charge did not introduce. The briefing concerned contingencies in "hostage situations" where the perpetrators had political objectives. If the taking of hostages was not conspicuously public, the terrorists were to be allowed to proceed unchallenged to wherever they wanted to go. They were to be followed only, by no more than four officers in civilian clothes and unmarked cars. When the terrorists made demands known, the officers were to respond by saying they were not authorized to negotiate. Wesley was given a telephone number to call to report the situation. Personnel at the number would instruct the local officers to wait to be contacted at the site by individuals who would identify themselves by an "enabling phrase." These individuals would be in command of all operations. There were three objectives, in this priority: Concealment. Containment. Delay. If any media inquiries were made, describe the incident as a hoax.

After finishing his instructions and asking for questions—the directions were so clear and unequivocal that the policemen had nothing to say or ask during the five minutes they were in the office—the briefer left. It was exclusively an oral briefing. They were left with no memos, no documentation, other than the phone number.

Wesley had followed the instructions precisely. The perpetrators had made it easier for him by taking the hostages quietly, from a motel meeting room, and by not contacting the police dispatcher until just before they'd secured themselves inside the Drummer's Hotel. The dispatcher had, according to police procedure, transferred the call to Wesley. And Wesley took the piece of paper he'd been given in the FBI office from where he'd folded it and put it in his wallet, along with the new enabling phrase he had been given over the phone only four days before.

Wesley picked up the hand communicator from the seat beside him and keyed it on. "Don, you see anything?"

"Yeah, eighth floor. I think I can see where they might have drilled a hole through the plywood over the windows so they can see out." Wesley rolled down the window, put his own binoculars on the eighth floor. "Don't see anything on this side . . ." There was a sudden glint on one side of the image inside his binoculars. He pulled them down. The glint was a reflection from a pair of opaque-silver sunglasses. They were worn by a man who was leaning, grinning, on the door of Wesley's pickup.

"I'll bet you're a policeman," said the grinning man. Wesley saw that the man was dressed lightly for the cold: a number-69 football jersey inside his quilted jacket, the obligatory cap with a Wayne Feed insignia on the crown. "Me and my buddy saw you parked here using that walkie-talkie gizmo and I bet him you were a policeman."

Wesley looked at him levelly. "You go tell your buddy that you're right, and then both of you get your asses on down the road. This is police business."

"Good," said the man as he opened the pickup door. "We're the guys from Copper Creek."

Wesley stared at the man. He felt himself flush, his palms moisten. He sensed the same cold fear that radiated from the Secret Servicemen who surrounded the President when he came to town in the fall.

The man noted Wesley's immobility, and the fact that he'd established his dominance over Wesley within two seconds of their meeting. "That *is* the enabling phrase, lieutenant. Can you scoot over a little, please?" Wesley crabbed over on the seat. The man got behind the wheel, closed the door. "Going down to fifteen tonight, I hear. First of all, lieutenant—you are Wesley, aren't you? R.W.?"

"Right."

"R for Robert? They call you Bob or Bobby?"

"Bobby."

"I'm Sam." He did not offer to shake hands. "First of all,

Bobby, you handled this very well. I'm very pleased." He picked up Wesley's binoculars, inspected the building. Wesley started to tell this Sam guy about the other OCPD unit watching the north side of the building, decided that this Sam guy probably already knew about it. And that he should speak when spoken to. "Bobby, tell me about this old place."

"Yes sir, well, it's just an old ho-tel. It was a flophouse before the health department closed it down."

"Any particular reason why it's the only building left on the block?"

"Well, the city owns all this land, and they're going to turn it into one of those miniparks, you know? But some historical society decided that the ho-tel ought to be saved on account of it's got some kind of special architectural design or something. They got an injunction, and the city's fighting it. I can't see that it's anything special except a wino firetrap."

"Seen any of them?"

"No sir."

"And they didn't say anything that would suggest how many of them there are?"

"No sir."

Sam took from his jacket pocket the kind of telephone headsets Wesley noticed the police dispatchers used. The earpiece was molded into the ear cavity, and a thin white tube of plastic curved out to in front of his lips. Sam adjusted it into place as he spoke and smoothed a thin silver thread of wire—an antenna?—into the flow of his hair. "Wesley," said Sam, "here's what I'd like you to do: Nothing."

"Yes sir."

"That's *nothing*, Bobby. Not a thing."

"Yes sir."

"You might see some men get out of those vans over there and go inside the building with me. But they might not. But if they do, Bobby, tell me what you're going to do about it."

"Not a thing."

"Way to go, Bobby." Sam opened the door and slid out of the pickup. As he walked across the street, he adjusted the boom microphone in front of his lips and spoke into it. "We're not going to show what we have until they show us what they have. If they break, let them leave. No firing, no return of fire. I'm going to see what we can do for them."

The pieces of two-by-four that had been nailed across the door of the hotel had been crowbarred off. Sam pushed the door the rest of the way open and stepped into the dark.

As his eyes irised open, he kicked pint bottles of 20-20 and Thunderbird wine ahead of him. The cold did nothing to abate the stench of ancient alkali plaster, of pigeon shit and walls wainscoted yellow up to waist level by wino urine. Sam had to breathe through his mouth for a moment. From ahead of him, beside the splintered registration desk, light. It was a stairwell. The light came from above, apparently from the second landing.

"They aren't on the first floor," said Sam into the microphone. "Which makes sense. The position is easier to defend several floors up. They've turned on a light upstairs, which is obviously where they want contact to be made."

Sam had taken five steps up the stairs when he realized the muscles in his face were clenched. Awaiting a blow, thought Sam, and made himself relax. He reached the first landing, turned to make the spiral upward.

"There's a barrier here. Doors nailed across the stairway, old pipes, junk piled up. Not strong, but you'd take a lot of casualties getting through it. The building's probably fortified all the way up. They've been working on this one for a while."

The ascending flights of stairs, as they switched back, defined a column. Sam looked up into the volume of space and saw a thin white wire descending from the dark. His eyes followed it down. It wrapped around the stair rail a couple of times, continued on downward. At its end was a standard telephone handset.

"Telephone call," said Sam, and switched off his transmitter. He sat on the stairs beside the phone and leaned back to look up the space between the stair flights. He could see nothing. There was no switch on the handset, so Sam assumed that someone was continually listening on the other end, or perhaps it was connected to a speakerphone.

"You people have been doing quite a bit of improvements around here," said Sam into the telephone. "You have a building permit?"

There was quiet on the line. Then a voice, intense and cold: "Who is this and what's your authorization?"

"You first, asshole," said Sam pleasantly.

"We are members of the People's Department of Justice and—"

"Jesus Christ. Spare us all from assholes who call themselves the people's anything."

"Look. Your mouth is going to cause these people up here a whole lot of pain. Shut it up and listen, don't talk." Good, thought Sam. Macho, and an ego. Work on it, and he might stop paying enough attention to what he's doing.

"You got it," said Sam.

"You probably already have the names of the men we're holding."

"You got it."

"Six of these men are from the Energy Resource and Development Administration, and four are employees of Gulf Nuclear Corporation. We discovered them in the act of committing a crime, and made a citizen's arrest."

"Are they—?"

"You *shut* that fucking *mouth*. Here are the rules. Make any aggressive move on our position and we start throwing people out the window. Turn off the electricity and we start throwing people out the window. Miss any of our deadlines by as much as ten seconds and we starting throwing people out the window. Now, I say again: What is the extent of your authorization?"

"Asshole, I can get you any little thing your heart desires, but you don't have shit chance of getting it."

"The men from ERDA and the Gulf Nuclear were engaged in a conspiracy in which a breeder-reactor power station would be built at Lake Chickasha. The construction of any nuclear reactor anywhere is immoral and no longer permissible. We will try them for their crime; they will explain why what they intended to do is wrong. You will arrange for this trial to be nationally televised. By six-thirty there will be an electronic news truck capable of transmitting a live broadcast parked on the street. We will send down a rope, you will attach a portable television camera to it. We begin in two hours. *All* networks."

"You sure you want all three networks, asshole? There's a playoff game on tonight. I'm sure people could care less if you started throwing engineers out of windows, but if you preempt the playoff game, there's not enough cops in Oklahoma to keep them from tearing your hearts out." Sam looked at his watch. It was four-thirty. "Well, don't go away. I'll be back in half an hour."

"Do not come back with a counteroffer. Counteroffers aren't going to do any good, and it's going to cost you guts all over the sidewalk. It's not going to be hard for you to do what we want when we want it, if you start now. You *do* it."

"Ooooo," said Sam. "I love it when you're assertive." He kissed the mouthpiece of the handset and dropped it. It banged against the railings and then slowly pendulumed, twisting on its cord in the gloom.

He walked outside toward the two vans, talking into his microphone. "They want TV time. East Coast prime time, the assholes."

"The chopper just dropped Sutton and the panel truck," said a voice in his ear. "Twelve blocks away."

"This is Sutton, I'm on line now," said another voice in Sam's ear. "Chopper's lifting off and I'm en route. Five minutes."

Sam slid open the side door of the first van. Ramsey and Sandoval were sitting on the floor among the gear, holding their weapons. Dana and Carmi stood behind them, slightly stooped. Lanark and Hardin were in the other van parked just ahead. All, including Sutton in the panel truck, just brought in by helicopter, were interconnected by the radios, which were encoded and operating at a frequency where one would not expect voice transmission.

Sam was a little annoyed with himself. He'd overreacted by a factor of two; the operation was twice as conspicuous as need be. "They're making it easy for us," he said, sitting down cross-legged on the floor of the van. The response for this situation was obvious enough already that Dana and Carmi began to get their equipment organized. No real need for the extra van or the men in it, but they were already here, so there was no need to remove them. But Sutton didn't need to be on site to do what he needed to do. "Sutton."

"Yeah."

"Hold short."

"Roger."

"And give me phone patches to DC. I'm going to need the liaisons in Commerce, Interior, and HEW. Get them on line and standing by, but do not interconnect them."

"Working."

"Lanark and Hardin, stand by and stay inside."

"Understand."

Dana was in charge of his two-man team. "How much time?" asked Sam. He had trained his men to respond to such questions as accurately as possible. They were neither to give unrealistically long estimates of time, to insure that they could complete the task within their prediction and please him, nor to give impractically short estimates as an advertisement of their skills. In return, his men knew that Sam would accept the estimates and plan for them.

Dana glanced up. "Without going inside first?"

"Afraid so."

"And without plans for the building or jackhammers." Dana looked at Carmi. "Two hours. No. Two and a half."

"Problem," said Sam. "They want to be on the air in two."

"Think they'll make noise if they're not?" said Ramsey.

"Lots," said Sam. "They've thought this out pretty well. They've almost certainly got a television set up there. We could give them cameras, but they can tune in the local stations to see if they're really on the air. We can't fake it."

"Sure we can." It was Sutton, holding short in the communications truck. "An RF generator. It's what they put in home video recorders to play back through regular TV sets. Puts out a very low broadcast signal on a preset channel through the antenna leads. But kids have learned that if you connect the RF to an outside antenna, you can maybe punch a signal through so you can pick it up halfway down the block. Drives the FCC crazy." Sutton was starting to think it through as he talked. "We take their video and audio output, RF it, then send it back to them through the microwave dish on the TV station's remote truck . . . It'll be a tight beam, so it won't spill. I'll need crystals . . ."

"How long?" said Sam.

"Two hours, if I'm lucky with the Yellow Pages. Don't have an RF on board. I'll . . ." He stopped. "Shit. Stupid. Won't work."

Carmi and Dana stopped stowing their gear.

"There's already a signal on the channels," said Sutton. "They'll see garbage. They'll know they're being fucked over."

"No problem then," said Sam. "We take the station off the air. Lanark and Hardin."

"Listening," said Lanark from the second van.

"Locate the transmitter of the local network affiliate that's the furthest from their studio and hold short."

"That's probably the ABC affiliate," said Sutton. "I saw the transmitter site inbound from Tinker. Channel Five."

"Working," said Hardin. Sam heard the motor of the other van start and the vehicle pull away. "Sutton," said Sam, "come to the site and park across the street from our van, behind a pickup truck." He looked at Dana. "You guys ready?" Dana nodded. "Go to it."

"Right."

He touched Ramsey and Sandoval on the knee. "With me. Handguns, no rifles." He slid the door to the van back open and all five men got out. Dana and Carmi walked toward the building, carrying their gear in sacks. Sandoval and Ramsey, pistols jammed into their belts, followed Sam.

"You guys get the remote truck," said Sam as they crossed

the street. "Very quietly. No casualties." Sam opened the door to Lieutenant Wesley's pickup. "Bobby, we're going to need your truck." The policeman slid instantly out.

"Okay, Bobby," said Sam. Wesley watched the two men start off in his pickup and disappear around the corner. "Here's what you do. First you give me this." He took Wesley's hand radio. "Be sure to get yourself another one. You walk over to where your buddies are. I want all of you back in forty-five minutes in two regular marked police cars, everybody in uniform."

"Well, sir, I haven't worn a uniform in ten years."

"Find one that fits, Bobby. On my signal, I want you and your men to cut off traffic on this street and the one to the north, two blocks back. But until I give the signal, what do you do, Bobby?"

"Not a thing, no sir."

"Bobby, you're just getting better and better."

Molly Rice of *The New York Times* meets Larry Amble, director of media relations, EnconAmerica, in the lobby of the Holiday Inn in Ontonagon, Michigan. Jesus. Chatting and smiling at one another, she had allowed both of them enough time to compose lies and arrange strategies for a sprightly game of *What Does He Know I Know?*, using their simultaneous presence in this unlikely place as tokens. Certainly Amble would need no more than sixty seconds. One did not become director of media relations for a megacompany without landing on one's feet the first time, every time. In any event, the presence of Amble, whose job was to keep the press from knowing about his company's operations, meant the effective end of any eavesdropping. And pinning Amble up against the wall with what she called an "Ah-*ha*!" question—"Okay, buster, what are three hundred corporate jets doing parked at an airport on the north side of nowhere that isn't supposed to be here and what are *you* doing here yourself?"—would only result in Amble's increasing the size of his lies geometrically. That might be temporarily amusing—it was generally conceded among reporters that

Amble's lies were the most breathtaking in the New York market. But it would serve only to alert those gathered at the Federal Motors retreat that *The New York Times* was following them around. They'd go even deeper underground before Molly would have a chance to find out whatever it was they were hiding.

And Molly realized that even if she hadn't run into Amble, what really could she do here, incognito or out? Rent snowshoes, schuss out to the chalet, and stick a drinking glass and her ear to the wall? Even if she weren't eaten by timber wolves en route, she'd probably run into two security men per square yard.

When the elevator opened and Amble came back, precisely when Molly thought he would, he was smiling dazzlingly and saying "My God, that *was* Molly Rice, I guess my brain's been frozen." Molly decided to let the natural playing of roles happen. Amble became the pluperfect corporation flack sucking up to an important media type. The Holiday Inn was booked up, of course, but Amble told the clerk to let her have the room reservation of one of the guys in his party. Amble clapped his hands on her shoulder and steered her toward the bar. He said that he wasn't even going to offer to pick up her hotel bill because he knew the *Times* would have one of their piety attacks if he did.

They ordered drinks. He asked after Harland. He said he'd tried to learn how to snowmobile but the damn things scared him. When he finally smiled and very casually said, "And so. What're you doing here?" Molly realized that she'd forgotten to work out why. She was concurrently pleased with and appalled by the lies that slid effortlessly and, apparently, instinctively from her mouth. The pension fund of the iron-ore miners. Going broke. Mismanaged. Old retired miners getting ripped off. *Times* sent her up here to personalize it.

Amble immediately volunteered that Encon had sent him up here to FedMo's executive retreat for a training seminar. A think-tank conducted for its upwardly mobile younger executives. Bunch of other young execs from several companies here with him. Amble said that he guessed it meant the company had plans for him; he'd heard this cost the companies who sent guys here twenty grand a pop. Molly said congratulations, and Amble said thanks, but please not to print anything about his being here because it really meant that he was being anointed; and you know how it is in corporations, there were guys back in the office who'd push him out a window if they thought he was about to pass them on the way up.

So Molly improvised some more background on her pension-fund story, and the conversation was sustained the length of one more drink by New York media gossip. When their eyes met for the last time as Amble got off the elevator on his floor, there was admiration in hers and his for how well the other had played.

Sam scrubbed some of the pigeon droppings off the stairs with his shoe. He sat down and he took up the phone headset. "Well, asshole, you did better than I thought you would. ABC's going to put you on live, coast-to-coast TV at seven our time. The other two networks turned you down."

There was quiet on the line. Then: "We want all three. I said it wasn't negotiable."

"Look, asshole, you're lucky. All three said it was policy not to give in to any terrorist's demands for airtime, and ABC says it's carrying only on the basis of a news judgment. The other two will be taping and running highlights. I'm doing the best I can. I'm telling everybody you're hardened committed radicals who're prepared to carry out threats, although I imagine the truth is that we're dealing with a bunch of cocksucking invert candyass gutless wonders, huh?"

Sam heard a clatter on the line, then a new voice. "Look, man, where's the fucking TV trucks? We don't see no fucking TV trucks out there."

"On their way."

"You get the TV trucks here, you sumbitch. How'd you

like it if we kicked the plywood off these fucking windows and started blowing people away in downtown Oklahoma City?"

Sam waited a few beats, and then he spoke in tones of annoyance and impatience. "Come *on*, you guys, think this *out*. Think about how you're going to leave this hotel. A, you can come out walking, having had your TV show. If nobody's hurt, you're going to get five or six years in a minimum-security prison, tops. Shit, the way they kiss-ass people like you these days, you might get probation. Right now, somebody else is running this show. I'm just a messenger boy, reading the mail. But guys, you fire one shot out the window—at a person, a fucking pigeon, anything—and it's *my* show. That's B. One shot, and we take you out. All the way out, fuck the hostages. I got twelve guys in my squad, and they haven't killed anybody slowly since Nam, and they're *hungry*." Sam paused, then said in almost a croon: "We've already worked out the story, guys. See, we'll say afterward that you resisted, and we had to use tear gas, and the tear gas caught this shithouse on fire and you were so heroically committed you still wouldn't surrender. But what's really going to happen is that those of you we don't have to kill, we break your arms and your kneecaps, and then . . . Thermit, guys. We got five *pounds* of fucking Thermit, just for you. You won't believe it can take that long to die." Sam kissed the mouthpiece again and dropped the handset. It banged against the stair rails.

It had taken Lanark and Hardin, with the traffic, almost half an hour to find the transmitter site. "I want no signs of forcible entry, no signs of damage or vandalism," Sam had told them. "We'll keep the station off the air no longer than we have to. I want the station's signal to come back on as quickly as it went off." Hardin and Lanark acknowledged and held short.

Ramsey and Sandoval were having a harder time. They tried to locate a TV news truck out on the streets by calling the stations' newsrooms and saying they were an electronics-supply house, that the news truck crew had called and ordered some gizmo sent out immediately, that the delivery boy couldn't find them, that . . .

The first two stations had raised their news trucks on two-way radio. Sandoval heard the conversation; when the man at the station mentioned the electronics parts and the remote truck crew answered by saying they hadn't ordered any parts, Sandoval hung up.

But at the third and last station, the woman on duty in the newsroom simply asked the truck its location. Ramsey and Sandoval found it in Will Rogers Park. One of the men was stowing the small video camera, the other was coiling cable. Sandoval and Ramsey pulled up behind them in the pickup and approached, smiling, and displaying their weapons only when they got close.

Sandoval stayed in the back with the terrified TV crew while Ramsey drove. "Be on site in about twenty minutes," said Ramsey into his microphone. "Traffic's terrible." It was six-oh-five. Sutton had specified half an hour to rig up the RF generator. And that would put the truck at the site after the deadline. "Sandoval's going to anesthetize them," Ramsey reported.

"Negative on that," said Sam's voice. "They might need to help Sutton on the operation of the TV gear before you put them out."

"Roger," said Ramsey.

"Sutton."

"Yes, Sam."

"Put me through to Interior."

At six-twenty-nine, Sam looked out through the front door of the Drummer's Hotel and saw Ramsey pull up at the curb in a large panel truck. He had forgotten to tell Ramsey and Sandoval, but he was glad to see that they had anticipated him: The signs that identified the vehicle as a TV remote truck had been messily but effectively spray-painted over.

"Dana?" said Sam.

"Going as well as can be expected. Forty-five minutes."

"Lanark."

"Listening."

"You and Hardin secure and stand by."

The door to Channel 5's transmitter shack was locked. But it took the engineer inside only a brief look through the security viewport to satisfy himself it was okay to open. It was probably the logo on the hardhats and gray windbreakers Lanark and Hardin wore. The civilian design firm had been commissioned to develop a logo that meant nothing, was hard to remember, looked like that of the phone company, or the light company, or the gas company, or all three at once. And it did.

"Truck broke down," said Lanark. "Got a phone I can use to call my dispatcher?" The engineer let them in. After he determined there was no one else in the shack, Lanark pulled out his weapon. He aimed precisely at the engineer's throat. "Please walk directly over to the panel and put your hand on the switch that takes the station off the air," said Lanark. "Do it now." Never taking his eyes off the gun, flushing, gasping, nauseous with terror, the man felt his way backward toward a console, reached back, played his fingers over several switches, came to rest on one.

"Okay, okay," said Lanark. "You can sit down. You'll be fine. Just put your head between your legs and take some deep breaths and you won't feel so sick." Hardin switched his microphone back on. "Secured and standing by."

"Roger," said Sam. He walked into the Drummer's with a battery-powered television set from the remote truck. He went up the stairs and picked up the phone handset. "Okay, asshole," he said cheerfully. "You ready for your camera?"

"We're going to push out the plywood a little bit and let down a rope. Anybody extra we see on the sidewalk just below us gets blown away."

"Plywood's moving," said Sandoval in Sam's ear. "Rope's coming down . . . We're tying the camera cable to it . . ."

Sam put down the handset, cupped his hand over his microphone: "You put the plastic bag over it?"

"That's affirmative." A television camera being lifted up the side of an abandoned building could attract too much attention.

It was six-fifty. "Dana?" said Sam.

"I think I'm going to be able to give it to you early," said Dana. "Twenty minutes."

"I'll be ready in ten," said Sutton.

"Lanark," said Sam. "You hold in position. You might not have to pull the station off the air after all. I might be able to stall."

"They've got the camera inside," said Sandoval.

"They got the lens cap off," said Sutton from inside the remote truck.

Sam would not be able to see the picture the camera was taking until Sutton broadcast it out over the RF generator he was still setting up. Sam turned on his portable. Channel 5 was showing a game show. Sam picked up the two-way hand radio borrowed from Lieutenant Wesley. "Bobby? You there?"

"Yes sir, sure am."

"Let's stop the traffic, please." He put down the police radio. "Sutton? Can you see how many there are?"

"Negative, they're still moving the camera around too much, and it's too dark . . . Wait, they've turned lights on. Still can't see . . ." Sam heard a miniature voice calling over the handset. He picked it up.

"We're ready, we're ready. Let's get it on." Actually getting the camera had put the people upstairs in a more buoyant mood.

"Uh . . . it looks like they're having some trouble with the transmission lines," said Sam over the phone. "They're just not going to make seven o'clock. Sorry about that."

The gunmen upstairs had rediscovered their commitment. "You are turning us on, man, and you are turning us on right *fucking* now."

"Sandoval here. Looks like they're kicking out two of the sheets of plywood. Eighth floor."

"Tell them two minutes," Sutton answered.

"Okay, okay," Sam told the terrorists. "They're just about ready. One minute. They tell me one minute."

Sam heard a thud on the sidewalk. "Plywood came off," said Sandoval. "I can see them at the window. Two of them. They've got M-16s. Oh Jesus. They've got grenades."

"Traffic stopped yet?"

"That's affirmative."

Sam said into the phone: "Okay, so it's not going to be a minute. It's going to be more like two minutes, maybe three—"

"You don't *have* another fucking minute, man."

Sam heard three sharp cracks. "They're firing into the air out the window," said Sandoval. Three shots. Three shots might get lost in the background noise of the city. But if they were to start firing again . . . Sam stared for a second at the television on the stairs beside him. The network movie, *The Deep*, was just beginning. "Lanark."

"Listening."

"Pull the plug."

The credits for *The Deep* were suddenly replaced with loud static on the screen. Over the phone, Sam heard cheers, hand-clapping from upstairs, someone saying "Aw-*right!*"

"Sutton, you ready?" said Sam with surprising evenness, considering there was no alternative to an affirmative answer.

Sam heard Sutton's voice in his ear and over the TV set: "We . . . interrupt this program to bring you a . . . uh, special broadcast from Oklahoma City, Oklahoma."

Sutton sounded nothing like a network television announcer, but the people upstairs were too euphoric to notice. When the picture appeared on the screen, dodging about as the camera was held in someone's unsteady hand, the man talking into it seemed convinced he was talking to the whole nation.

Four middle-aged men—some of the hostages—sat in a row on half-broken derelict furniture, shading their eyes from the brutal lights. Three people—two men and a woman—stood by proudly with their weapons, guarding them. More figures moved in the murk at the edge of the lights. Terrorists didn't look like terrorists anymore, Sam thought. They were young, neutrally dressed. All average. The low power of the RF generator made the picture on the screen ghosty and snowy on Sam's TV; it would look that way on the set upstairs too, but Sam doubted they would notice that either.

The camera zoomed in clumsily to the young man, who was telling his audience that they were witnessing proceedings of their own people's court, the last place of true justice in this country, and that the defendants would confess their part in a conspiracy between business and the government to destroy the whole country in exchange for a few kilowatts of electricity.

Sam didn't need to ask Lanark if the phone in the transmitter shack was already ringing. It would be. How long before a confrontation? Maybe two minutes for the engineers at the station to decide that the transmitter shack wasn't going to answer. Then how long? Ten minutes? Fifteen minutes until someone got to the transmitter to find out what was wrong?

And then suddenly Channel 5 was back on the air. *The Deep* and the image of the terrorists were layered on top of each other, a surreal montage of Nick Nolte swimming through a hotel room full of bewildered looking people.

"Shit." It was Sutton. "Fucking back-up transmitter. They must have a low-power emergency transmitter at another location."

Over the phone headset, Sam could hear the immediate reaction: Shouts, outrage, fear, something smashing. "*What is this shit?*" was screamed into the phone, then it was yanked away and another voice screamed: "You *fucking* us around?" The phone was dropped and Sam could hear fierce argument and panic: They should waste a hostage. They should waste all the hostages. It was a trap, and they should forget the hostages and get out.

There was a fury of small explosions on the stairs beside Sam, and the portable TV blew apart. Sam rolled away without thinking of what he'd done. They were firing down the stairwell.

"Sandoval, are they firing out the windows?"

"Not yet."

"Do not return fire. Dana, we're going to have to go now. If we go now, will it work?"

"It won't work now. If you give me thirty seconds, maybe it'll work."

Sam pulled his six-shot pistol out of his belt and wished for his .22 machine gun with the laser sighting. He heard people coming quickly down the stairs, ran down around the landing as another burst of automatic fire was fired down the stairwell. He half-stumbled into the reeking lobby and tried to make his eyes work. There was only a metallic blue column of light coming in the door from the mercury-vapor streetlights outside. On the ceiling above him, sounds of several people, running. The sounds crossed to his right to a point behind the old registration desk and descended. *Another stairway*.

Shoulders were being thrown into a door behind the desk. The wall vibrated. The warren of mail boxes worked loose and crashed to the floor. The door gave and a man with an M-16 rifle stumbled through and caught himself from falling by grabbing the edge of the registration desk.

To Sam's left, two shadows: Dana and Carmi. "Hold short," said Sam, and they pulled back into shadow. Sam knew the man with the M-16 would fire at his voice, so he was already starting down. The burst hit the wall above him. Sam stuck his pistol out and fired three times in the direction of the noise. He knew he wouldn't hit anything—the man with the rifle had dropped behind the registration desk. He wanted to give Dana and Carmi a safe path out the door.

"Go," said Sam. "Right behind you." He fired two more shots as Dana and Carmi ran past and out the door.

The man with the M-16 wanted out more than he wanted Sam, and he was closer to the door. He stood up, fired another burst in Sam's general direction, and made for the door. Sam raised himself on one elbow and fired his last round, a fair-to-middling shot that knocked the man's legs out from under him and made him scream with pain.

It was thirty feet across the lobby to the rectangle of cold blue light outside. As Sam pushed himself into a crouch, slipping in something unspeakable, he saw that the man was pulling himself into a sitting position and leveling the M-16. Sam ran for the light. He weaved and kept low. He knew evasion was useless this close to an M-16, but it made him feel better. Through the door Sam saw that Dana and Carmi had stopped in the middle of the street. He saw the reflection of the sterile street light describe a slab of blue silver in Dana's hand.

"*Shoot it,*" Sam screamed. "*Shoot it, shoot it.*"

Movement in Dana's hand. He held a box.

Sam sensed the firing of the M-16 as a bright pressure from his right, and a contrapuntal explosion from his left that chipped shards of glass and wood into his face as the slugs hit the door jamb.

But more he sensed the great growing swelling from beneath him, the compression of all the air around him into a smothering density that would drown him if he didn't get out on the sidewalk, out into the street—away.

Sutton, looking at the monitor in the remote truck, saw a cubist fantasy. Before the lights in the Drummer's Hotel went out, the walls and ceilings of the room, still full of frightened hostages, went gently out of plumb. They drifted away from each other; right angles became acute or obtuse, and there was a sudden frost of plaster. The horizon tilted slowly, the faces of the hostages contorted as they floated gently up from the floor. They became lazy, silly balloons, their arms and legs flailing, crashing into each other and the furniture as the screen went dark. Sutton heard the audio for another second: grinding noises, and screaming.

Lieutenant Wesley, two blocks away, felt it through his feet. He saw fistulas of dust escape from the base of the Drummer's and then saw the old building begin to fold in on itself, its middle descending straight down, the sides leaning over to occupy that space, the whole structure dropping without preamble or reason into the boil of dust that consumed it.

The instant creation of void made an acrophobe of Wesley

on the spot, and he was slammed with a sudden spatial disorientation. That, the cold, sweaty fear and confusion, the simple refusal of his mind to accept what he'd just seen, all combined to pass vertigo over Wesley at the same time that the dust cloud reached him. He staggered to the curb and sat heavily upon it.

Wesley had not moved from that spot when the silver van, followed by the remote truck, emerged from the settling cloud of dust. He stared in the direction of the Drummer's and thought that somewhere under there were . . . twelve people? Twenty? He kept staring even as Ramsey stopped the van and Sam got out.

"Bobby," said Sam. Bobby was aware of sirens, lots of them, approaching from several directions. "You're going to have a hell of a mess here, but we've helped you out a little. When the media asks you what happened here, you can tell them this story, and it'll check out right down the line. Bobby? Are you listening to me now?"

Wesley felt his head nodding.

"You tell them that this afternoon the judge lifted the injunction against the demolition of the building. That the city decided to go ahead and bring it down immediately to avoid further litigation and possible confrontation with protestors. They got explosive-demolition contractors in from out of state, and it went off perfectly. Which it did. I don't think my men dropped more than two truckloads of brick on the sidewalk."

"Those people . . ."

"Tomorrow, Bobby, the city's going to announce that they've gotten a grant from the federal government for landscaping these miniparks, that instead of paying for what's left of the hotel to be hauled away, they're just going to cover it with dirt and contour it and seed it and make a nice little grassy knoll for the office workers to eat their lunch on." No need, thought Sam, for the cop to know about the hallucinogen that was given the TV remote truck crew and the transmitter engineer that would make them recurrently psychotic for two to six weeks and hopelessly jumble their perception of what had happened to them for a good week on either side of today. Unpleasant, thought Sam, but he was sure they would prefer it to the traditional alternative.

"And here's the keys to your truck, Bobby." Sam was holding them out. "It's out in Will Rogers Park. Bobby?" The policeman made no move to take them, so Sam dropped them into the pocket of his coat. "You did a terrific job. Really. You—"

And then Wesley had Sam by the jacket front, twisting the fabric to match the risus of revulsion and sick fear on his face. "*Jesus Christ, who are you people? Who the shit are you?*"

Sam smiled and very gently untangled Wesley's fingers from his jacket.

"Consultants, Bobby," he said. Sam got back into the van, and they pulled away. They were just about out of sight when the fire truck and Channel 9's remote news truck pulled up.

6

HARLAND COULD SEE THROUGH THE GRILLE OF THE MAILBOX IN
the lobby of his building that it hadn't been emptied; and that
meant that, despite most of an afternoon of his wishing for it,
Molly hadn't come home.

Had she come home before him, she would have taken the
mail up. Had they walked into the building together, Molly
would have sped up a couple of steps to beat him to the
mailboxes.

"Jesus, what is it?" Harland had said after they'd started living together. "You're compulsive about this. Do you think I'm
going to microfilm your mail?"

"All right. You got it. I'm compulsive about mail," Molly had
said, roiling up the contents of her purse. She could never find
the mailbox key. "It's a childhood thing. I was always writing
off for things. Books. Pamphlets. Shit from the government,
and I got a bigger rush if I got it out of the mailbox myself.
Opening mailboxes excites me. Will you get off my case?"

"Hmmmm," said Harland. "Have you seen a shrink about
this?"

"Just give me the key, asshole," Molly had said.

Harland had learned to be ready for the contents of the mailbox to leap out upon being opened, spring-loaded by Molly's magazines crammed inside. She was also compulsive about subscribing to magazines. They teetered in perilous stacks all over her study, unread. "I'll *get* to them, I'll *get* to them," she would say. Most of Molly's pleasure came from their reception. He had counted her subscriptions once: thirty-three. She usually tried to cover for her addiction by saying that she was thinking of doing a story on whatever subject the newly subscribed magazine specialized in. For twelve months she'd even subscribed to *Casket and Sunnyside*, the trade magazine of the funeral industry.

Today had brought *The New Republic*, *Newsweek*, and a new one: *Byte*, which was full of schematic diagrams of computers. The bizarre mix of her subscriptions landed her on a welter of mailing lists of organizations that extrapolated her politics from her reading material. Harland saw by return address on today's direct-mail pieces that she was being solicited for funds by both the Save the Whales Committee and the Pro-Life Caucus.

Harland was careful about his address. He didn't mind billing computers exchanging it with other computers. He semi-hid behind his blandly common WASPish surname and the initials J. L. He corresponded with humans only on CBS stationery. None of the *Times* people had found out where he lived, and the strangers who buttonholed him in the building lobby had been even remotely pleasant. The buttonholers were either endlessly tedious nutcases, or they were simply fans whose effusions sent Molly into one of her "Jesus Christ, *show* business" tirades. Or into manic acts of impatience, such as when Molly dragged him away from four Cliffies with booming reminders of the really swell blowjob awaiting him upstairs.

He was a bit disturbed to see the handwritten envelope among the computer-addressed ones. Harland's correspondent had carefully included, as if to make a point that he knew it,

Harland's middle initial and apartment number. Not the Moonies, thought Harland as he sat down at his desk and took up a letter opener. Dear God, don't let the Moonies have my home address.

Inside the letter was a three-by-five plain white index card. Typed on one side: PHOTO OPPORTUNITY. Sundown. January tenth.

Had Harland received this at the office, it would have been sentenced to the wastebasket by now, guilty of being uninteresting. But because the correspondent knew his home address, it worried him a little; and that he was worried even a little annoyed him. It was almost certainly nothing to be worried about, and yet he was going to have to take some time and effort to figure out just *why* it was nothing to be worried about.

It was either A, a joke performed by a colleague, because the phrase "photo opportunity" was unused outside journalism and politics. It appeared on the itineraries issued by politicians' press offices: "The President will greet tourists at ten a.m. in the Portico. Photo opportunity." It meant an occasion when photographers and newspapers could shoot the politician doing essentially nothing and the stuff would still end up on the air. The press secretaries loved it; it got air time, and the politician would not have to say anything, since saying anything was always potentially disadvantageous.

Or it was B, meaningless, the utterly inconsequential act of a crank who'd copied it down from where he'd seen it and mailed it off to Harland and Chancellor and Brinkley and Walters and Reynolds for whatever eel-brained reason made sense to him when he did it.

Or it was C, for a reason not evident until later.

Or it was D, none of the above, and he shouldn't worry about it.

"D," said Harland. *And anyway*, he thought, looking at the day-by-day calendar on his desk, *it's already the—No. That was yesterday*. He laid the card on the page saying January tenth and turned the calendar. *It's five-thirty on January tenth al-*

ready. A case of someone putting too much childlike trust in the U.S. Postal Service.

What do you expect? Harland thought. *It's a nutcase.*

Harland was reading and had dozed off. The phone awoke him. He was pretty sure it was Molly. When one of them was on the road, he or she always tried to call the apartment about this time of night.

He picked up the phone by the bed. "Don't tell me. Only twenty-four hours away from me, and you can't take it anymore. You tried getting it off with a pro football player you met in the hotel bar, but it was no good. With anybody else, no bells, no rockets. Face it, kid, once a lady has been dorked by the champ—"

"How do you know that the only reason you get anything at all isn't that I'm screwing all the network anchors on assignment from *Ms.?*"

"You sound a long way off," said Harland, listening to the microwave links breathe over the connection. "Are you anyplace interesting?"

"I am *no*place interesting. And tired. What's the time in New York and what's happening back there?"

"You got a dun from Saks. They say that if you don't pay up, they're going to turn your account over to the Bonano family. It's a postcard, for maximum humiliating effect."

"Oh shit. Will you pay it? Put the bill in my checkbook." Harland missed her so palpably that he put his hand on the place where her hip would be when, taking a break from working in her study, she would come into the bedroom and lie with her head on his shoulder as he read in bed. "Any idea when you're coming home?"

"Nah. Why, are you thinking of giving away my clothes?"

"Selling them."

"I'm so tired I forgot why I called you."

"No you haven't."

"No, I haven't. I called to tell you I love you like a bandit."

7

As they could recall where they were when they heard that President Kennedy had been assassinated, they would all remember where they were on January tenth.

Jack Bethune was heading north on State 23 in his new half-ton pickup, wasn't more than two months old, had less than four hundred miles on it. Each time he'd retell it, he'd move himself and the truck a few yards closer to the track.

Mabel Orchard remembers that it was starting to get cold and it looked like snow. She will start to say after a few retellings that she had a funny feeling at the time. You know, like something was going to happen.

Bill Kellersberger knows that he was heading south on State 23 and he had just crossed the tracks, because he remembers looking over at the Fina station and seeing poor Pokey Bower standing there at the self-service pumps, filling up the auxiliary tanks on his camper. Poor old Pokey had waved at him. Bill Kellersberger will shake his head and say Boy, if I had been just half a second longer at the Western Auto store . . .

Harry Lemon wouldn't remember anything. He was the first one in town to die.

Harry was heading North on State 23, a few hundred yards ahead of Jack Bethune, when he saw the warning signals on the MKT tracks start flashing. Like everybody else who lived in town, he knew the rhythm of the signal, knew how long he'd have before the barricade arm dropped over the road. It clanged and flashed annoyingly often for the temperament of the citizens; the town was effectively divided in half by the MKT tracks. Damn coal trains, thought Harry. All times of the day and night, taking that Western anthracite east. We get all the noise from coal and none of the bucks. Seems as though everybody west of Kansas City was getting rich off Western coal except Kansas. Harry thought about getting up another petition to get that coal moving by a slurry pipeline, preferably one going smackdab through his nine hundred acres. Somebody besides the damn railroads ought to get some of all that money those New Yorkers were paying for electricity.

He could have beaten the barrier arm, but he dropped the pickup out of gear and coasted up to the tracks. He had time. He looked left, to the west, and saw the glimmer of the train's headlights. Might be a coal train, thought Harry, not without pleasure. He was always impressed by the simple mass of the huge trains.

Yep, coal train. Looks like six or seven engines. Jee-sus. *Look at that sumbitch.* He could feel it now, a bass rumble resonating in his sternum. Harry thought he saw a brief light, fifty yards away from him. Reflection of the headlight off the tracks. But there was a puff of smoke with it, what looked like rocks flying up. The tracks looked like plastic, like . . .

There was the briefest scream of metal trying to brake on metal, and then Harry saw the engine nose down off the tracks, saw the front bite into the roadbed. The lead engine lifted easily off the ground. Harry, unmoving, followed it up into the air with his eyes, peripherally aware of the second engine leaving the tracks, starting to spin on its axis, the third beginning to leave the tracks behind it. Harry thought of the time his older brother, back in Ogallah, had thrown the engine of a toy train at him. It had floated like that.

The engine came back to earth directly on top of Harry Lemon's pickup.

There were seven engines in all, and one hundred and seven cars full of anthracite, and a caboose. When the engineer had started braking after he'd seen the rails blow up in front of him, pitiably late, the train was traveling east at fifty-four miles per hour.

Jack Bethune reflexively stomped on his brakes and turtled his head between his shoulders, not knowing exactly what had happened, aware only of an impossible mass entering his field of vision. He saw Harry Lemon's pickup stick briefly to the side of the lead engine as it started to spin, then saw centrifugal force expel it, like a tin can briefly adhering to a tire, in an arc eastward down the tracks. The second and third engines followed the leader, both staying roughly upright. But the fourth and fifth fell off to the north of the tracks, through the storefronts housing the county agricultural extension office and the barber shop. The sixth crashed into the second and third. And the seventh fell to the south and passed through the space occupied by the Fina station and poor motionless Pokey Bower, still filling his camper tanks at the self-service pumps. There was a flash of orange flame as the exhaust manifold sizzled in the spume of gasoline.

The engines had dammed the tracks, and the train was turning itself into flotsam. The first twelve cars were melded within two seconds into a drifting mound of coal and transfigured metal almost forty feet tall, spilling over the space just occupied by the Fina station. The next dozen or so cars compressed and distorted and spewed their cargo forward, but they didn't break their linkage. It was two hundred yards behind the first wreckage that the cars started leaving the tracks again. Some skidded into the support of the water tower, whose metal latticework screamed and folded. And one leaped a drainage ditch and entered the schoolyard.

Mabel Orchard remembers it heading directly toward her, this absurd escapee car with its steel wheels skiing through the dirt in search of rails. She had no time to do more than grab the child nearest her and pull him to the floor with her. The car turned over and caught a utility shed and several trees no less than fifty feet from the school. It stopped there, but it sent a horizontal hailstorm crashing through Mabel Orchard's classroom window. The coal bounced off the walls and floors among the screaming children, endlessly.

There was a floodtide of hard blackness through the town. It pushed in the front of the Western Auto, buried cars in front of the post office. Jack Bethune didn't see it happen, heard only an impossible noise, a sentient thing, and felt his pickup being pushed to the right, saw his windshield and rear window shatter. When he started breathing again and tried to open his door, he saw that his truck was half buried in blackness.

The fire that started at the Fina station had been smothered under fifteen feet of coal, but the wrenched steel of the coal cars allowed it draft. Within fifteen minutes, the interior of the drift of coal was burning with the intensity of a coke oven. The dazed Sundown volunteer fire department sprinkled the pile with what little water could be coaxed from the tilted water tower. It suffused State 23 with red as snow clouds brought darkness faster.

They were not professional firefighters. None of them thought about the gasoline storage tanks directly beneath it. Just after dark, the concrete cracked from the heat, and the fire collapsed upon the fiberglass gas tanks. Ten seconds later, five thousand gallons of gasoline exploded.

The train killed eighteen people that day.

It was to have been the first of the four consecutive assignment-free days Harland had been promised so he could finish the Vandellen piece. It was about two o'clock when Jerry Lee came in.

"Spool it up, kid," said Lee. "You're going to work." Harland turned around, prepared to be annoyed at the breach of managerial promise. But he saw that although one side of Jerry's mouth was turned up in the cynical grin that greeted news of the President's daughter's toothache or of war in the Middle

East, his eyes were scared; and Harland had never seen Jerry scared.

"Chicago's blacked out."

"Jesus," said Harland.

"Indianapolis is blacked out, Cincinnati is blacked out, Milwaukee is blacked out."

"*Jesus.*"

"They're trying to save Detroit." Jerry held the door open for Harland. "I hope you've been buying Krugerrands."

At two minutes after three, they lost Detroit.

Harland had wanted, instinctively, to go to Chicago, while it was still light. Maybe a charter plane could land. He loved working stories where thousands of persons were uniformly affected, where the competition among his colleagues was at its most intense. It was the one time when he felt the power of his name and of CBS News. Because they helped him do his job better, he felt no embarrassment in their use.

"You're staying here," said Len, the *Evening News* producer. "Walter's going to hand off to you, and you'll subanchor the coverage."

"That's what Upstairs wants?" said Harland.

"Star time, ace," said Jerry Lee, passing.

Harland worked hard. He watched the newstape from affiliate stations in the blackout area, ghostly and snowy from being transmitted using inadequate emergency power, and wrote his lead-ins for them. He looked over the backgrounders the research girls had brought in on the Federal Midwestern Power Grid Act. He went through three drafts to explain it in the very few words television journalism allowed him. He read it aloud to time it:

" 'The cities' going black one by one, like lights on a Christmas tree, was made possible by the same system created to prevent it. The interconnection of the cities' power-generation capabilities was forced by the federal government despite the objections of the power companies, which didn't like the idea of sending the electricity they made beyond their own billing areas. It was supposed to give one city the capability of drawing surplus power from other cities to see it through emergencies. Instead, chaining the cities together meant that one dragged down the next, like a drowning man taking his rescuers with him. And all because of three bolts of lightning . . .' "

A little after four, Jerry Lee came over with two cups of coffee and put one in front of Harland. "It's sabotage, Johnny."

"Can't be. Rotten luck, and rotten design, yeah. That system has two hundred and eleven separate generating plants. You can't . . ." Harland could tell from Lee's expression that he was not speculating. "You talked with somebody?"

"Guy I know in the Department of Energy. The lightning story is a cover. Some chutzpah, huh, trying to get God to take the fall?"

"But sabotage . . . Jesus, you'd need an air force."

"If you know how the system works, all you need are wire cutters. Shit, bobby pins. The guys who brought the system down did it with five routine outages at exactly the right places, at exactly the right intervals. They're scared at Energy. Nobody is supposed to know what these guys know. Nobody."

"Any idea who?"

"Commies. Extraterrestrials. Republicans. The Toronto Blue Jays. They'll speak up and take credit. They didn't go to all this trouble not to raise their little hands and grin."

Credit was taken shortly after five o'clock. Simultaneous calls were made to the New York and Washington newsrooms of *The New York Times*, the Associated Press, United Press International, and the networks, telling them where to find dupes of the same audio cassette at drops near their offices. CBS's copy was taped under a table in the restaurant in the building lobby.

"This is Green Earth," said the woman's soft, intense voice from the cassette player. "We claim responsibility for the interruption of electrical service in the Midwest, and for stopping the transportation of illegally mined coal . . ."

"What's this coal bit?" someone said.

"Just came over the wire," someone answered. "Blew up a coal train out in Kansas somewhere. Bunch of people killed."

"My God . . ."

"... and our resistance will become more severe. We have no reason to regret what may appear to some as the suffering of innocent people. In a nation that permits its environment, the irreplaceable natural beauty of its last pure places, to be raped for anthracite coal, there are no innocents. This is Green Earth."

"These guys are cuties," said Jerry Lee into the brief silence that followed the end of the tape. "I mean, they know their media. They obviously could have taken out New York if they wanted to, but all the national media are here and they didn't want to cut into their coverage. So they go to work in the Midwest and give us plenty of lead time to get our coverage together. And we give them maximum minutes. They're playing us like clarinets."

A few seconds before they were to come back to Harland at the end of the newscast's first commercial, the director spoke to him through the earphone he wore throughout the show. "We just got a live feed from Kansas on the train crash. Go to it instead of the Washington reaction. You're going to have to ad-lib the lead-in. The reporter's name doing the mobile stand-up on the video is Bill Kokesh."

Harland had time only to write down Kokesh's name on his news script before he heard the audio monitor cut out as the commercial ended. He looked up for the camera's lens just before the red light went on. "We now have first film from Kansas, where the terrorists who call themselves Green Earth claim to have sabotaged a coal train yesterday, killing eighteen. Here is CBS correspondent Bill Kokesh."

He saw from the corner of his eye the studio monitor switch smoothly to pictures of piles of coal and twisted metal. Harland reached under his studio podium and picked up the phone that connected him to the *Evening News* producer in the control room. "How long is this?"

"Forty seconds plus change."

"After it, do I do the Washington reaction or go back to Walter?"

"Do Washington reaction. We'll trim later in the show."

"Gotcha." Harland hung up and reviewed the two sentences that would lead into the Washington feed. "Coming to you in fifteen," said the floor man. Harland nodded. His eyes wandered back to the studio monitor. They hadn't cut the audio back on in the studio, but the pictures made sense without words. A jumble of metal twisted beyond comprehension of its original form. A railroad car overturned very close to a school. Smoldering piles of coal.

Twisted stanchions of a water tower, listing madly. *Looks a lot like the water tower back in Angleton*, Harland thought as the camera tilted up. Kids had climbed it, written "Seniors '73" on the side, next to the name of the town.

Sundown.

Molly was at the dead end of another ad-libbed day, and in a Holiday Inn without even a toothbrush or a change of underwear. The toothbrush she bought from one of those depressing vending machines in the lobby, the underwear she washed out. She was too tired to work, so she guiltlessly turned on the television, and saw John Harland looking back at her from the screen.

"Well, Harland, what are you doing at this time of night?" said Molly, who always talked back to Harland when he was on television, especially when he was on videotape and they were in the apartment together and she knew he could hear her.

"Son of a *bitch*," she said after a few moments' watching. She had heard, peripherally in the bar, about Detroit blacking out. The outage stopped short of the upper peninsula. But she hadn't realized, until she saw Harland on the CBS News special report, the extent of the blackout, or that it had been the work of terrorists. Harland was talking about the kind of looting that was going on in darkened Detroit and Chicago—not the communal exploitation of a New York summertime blackout, but the desperate grasping of cold, frightened people trying to improvise their own survival: portable heaters, blankets. Death from carbon monoxide poisoning as people burned charcoal in fake fireplaces. As water pipes began to burst, the city faced the destruction of its sanitation system. The overnight low in Chicago was expected to be nine degrees. The President was thinking of declaring a national state of emergency.

Green Earth said that the outage was designed so that Detroit and most of the blacked-out area could be brought back after eight hours. But Chicago, because the city was building three "irresponsible" new nuclear plants, would need three days to come back alive.

It would take four. From Columbus to Milwaukee to Cleveland, more than eight hundred people would freeze to death.

Molly thought of calling in to the *Times*, telling them where she was and volunteering to help work the story. But she couldn't get an LD line in any direction but west; and anyway, there wasn't much she could have done.

The Michigan television stations were staying on the air twenty-four hours with blackout coverage, and Molly went to sleep watching it.

Detroit's power was back on by the time she woke up. That the weather had stayed clear and snow-free was the one thing that had kept the blackout from becoming utter catastrophe. Unfortunately, there was snow on the upper peninsula. Molly had awakened to it. She cursed, called the FBO at the airfield, and was told what she had feared: There was too much snow for a pilot with her limited cold-weather experience even to think about flying.

She had to kill the rest of the day. It died hard: Three meals, the third of which she ate exclusively from boredom. She bought shampoo and washed her hair. She bought two crummy paperback novels and read them. She watched crummy prime-time TV. She washed out her underwear again and slept.

The next morning was clear, and the FBO had his strip plowed early.

Molly flew the Cessna back to the Detroit area smoothly. But landing at Detroit City, an uncontrolled field where hundreds of aircraft were making up for delayed arrivals and departures, was one of the most harrowing things she'd ever done in an airplane.

On the way back she'd given intense thought to Fourteenmile Point. Whatever was going on there, Encon was in on it, and Larry Amble knew about it. He might not be part of the process; the deals being cut at Fourteenmile might be of such consequence and secrecy that media-relations vice presidents were around just as towel boys. But Amble knew about it. Molly decided to move in on Amble. Might as well. She knew of nowhere else to move in.

The Pinto's radio was still full of blackout coverage as she drove back to the car-rental agency. She saw a few looted shops, but not as many as she'd have thought. The *Times* Op-Ed Page's instant sociologists were certainly at this moment cranking out interpretive pieces explaining just how the pathology of a winter blackout is different from a summer blackout.

The cabdriver who took her from the car-rental agency back to her hotel said he couldn't wait for the next blackout because he'd made a fortune, been up for thirty hours straight now, that if somebody hailed the cab with a new TV under his arm that still had the tags hanging off the cords, he didn't ask no questions, he just charged 'em twenty bucks flat to take 'em anywhere they wanted, provided they was white.

Back at the hotel, Molly changed her underwear just on principle and decided she'd better call in to see if she still had a job.

"Well, hello, Lennie," said Molly when her editor, Leonard Gass, picked up his extension. "I see the phones are still working. Does that mean we publish tomorrow?"

"I have enough paranoid people right here in the city room without getting it long distance," said Gass. "Where are you?"

"Detroit. Who's supposed to be buying us today?"

"If you believe the *Daily News* this morning, it's Knight-Ridder. If you believe *Newsweek*, as leaked to Associated Press, it's Atlantic Richfield."

"Atlantic Richfield? Shit, that's right, they bought that English paper."

"They're buying the *Times* already, a page at a time, with those ads telling the country how good three-dollar-a-gallon gas is going to be for us. I guess they figure they might as well get the whole thing. Or, if you believe what I heard from an anonymous source in the next crapper in the men's room, it's Murdoch. He's buying the *Times* and folding the *Post*." Gass was trying to match Molly's tone, but she could hear in his voice the force necessary to make it sound light.

"Geez, Lennie, then I guess I'd better stop things like expense-accounting two hotel rooms the last two nights. The paper's cash-flow is gonna look so grim the Sulzbergers aren't going to be able to unload this turkey."

"Two hotel rooms?"

"I was chasing somebody and didn't have time to check out."

"Well, live it up, dear. There's no tomorrow."

Molly felt Gass's fear start to seep out of the phone; to stop it from spreading to her, she would talk about the story.

"I'm onto something."

"That's nice."

"However, I don't know what 'something' is. But . . . it roughly confirms what our Mr. Nervous was hinting at, and I'm going to chase it a little more, if it's okay."

"It's okay."

"Favor: Ask a newsclerk to check out with the FAA these aircraft registration numbers and see who they belong to. These are big-mother, corporation jets." Molly read off the numbers of the only two planes stuffed into the FedMo hangar at Fourteenmile Point she'd been able to remember long enough to scrawl down on her sectional map.

"And so now I'm going on to Houston," said Molly.

"Fine, dear," said Gass. "Call in after you get there. And do something for me, dear?"

"Virtually anything, Lennie."

"Fly first class. If Atlantic Richfield buys us, I think we have a moral obligation to cut as deep as we can into their first-quarter earnings."

She flew first class, which *Times* wage slaves were not supposed to do unless firsts were the only seats left on the only flight remaining. She'd called ahead to Houston before she left. Tom Evan's secretary said he was out of the office until Friday and who was calling, please? Molly said that she was Ethel Griffies from the Philadelphia *Bulletin*, and that she'd call back tomorrow to confirm an appointment, if she could be positive that Mr. Evan would be in Friday. Positive, his secretary said. At nine o'clock.

Molly decided to be waiting in ol' Tom's Encon Building office at nine Friday morning and just let ol' Tom walk in and discover her there.

One reason that ol' Tom Evan worked for Larry Amble and Larry Amble didn't work for ol' Tom Evan was that ol' Tom Evan didn't always come up on his feet.

8

Long ago, Harland realized that the most depressing thing about traveling was the ride in from the airport. No matter how new and glorious the airport, the route to his hotel always took him through the armpits of a city. On pain of motion sickness within three paragraphs, Harland could not read in buses, cars, or on choppy plane flights. He had no choice but to stare out the windows at whatever aesthetic horror show was going past the freeway: a wastepaper plant beside a torpid gray-green river of some sort, a ghetto, and then, for an alarming amount of time, nothing but concrete slab as the freeway dropped below ground level into an endless interchange complex. The city slid past over his head.

So much, thought Harland, for the promise of four days to work on the Vandellen piece. One of his colleagues had come down with a sudden virus, and Upstairs had decided Harland should cover the high-level conference in her place.

"Know why?" Jerry Lee had said; Jerry Lee claimed to know the dark, true meaning behind everything Upstairs did. "Because, for a change, they expect some good news about energy to come out of this. The guys up in Strangelove"—

Lee's name for the psychological-testing firm CBS was alleged to have retained for predicting news viewers' likes and dislikes —"they figure that Harland needs some cozying up with *positive* values after all this negative association he got anchoring the blackout coverage. Upstairs can't afford to let their chosen boy turn *off* Mr. and Mrs. America because he brings them nothing but *bad* news, can they?"

Harland had laughed it off. But he knew for a fact that at frequent intervals the consulting firm would show videotapes of Harland, other CBS correspondents, and rivals at other networks to people with galvanometers attached to their palms. And every time, the readings indicated that more and more people liked John Harland best. And that, and not his thirteen years in the business and his Emmy and the respect of his colleagues, was why he was maybe going to replace Mr. C. And he did not like the way that knowledge made him feel. Namely, pleased.

As Harland was paying off the cab in front of the hotel, he saw the first familiar face—the energy reporter from *Newsweek*—and waved at him. Harland had once described the national-correspondent business as one long out-of-town game; the same faces assembling, disassembling after the event was over, reassembling again at an unlikelier place later. You wouldn't know where, or when, or why; but you'd know who'd be there.

There were two ahead of him at the registration desk. As he made the first scooch forward of his suitcase with his toe, there was a completely recognizable voice behind him: "We can't go on meeting like this." Trish Denning, ABC News.

Harland turned to smile at her, already knowing what he'd see: the tumble of carefully casual blond hair; the aviatrix glasses, lightly tinted yellow; the beige pantsuit, two buttons too many open at the neck; two strands of ultrathin gold chain around the neck. Harland smiled to keep from laughing. If a movie producer had sent for actresses to play a successful woman network news correspondent, Trish Denning would have been rejected immediately as too on-the-nose, and the producer would look down the line for someone who looked less like a living cliché. Her egocentrism, abrasiveness, and naked ambition were legend among the transmedia traveling squad, even though her professionalism was unquestioned. And she worked harder than anybody on the tour. Molly, who was a member before the *Times* put her on investigative projects, had once predicted that "sometime, somewhere, somebody is going to slip that nerd an explosive Tampax."

Consequently, no one but Harland, who was fascinated by Trish's ongoing self-creation, would speak more than three consecutive sentences to her. She responded with flagrant attempts at seduction and self-serving, bitter monologues about her industry rep: "My God, do you know how much shit I have to take to get taken seriously in this business? Okay, so I'm pretty. Jesus Christ, I can't help it if I'm pretty. Would I make a better reporter if I had my face put through a windshield?"

Once a rumor had gone around that her unlikely Cosmo-girl slick-fiction name was the invention of her first news director; in response, Trish had taken to carrying around a Xerox copy of her sixth-grade report card. "There it is, 'Trish.' It's 'Patricia' on my birth certificate, but I swear to God, my mother and everybody always called me '*Trish.*' Jesus H. Christ, what do people *want?*"

Harland would eat dinner with her, and marvel at her, but he was far too sane to take her up on the standing offer to bed her, not entirely out of affection for Molly; mostly because he'd feel silly if anyone found out. Trish fumbled through her pocketbook as they advanced toward the registration desk.

"What's going on tomorrow? I haven't looked at the itinerary," said Trish. "Is it going to be awful?"

"Well, they send around press buses, and we get on them, and we go out to the conference center. It's out in the boonies, you know."

"I didn't," said Trish. Harland noticed a furl of concern in the flesh between her eyes, likely attributable to her sudden concern over finding hairdressers at short notice in the boonies.

"At a conference center. Don't worry, it's in a big resort development. All the amenities. Indoor plumbing, hairdressers."

Trish brightened. "Dinner tonight, John?" Her smile widened perceptibly. "Late?"

"Early," said Harland. "Press bus leaves at eight in the morning."

"Thanks a *lot*," said Trish to the invisible Department of Energy press office responsible for the itinerary. "We'll talk. Two-oh-two," she said, holding up her room key.

"Two-oh-two," said Harland, and Trish went off toward the elevators, trailing the attention of at least six men in the lobby.

Harland signed the guest register and was handed his room key and a couple of envelopes that had been held for his arrival. He fell in file behind the bellman to whom he'd surrendered his bags and saw that the larger envelope was a packet of backgrounders on the conference. It had been assembled by the Department of Energy press officer and provided to each reporter in attendance. He tore open the letter-sized envelope with his name, all caps, written in red felt-tip pen.

Inside was an object whose immediate function was unclear. Then Harland realized it was a Xerox of a Xerox of a parody of a dollar bill. In place of George Washington was an engraving, in Treasury Department style, of an immediately recognizable person—Thomas Edison. In the corners, instead of the "1" denomination, was "1 KwH." On the back, lots of filigree, the familiar "ONE" but beneath it appeared "American Energy Unit." Stapled to it in the margin was a piece of paper. The message was typed, then photocopied: I KNOW WHERE THERE ARE 500,000,000 OF THESE. Below it, a telephone number, but Harland's eyes didn't even get that far. He shook his head. *This town is full of crazies.* Harland tore off the attached note and stuffed the bill into his pocket. Molly might get a kick out of it. The other correspondents who'd been given the same envelope and message were less amused. The ashtray beside the elevator was overflowing with the crumpled Xeroxes. Harland rolled the bit of paper into a small ball. As the elevator dinged its arrival, he tossed it into the ashtray neatly, to make sure it would stay in.

Molly knew, even before she punched 8 for long distance on the phone in her Houston hotel room, that it was too early to call Harland. It was barely eight o'clock and she was almost sure he would still be down at CBS, working on that Big Piece that she didn't ask about and he didn't talk about, except to say that it was guaranteed Emmy time. And if he wasn't home, she already knew she was going to call him at the studio, even though she herself hated being interrupted at work. She wanted to hear his voice badly enough to risk a selfishness rap.

The phone didn't answer the first three rings, but it did the fourth. It was the service, answering with the last four digits of their phone number.

"Not in, huh?" said Molly. "Okay, I'll get him at the office."

"Ms. Rice?" said the service.

"Yeah."

"Mr. Harland is out of town." *Son of a bitch*, thought Molly. "But he left a number he said to give you if you called in. It's his hotel."

"Oh, sensational," said Molly. She thought, as she felt for the notepad and the eraserless sliver of a dwarf pencil the hotel provided on the night table, that the woman must surely think she sounded like an eighteen-year-old calling her steady on her first night away from college. Molly was at times still embarrassed by the mindless, enveloping, little-white-cottage-with-red-roses-'round middle-class way she was in love with John Harland.

She got the number, pushed down the receiver, and dialed 8, then the area code. Before she got to the next digit, she got a recording: "When dialing long distance inside the 713 area code, it is not necessary to dial the area code before the number. Please—"

Harland was somewhere inside the same area code, probably

meant he was here in Houston. Molly felt her face break with a smile so wide and silly she was glad no one else was there to see it.

The object of putting a restaurant on the top floor of Stouffer's was that the hotel could jack up the price of the food in exchange for a really spectacular view of the city, glittering below. When the hotel opened, Houston probably did glitter. Now it didn't, but then no city really glittered at night anymore. *The lights are going off all over America*, Harland thought as he looked west. The response of Houston, "Energy City," to mandatory percentage reductions in public and private use of energy was to turn off every other streetlight and to dim the remaining ones. Billboards were unlighted. The outside of the sports area just across from the hotel, where people were arriving to see an NBA game, was unlighted, Harland guessed there were half as many lights burning in the area concourse as had been designed.

Keep this up and we're not going to be a twenty-four-hour-a-day culture anymore, Harland thought. *There won't be anything left to do at night but sleep. But tonight we live.* He ordered the Texas-sized sirloin.

Trish was wearing some sort of clinging black jersey number when he called for her at her room. It seemed to Harland a bit incongruous that she'd take something like that on an out-of-town assignment that didn't involve a state dinner or the impersonation of an oilman's mistress.

"It is no big deal that I brought along this dress," said Trish, eternally defensive. "This thing takes no room to pack—"

"I believe that."

"—and I can hang it up in the bathroom and steam out the wrinkles in no time. Look, do I have to apologize for bringing along a halfway good-looking dress? There are places that won't seat women in pantsuits. You're wearing a coat and tie."

When they'd finished dinner, Trish brushed a few errant

crumbs off the dress, then knotted her napkin and pulled on the edges, her face a grimace. "These are the worst times, just before dessert. Three years, Jesus, and I still miss them."

"Cigarettes?"

"You wouldn't understand, you've never smoked. I think they ought to *make* everybody smoke so they'd understand."

"Excuse me?" A voice from beside the table. A guy and his wife, standing there. Harland had seen them three tables away, sneaking looks at him most of the night. "You're John Harland, aren't you?" said the man.

"Right," said Harland.

"We won't bother you," said the man. "We just wanted to say hello to you and tell you how much we enjoy you on the news shows. We think you're the best newscaster on television." Harland said thanks, held out his hand so the guy and his wife could shake it, and they left. Harland dropped his eyes to meet Trish's.

"That's right," said Trish. "I'm doing a slow burn because they recognized you and not me."

"It's the dress, Trish. I'll bet they thought you were a working girl."

"No, it's the *People* cover. Speaking of which." She looked at Harland and smiled as he picked up a spoon to address the strawberries Romanoff that had just arrived. "How *is* old Molly?"

"Old Molly is fine."

"Your thoughts are forever with her?"

"Forever with her."

"Even two thousand miles away?"

"Near or far."

"Stop it, you're starting to sound like a song cue. John, you're a toughie. Have I been too subtle here, kid? If it's hearth and home you're worried about, forget it; it's no problem. If you haven't caught my drift by now, you happen to be a terrific-looking guy, and all I'm interested in, I swear to you, is a little minor-league action. Give me a break. You could be a real confidence-builder. John?"

Harland covered his mouth with his napkin, but it did an inadequate job of concealing his laughter. Trish frowned.

"Hokay, I'm gonna change the subject. No, I'm not. How much of that crap in *People* was true? I mean, how can you expect anybody to believe that true-love stuff if in the next paragraph you're asking us to swallow that garbage that you and Molly never talk about each other's stories?"

"Absolutely true. I don't care that much, but Molly does. We work for competing media, and she believes that competition is one of the principles of free press."

"You could sneak looks. I mean, Jesus, you live in the same apartment, you both got files there, right? You guys take leaks together?"

"We could look. But we don't."

"Lips are sealed, huh? Even in moments of passion? I mean, are you sure you haven't *ever* put it to her so hot and heavy that she started screaming out sources when she hit orgasm?"

"*Jesus*, Trish," said Harland, and laughed hard enough to choke on the strawberries. The waiter appeared with the bill and she scooped it up.

Harland let Trish get the check. "Let's let ABC pay for this one," she'd said; and Harland had thought, if it makes her feel tough, fine. He'd been back in the room no more than five minutes, staring balefully and inertly at the packet of press-kit backgrounders that seemed to thicken before his eyes, when the phone rang. Rescue, he thought.

"Harland," he heard Molly say. "What hotel is this?"

"Stouffer's."

"And how far away is it from the Houston Oaks?"

"Mile, maybe. Mile and a ha—"

"I'm *talking* to you from the Houston fucking Oaks."

It took Harland fifteen minutes to get a rental, ten minutes to pick his way out a moderately well-remembered Southwest Freeway to the Galleria, and five more to make his way to Molly's door and knock on it.

"It's open," said Molly.

Harland pushed aside the door to see a shape in the bed, completely covered by bedclothes. A pair of hands snaked out of the top of the pile and Molly uncovered her face.

"My God," said Harland. "You don't have any clothes on, do you?" Molly, eyes closed, split her face in a tight, close-lipped grin and shook her head vigorously enough to spill her hair across her face. "That could have been somebody else at the door, you know."

"I know, but I can't expect to get lucky every time."

Harland felt heat in his face. Molly suddenly pulled down the covers to expose one breast. "Look at the size of that thing," she said. "Instant hard-on, huh?" Harland moved to her, intending to use his repertoire of cracks about the lack of largeness of Molly's tits. But he knelt beside the bed, knowing that unless he were able within three seconds to get his face buried in that warm place between Molly's neck and shoulder, he would probably pass out from the longing to do it.

"My God," Harland said from that sweet place as he felt her start to rub the back of his neck. "You're such a gift."

Molly wanted out of hotel rooms, and out of hotels. So Harland took her rolling aimlessly over the rim and spokes of Houston's freeway system. "My God, I don't believe this," Molly shouted over the wind. "January, and you can roll the windows down in the car."

"One of the few nice things you can say about Texas," said Harland.

"Will you look at that?" said Molly as the huge glass monoliths slid past. "Is any part of this town more than four years old? It all looks like it arrived here this morning by United Parcel." But after a while, she rolled up the window and was quiet. Harland noticed it, and rolled up his window.

"What's up?" he said. "Post-coital depression? I've always heard the best thing for post-coital depression is a little hair of the dog."

She smiled, wearily.

"You're tired, baby. Can't you take some time off so we could go up to the place?" It had been months since they'd spent any time at Harland's weekend house in Vermont.

"Naw, I'm on a story," she said.

"Then after."

"Maybe after."

"Promise."

"Promise." Then she was quiet again. After a moment, without looking at him, she said, "What have you heard about the *Times* recently?"

"The same old rumors that you've been hearing about the *Times* for the last three years. That everything else in the Times Company makes money but the *Times*. That they want to dump it, and that everybody from Citizen Kane to Kuwait is going to buy it. What's the matter? You're afraid the new owners are going to let you go?" Harland smiled. "No, you're not. You're afraid that *you* might have to let *them* go."

"The *Times* is the Lone Ranger, Harland," said Molly, staring off into the lights. "Everything else is turning into show business. The fucking conglomerates. They all seemed to be called . . . 'Twenty-Second Century Communications Group,' and you never see them, or know who they are, except for the lawyer clones who announce the sale at a press conference. And they're turning them all into the *Post*. One by one."

Harland was startled by the look on Molly's face. He wanted to joke about it, but he knew it wouldn't take, not now. So he reached out and stroked her arm. "I'm going to have to get you to Guidry's, and get you there quick."

Harland's sense of the way to the huge country-and-western dance hall was vague. He'd gone there often when he was with the Houston bureau, but it had been four years. He knew it was vaguely south and east of the city, on the other side of the refineries along the ship channel.

On the Pasadena freeway, the refineries lined both sides of the road, mile upon mile of them. Molly marveled at the stalagmites of cracking towers defined against the dark by their Christmas-tree illumination: "God, it's like *Oz*." At one point, Harland pulled off on the freeway service road and turned off the engine so Molly could hear the place ingest its oxygen and exhale, in hissing flares, its waste gases. "Jesus, the *smell*. Do people breathe this stuff?"

"Most people in southeast Texas grow up downwind of one of those things," said Harland as he restarted the car. "I was eighteen years old before I learned air *didn't* smell like that."

Harland navigated, correctly on the first attempt, to the X a gas-station attendant had drawn on their roadmap. That was where he was sure Guidry's lay. Molly surveyed the acres of parking lot full of elaborately customized pickup trucks with gun racks over their back windows and plastered with bumper stickers that said, among other things, "Cowboys do it in the dirt." There were several Mercedes parked next to primer-painted '64 Chevies with their trunks wired shut.

"I don't believe this," said Molly.

"Don't sweat the small stuff," said Harland as he led her to the door. "There's a lot of things you're not going to believe before this night's over."

He paid their cover charge and shoved open the front door. "Behold," he said, "my ethnic heritage."

Guidry's was full at the moment with maybe five hundred people. Half were primarily interested in getting drunk; half were interested in getting drunk and dancing to a band whose lead singer wore Hank Snow boots, faded Levi's, a Hoss Cartwright twenty-four gallon hat, and a T-shirt bearing the Champion spark-plug emblem.

There were three bars, one of which solely dispensed immense pitchers of beer. Maybe a dozen pool tables. From corners of the place would come frequent screams and inexplicable crashes, all of which were ignored.

"No place but Texas," Harland shouted in Molly's ear.

"Shitkicker chic. I guarantee you that by midnight there's going to be a fist fight between a pipefitter and a downtown tax lawyer who pulls down a hundred and a half a year."

"I love it," said Molly. "I *love* it." And she did. To Harland's relief, her spirit immediately brightened.

By the time they left at two in the morning, Molly had gotten medium drunk, learned how to dance the cotton-eyed-joe with a welder who worked at the Diamond Alkali plant, and reported in amazement after a trip to the ladies' room that she had seen a woman exclaim "I'm *tired* of this shitty thing" and throw her wig into the toilet. Just before they left, they witnessed the fight Harland had promised. The combatants rolled around among the pickups on the parking lot without damaging each other.

Molly was staggering with laughter when they walked into the lobby of the Houston Oaks, and Harland was nearly as bad off. Molly had to ask for another key, since she'd left hers in her room. Both Molly and Harland saw from the room clerk's look as he provided the key—they were familiar with that look by now—that Harland was about to be recognized. "It's okay," said Molly back over her shoulder to the man as she and Harland made for the elevators. "I'm a geophysicist and Mr. Harland is going to interview me in my room. About plate tectonics."

"Oh *shit*," said Harland. He threw his arm up against the wall of the elevator bank and buried his face in the crook of his elbow.

The room clerk smiled weakly and nodded his head. "Uh, right."

"It's easier to do at night," said Molly. "I'm not lying. The gravity waves die down."

"Sure, I understand," said the room clerk, nodding vigorously.

"Honest to shit," said Molly as she and Harland entered the elevator and the doors closed.

"This thing had better not stop more than once," said Harland. He ran his finger down the V of her knit top. "Or anybody who gets on is going to have his eyes opened."

Molly felt for Harland's crotch. "Mother of God," she said. "He's a *pistol*."

They made effortless love in her room, laughing and gasping alternately. "Jesus, that feels weird," said Harland.

"What?"

"When you laugh when I'm inside you."

"You don't like it?"

"No, it's sensational."

"Maybe I could play to it."

"Huh?"

"You know. Get Henny Youngman to stand by the bed and—" Both of them exploded at that, Molly with such force that she almost expelled him.

9

THE WAKE-UP CALL CAME VICIOUSLY EARLY. THEY HAD NO TIME
for breakfast. They'd decided that Harland would take a cab
back to Stouffer's to dress and catch the press bus to the conference center. Molly would use the rental car to make her
appointment, then return it to the airport. He held on to her at
the door to her room, his tie bunched in one hand. Then he
looked her in the eyes, and squeezed her slightly for emphasis.

"Vermont," he said.

"Vermont."

"As soon as you finish the story."

"As soon as I finish the story."

Then he had to leave her.

Tom Evan had once troubled Molly. At one time, before
she had taken up with Harland, Molly felt herself approaching
that point where she had to decide whether or not she was
going to sleep with Tom Evan. He had been with *Newsweek*
then. They had run around together, and Molly was growing
fond of him. But Evan took a job in Encon's press-relations
office, at twice the money *Newsweek* paid him. Molly wasn't
fond enough of Evan to go with him to Houston, and Evan
wasn't fond enough of her to ask.

Molly sat, at a quarter of nine, in Evan's outer office, waiting for him to arrive and feeling his secretary's who-*is*-this-crazy-woman? stare fall upon her still again. Molly wondered if Evan might have any residual feeling for her. It would be helpful; but then she decided that no, she hoped he didn't. Although Molly wanted what she wanted badly, she always played fair to get it. It wouldn't be fair, not if Evan was still fond of her.

But from the half-second look that Evan wore, while he stood there just inside the hall door of his office after he saw her, Molly knew that she would have to play unfairly, or not play at all.

"Molly."

"Hey, he remembered my name."

"If you'd called, I wouldn't be having a coronary now."

He walked toward her, unsure of what to do. Molly took the opportunity to set the tone. She kissed him quickly on the cheek. *Old friends of the opposite sex*, she wanted the kiss to say.

"I was in the neighborhood." She was following Evan as he walked to the door of his inner office.

"Uh, Tom," said his secretary. "George Delft at nine-thirty?"

"Tell him I'll call him," said Evan.

"And you've got an—" Evan closed the door on her.

Evan's office was leather, chrome, rosewood closet doors. A rack beside the outer door that displayed current issues of magazines appeared to be made of teak. "Cripes," said Molly. "No wonder a gallon of gas costs a buck ninety-five."

"If only you'd called. When did you get in?" Evan sat on a visitor's chair in front of his desk, Molly on the sofa.

"Last night sometime. Too late."

Molly remembered Tom's defeated smile. "And how's John?"

"John's terrific. Uh, here's where I ask how your wife is, but I have to admit I don't know her name."

"Susie. She's fine. We aren't, though."

"Well, that's . . . I'm sorry to hear that."

Evan's intercom buzzed. "Tom," his secretary said, "that ten-o'clock, in case you've forgotten, *is* that meeting with—"

"I'll get back to you, Helen." Evan cut her off.

"Tom," said Molly, quietly, "make your meeting. I won't take long."

Evan was fiddling with an object on his desk. "Work, huh? Not a social call." The smile again. Molly was wishing for an anesthetist. "You weren't in the neighborhood."

"I was in Michigan. Fourteenmile Point."

Evan met her eyes. Three beats silence. "And how *is* Larry?" He got up and looked out upon his twenty-eighth-floor view at the virulent green, which, from that height, hid most signs of Houston's habitation. He leaned over his desk and turned on the intercom. "Helen, call Granger's secretary and tell her I can't make the ten-o'clock."

"Tom, I really think that—"

"Give her anything plausible for a reason, just be sure to write it down so I'll know what you said." He sat back down in the visitor's chair. "I did not want to go to that meeting. I don't want to go to most any of the meetings around this place." He sort of laughed. "You know if they got any jobs at the *Times*? News assistant? Copyboy? I'm not proud. I've . . . had a lot of practice recently at not being proud."

"Tom, I want you to talk to me. There's absolutely no advantage to you in talking to me, so I really have no idea on . . . what to base an appeal. I—"

"How about for old times' sake? That would be enough for me, Molly."

"No, Tom, I can't. Not for old times' sake. But how about this? How about that I've found out some things—Fourteenmile Point is one of them—and they scare me. But it's the things I *don't* know that scare me really shitless. And maybe if you would talk to me, I wouldn't be quite so scared."

"I know little pieces of things about Fourteenmile Point," said Evan. "Lots of guys around here at my rank know little pieces of things, but . . . ." He shook his head. "You gotta be a Larry Amble or above to know *big* pieces of things, and how they fit together."

"I'm gonna ask for everything you got, Tom. Don't duck me.

Let me have something you're not supposed to know. I've got a shot at making the pieces fit, Tom. You can help me. It is an *incredible* story, and when the *Times* prints it, there is going to be shit on the *walls*. Tommy, it is going to be *fine*."

After a moment, Evan said: "Molly, you sweet baby." There was affection in his eyes. "You do love it, don't you? Crusading girl reporter. After all these years in the business, do you still go down to the pressroom and watch them print it?"

"Yeah, sometimes. I'm embarrassed, but I do it."

"Nobody does that anymore, Molly."

"I know."

"Christ, you're lucky." He suddenly got up and went to another door, which turned out to be his washroom. When he came out, he had a file folder in his hands. "Be back," he said, walking toward the door to his outer office. The file folder went past her at eye level, and she could see written on the index tab: *2/15*.

He left the door open, and she could hear him ask his secretary for the key to the Xerox room. He was gone about three minutes.

He closed the door to his outer office and sat in the visitor's chair. He put the file folder in his lap, and was holding a sheaf of Xerox copies over his lips, thinking about something. "Okay," he finally said, "Here's something I'm not supposed to know." He held out the Xeroxes toward Molly, who arose and walked toward him. As she started to take the Xeroxes, his grasp tightened.

"But I want you to know how I got these. I really want you to know where this is all coming from." He paused, to make sure he was being careful about how he would say this. "Nothing I do here has any meaning. No one listens to what I say. No one wants me here. They want to fire me. But I make fifty-seven thousand, five hundred and forty-four dollars a year, and I want it. I need it, God help me. I have found out that you can keep from getting fired if you get somebody by the balls. So to get—"

Molly didn't want to hear this. "Tom . . ."

He tightened his grip on the Xeroxes. "—to get someone by the balls, I . . ." Molly tugged a little harder on the Xeroxes, and finally Evan let them go. She could see his eyes start to fill, and she had to get away from that. She stopped at the door, knowing she should turn and say something, but didn't know what. Her eyes went to the rack of magazines again, and saw that next to the *U. S. News & World Report* was the *People* with hers and Harland's picture on the cover. "I swear to you," said Evan behind her, "it's the only copy of that stupid magazine I've ever bought." Evan couldn't get entirely through the sentence. Molly went back to him, stood by his chair, and held his head in both her arms. He reached up a hand for her, but he stopped; and he never touched her. After she felt that the wetness was no longer spilling over her wrists when she cradled his face, she let him go and left.

Harland went to sleep on the press bus. Normally, he wasn't able to go to sleep sitting up, but the excesses of the night before being what they were . . . He found two empty seats, insulated his head against the cold, sweating windowpane with the Department of Energy press kit, and within five minutes of leaving the hotel . . .

When he woke up, the side of his face felt warm. When he focused his eyes, Harland was looking into the vanishing point between the cleavage of two nice-sized breasts. He sat up and force-fed himself consciousness. Although he had gone to sleep against a cold windowpane, he had awakened on the shoulder of Trish Denning. She, he was now beginning to realize, had sat down beside him and induced his head to tilt her way after removing his press-kit pillow. She had the kit in her lap now, making notes. Harland saw that George Tay, a *Times* energy reporter, was making note of Harland. Tay looked away when he noticed Harland was awake, and tried not to smile. This meant that this would get back to Molly for sure, thought Harland, and she'd give him a very hard time about it. Molly didn't feel the tiniest bit threatened by Trish's predations. The furious needling she gave Harland about it was her way of showing him that she wasn't, part of the style of challenging, oblique affection they showed for each other. At the moment all he could think of was the terrifying parallel to his ninth-grade school trip to Austin. He'd similarly gone to sleep, on Patsy Fleener's shoulder, and had awakened with a screaming erection. Patsy had noted it and made sure Melba Logan and Wanda Smiers in the seat behind them had noted it. Harland thought of mentally reconnoitering down there to see if, at age thirty-six, he was still subject to the Patsy Fleener effect, but then decided he didn't want to know.

"You're cute when you sleep," said Trish, reaching up to brush back Harland's hair from his forehead. "You clench your little hands into little fists."

Harland bounced his head back against the headrest. "Oh, for God's sake, Trish."

"Well, excuse me for living and for taking advantage of you in your defenseless state," said Trish, pouting a little. "You looked uncomfortable leaning up against that window. It's not like I gave you a blowjob."

Harland scrubbed his eyes with the heels of his hands. He peered out into the swirling gray murk that opaqued all the universe farther than ten feet from the roadbed. The bus growled along in a lower gear. "Has it been like this all the way out?"

"It's getting worse," said Trish. "I thought Texas was a desert."

"West Texas is a desert. East Texas is foggy in the winter."

"And the humidity is just *won*derful." Trish test-shook her hair, gauging its texture. "By the time I get out there and start shooting, my hair is going to look like rats have been sucking on it."

Harland looked over the seats and heads, out the front window. "Where's the scientists' bus? Did it get ahead of us in the—" Harland saw a thickening point of darkness in the membraneous gray. Then there was a man standing right in the middle of the freeway. In the quarter of a second before the busdriver half-screamed and the bus began skewing sideways off the road, Harland could tell the man was holding an automatic rifle.

The bus came to a halt pointed roughly in its original direction, but with the rear end tilted into a ditch at the side of the roadbed. Harland was half-lying on top of Trish in the aisle. A roll of videotape was unspooling itself as it rolled down the canted floor of the bus. A voice from outside was shouting at the driver, who was staring down into his lap and panting, to open the door. Harland started to raise his head to see who it was, but Trish caught his tie and tugged him back. "Keep your ass tucked, honey. I don't think he's a hitchhiker."

The driver was not reacting quickly enough to suit the man with the automatic rifle. He fired a short burst through the window in the bus door, into the ceiling. There were whimpers from the front and back of the bus. Harland bit his teeth against the noise. He felt Trish's nails dig into his upper arm. The busdriver didn't need to be told again. He opened the door. The man with the rifle stepped into the bus. He was wearing an old Army fatigue jacket and a ski mask.

"All right," he said. "Everybody back in his seat, eyes on me. Everybody, eyes on me at all times. Any time I look around and somebody's eyes isn't on me, it's big trouble." He grabbed the busdriver by the back of his collar and pushed him down the aisle, where he fell into a seat. "Anybody hurt? We don't want anybody from the press hurt. I know this gun is scaring the shit out of you, and it's supposed to. But if you'll just stay seated and quiet for about five more minutes—" The man looked around to make sure everyone was obeying him, and then took a very quick glance up the freeway into the fog. "—we'll be gone, and you people are going to have a very big news story to write about."

Harland sat immobile. The man panned the gun very slowly the width of the bus, back and forth. Harland closed his eyes when it oscillated to him.

"Okay, who *are* you cocksuckers?"

Harland, everybody jumped. It was Trish. In the stunned quiet, it sounded as though she were speaking through a public address system. Trish. With presidents and men with automatic weapons. Absolutely fearless.

"Very quiet, very still," crooned the man with the gun. He reached into a pocket of the fatigue jacket, came out with a packet of papers. "It's all in here," he said, holding the papers up. "Who we are, why we're doing it, what we want. Fifty copies, enough for everybody." He looked ahead into the fog again. "We should have the scientists transferred to our vehicles in just a few minutes, people, so just be very quiet, very still."

There was a sharp sound from the fog ahead. The man with the gun snapped his head around in its direction. Harland knew it was a gunshot. Within a second, there were three, five more from what would seem to be as many weapons. And then a steady pummeling of gunfire.

Panic and confusion came instantly to the man's face. He started to run out the door, then turned back. "Stay still," he shouted.

"Oh shit, they're *shooting* them," said someone on the bus, nausea in his voice.

"Nobody's shooting *anybody*," the man with the rifle screamed. He peered again ahead into the fog, but he could see nothing. The gunfire continued, dreamily, echoing from the pine forests that approached the edge of the freeway.

"Nobody is shooting anybody because it's not in the plan." He waved the papers over his head as if they could refute the reality of the awful noise behind him. "It's *not* in our plan, it's *not* in our plan, it's *not*—"

Harland thought he saw another deepening patch of dark in the fog, coalescing into the same kind of proto-shape that had evolved into the man with the automatic rifle. But it did not penetrate entirely out from the gray; Harland saw it only half-solidify into the shape of a man pointing something toward the bus.

But he did see a point of light.

The chest of the man with the gun leaped out from under the fatigue jacket and became a red mist mottled with darker red. Harland didn't see the man jerk forward and fall. He was watching, frozen, as Trish crawled backward down the aisle, half rolling, flailing her head and clawing at herself. A piece of that mottled red had landed in her hair.

They had been too far away from town to try a microwave link, so Harland grabbed the videocassette tapes his CBS crew had shot of the riddled bus and persuaded a Texas Department of Public Safety highway patrolman to take him back into Houston. CBS had broken into a soap to put Harland on the air, from a studio in the Houston CBS affiliate. He told what few confused details were known, ad-libbing narration for the tapes. He found himself apologizing on the air for explicitness in the carnage exhibited on the screen. He felt himself wanting to apologize for their obvious fabrication. This looked all wrong. It should have been a Mercedes coach, not a Greyhound. It should have been a road in Lebanon, or on the way to a resort near Haifa, or at an airport in a Fourth World African country with a funny name and an amusing dictator. This simply could not reasonably happen to fourteen scientists on a four-lane freeway thirty miles north of Houston, not in America.

No one was exactly sure what happened. All of the fourteen scientists who were to have been participants in the symposium were dead. Four Secret Service agents. Five terrorists. The bus driver. The first group of terrorists forced the bus off the road, disarmed the security force, and seemed prepared to transfer the scientists into other vehicles. The press releases mimeographed for those on the press bus indicated that they intended to hold the scientists hostage, with demands to be announced later. But when more terrorists—maybe five, maybe twelve—

arrived in vans, there seemed to be argument and confusion inside the bus. Then the shooting. Maybe some of the security force tried to take advantage of a lapse of attention and started firing. Or the terrorists fought among themselves. Everyone inside the bus was dead, several outside the bus, including the head of the security force, dead. An unknown number of terrorists slipped back into the vans and drove away into the fog, taking one of their dead with them.

New York decided that follow-up coverage should be left to the people at the local bureau, who were pissed off enough as it was that a national correspondent had been sent down to take a local story away from them. Harland reminded New York of the broken promise of time to edit the Vandellen piece, and New York's pledge was reinstated. Harland asked the secretary at the bureau to get him plane reservations back to New York that night, and he went back to Stouffer's to try to get a little sleep before he had to leave for the airport.

He'd been asleep about fifteen minutes when his phone rang. It was the hotel operator. "Mr. Harland, I know you had put in a wake-up call, and I really hate to do this, but this person is a police officer. He says it's important, and I did call him back to confirm he's calling from the police station. Shall I—"

"I'll take it, operator. Thanks for your trouble."

A male voice on the line: "John Harland?"

"Yeah."

"Billy Coombs." Harland vaguely recognized the name. He knew that he would probably be able to put together a composite on just who Billy Coombs was, but he was tired and it was going to take some time and effort. Coombs saved him both.

"Houston Police Department community-relations officer." The composite assembled itself. Billy Coombs. Lieutenant. Affected being the same species of redneck as the rest of the Houston cops. The affectation covered an active social conscience. A college degree in something besides police science. Had been honest with Harland during Harland's Houston-bureau stint when Harland was doing a police-brutality story;

had become an occasional drinking buddy thereafter, until Harland had gone on to New York.

"Hey, Billy."

"Woke you up, hoss, didn't I?" Coombs's voice sounded a little blurry. At six o'clock? And Harland didn't remember Coombs ever drinking more than a couple of beers. Well, it's been five years, and it's tough being a cop.

"I gotta get up anyway. Have to catch a plane."

"Lot of excitement today."

"Sure was." Quiet on the line.

"I was out there, hoss."

"You were? Didn't see you. How come you didn't—"

"Didn't see you either. Had to be ten thousand cops out there anyway."

"Real mess."

"Sure was." More quiet. Harland sensed that Coombs was wondering just how to slide into what he wanted to talk about. "Hoss, I was out there from the beginning. I was with the security detail. And I saw it all, hoss, I saw it all." Jesus, thought Harland, no wonder the guy was trying to get himself smashed.

"Damn, Billy, that's heavy duty."

Then the pretend-country was gone from Coombs's voice. "The guys who came up in the vans weren't terrorists, Johnny. I don't know who they were. But I'll tell you this: I'm afraid to find out. I been sitting here three hours figuring out what I should do. Think you could miss your plane? I got something I need somebody to take off my hands."

The smell of bourbon on Billy Coombs's breath was even stronger in the small room of the Houston Police Department training academy, which was, like any room full of electronics, too cold. Harland had noticed when Coombs picked him up near the hotel the Wild Turkey label on the quart bottle whose neck was sticking out—old home week—of the wrinkled brown paper bag. But the alcohol was doing an inadequate job of getting Billy Coombs drunk, because his brain was too well insulated by fear. Coombs had passed the new police parking garage and parked the car on the dark street behind the cop shop; he'd used a key to let them in a back door of the training academy.

Coombs had talked, pointedly, of nothing while he was taking Harland to the police station: He and his wife had had another kid. He was a captain now, only because they had to promote him because he'd done well on the civil-service exams. They put him in training, which wasn't like being a cop at all, and he loved being a cop. Coombs said he had got a reputation among his fellow officers for not believing with sufficient ferocity that any Houston cop was always right all the time, no matter what he did.

Harland didn't try to point Coombs toward the subject, whatever it was, even after he began to worry that Billy might never get to it. Coombs kept pulling on the paper cup he'd filled in the car with Turkey and repeatedly assuring Harland that he'd "kept up with you, Johnny" over the years by watching Harland on television.

Finally Coombs finished the cup, crumpled it, carefully aimed it at a wastepaper basket on the other side of the room, missed it. "Typical," he said. He took a deep breath, got up, and drew a reel of videotape from his coat pocket. It was a small reel, the kind that went on old half-inch black-and-white Sony portable videocorders.

"Johnny, you grew up in this part of the country," said Coombs as he threaded the tape on a playback deck. "You know what happens when somebody kills a police officer. They'll tear a town apart until they find who did it." He half-smiled. "Hoss, I got a feeling they could find me in Buffalo Bayou in six different pieces and it would get in the paper that I had an accident mowing my yard. I think I saw something I shouldn't have seen."

Coombs turned on the machine and provided narration for the details that weren't apparent from the fuzzy black-and-white images on the screen. Coombs had been allowed to accompany the Secret Service security detail to videotape them for academy training purposes. He had been in the trail car behind the scientists' bus when it veered off the freeway to avoid the accident, apparently staged by the terrorists, just ahead. "That damn fog, you couldn't tell what was going on. It was like smoke; one minute you couldn't see your hand in front of your face, the next a little wind would blow up and thin it out a little. By the time that ol' boy who headed up the Secret Service detail bailed out of that trail car, the terrorists had already got inside the bus. There were four Secret Service inside the bus, but they must have been jerking off or something. They paid for it, I guess. Well, I ain't never been smart, because I just jumped out and turned on the camera and just ran along with the head of the Secret Service detail. You can see the fog was still pretty thick then. We didn't know right away that there were people with rifles inside the bus.

"Funny, I never was scared while it was happening. Just after. You look at things just through that little viewfinder, it don't look real, and I guess you figure that something that isn't real can't hurt you.

"I had talked this guy who ran the Secret Service detail into wearing one of those wireless microphones, you know, so I could pick up his orders. I had a little gadget in my ear, so if I couldn't always see, I could hear sensational." Coombs turned up the volume on the monitor. The head of the Secret Service was in midsentence.

"—the fuck they *come* from?" On the screen, his poorly defined shape, little more than a silhouette in the murk, was waving at one of his men to fall back. "Jesus. Chip, don't fire, I don't care if you do have a shot. They'll waste everybody in there . . ." Coombs fast-forwarded the tape. "Next there's just more of that guy running around like a chicken with his head cut off." He punched the machine to play.

"I think this is where those goddamn vans come up . . ." Coombs had swung the camera around to pick up the vans, two of them, bouncing across the grassy freeway median after turning off the southbound lane of the freeway. "It couldn't have been six minutes, ten minutes at the most after those guys grabbed the bus, that those goddamn vans showed up and those men got out. I guess there were eight of 'em. Maybe twelve. They didn't wear masks, but they were dressed sort of like the terrorists, you know, sort of ragged but . . . very clean. They had these weapons, Jesus, I found out later they were those automatic .22s with laser sighting and they'll fire about sixty rounds a second. Those Secret Service guys, they were already about to pee in their pants, and then these ten boogers with automatic weapons come out of nowhere. It was just so fucking *strange* that nobody moved, except for one of the guys from the vans." On the screen, a shape was walking toward the Secret Service leader. "Jesus Christ, with five other Secret Service guys about to pee in their pants and holding guns on him . . ."

The man-shape on the screen did not shorten a single one of his strides, despite the firepower trained on him and the unease of the men at the triggers, as he approached the Secret Service leader. Coombs turned the volume back up to hear the Secret Service leader shout: "—stop right there and put down the weapons. I want to know who you people are, and I want some fucking *explanations*."

"*Listen* to this guy," said Coombs, almost shivering.

From the screen: "Sir. Are you with the Service?"

"Yes. I'm fucking with the Service. Now *you* tell *me*—"

"Thank you. We're from Copper Creek." Coombs had zoomed the little Sony camera in as tightly as he could, but the resolution was too poor to make out the Secret Service man's face or expression. But it came across in the silence preceding his reply and the quiver in his voice when he made it: "I—I—I understand."

"Very good. Will your men fall back? Over there, plea—" The playback suddenly shut off. "Ran out of tape," said Coombs, punching the machine to rewind. "I took the tape off the machine and stuck it in my coat pocket and was trying to thread up a new one and watch what was going on. The guys from the Secret Service fell back like they was told to, and . . ."

Coombs watched the tape reels spinning. "Hoss, there was no confusion. There was no breaking down in negotiations with the terrorists. There *wasn't* no negotiations with the terrorists. Those guys from the van took up positions around that bus; and without saying a word more to anybody, they started firing into it. About a million rounds. *Forever.*

"One of the people inside, somehow he didn't get killed right away, I guess, because he stuck out a gun, it must have been an M-16, and shot back, blind. It caught one of those people and the head Secret Serviceman, just about cut them two in half. So they shot some more into the bus. And then they stopped and listened to see if anybody was still moving inside, and then they thought they must have heard something, because they fired some more."

Coombs's consciousness had been drifting back to the freeway and the fog of earlier in the day, but he reeled it in again. "After they finished inside the bus, one of them walked over to me. Just before they'd started shooting, I'd gotten the Sony re-threaded and turned it back on. I guess I got them shooting. Shit, I don't know. He pulled the tape off the machine and put it into his pocket. Then he put about ten rounds into the tape machine. He asked me if I was a policeman, and I told him yes, and then he asked me if I had any more tapes."

The tape had finished rewinding and its tail was slapping against Coombs's wrist. "I didn't lie about the one in my pocket because I got steel for balls, Johnny. I said I didn't have any more tapes because I was too scared to remember it was there. Or I'd have given it to him. Oh yes. I'd have ate it if he told me to.

"And then they got back into their vans, put the dead guy in there with them, and they left." Coombs took the tape off the machine and sat down across the table from Harland.

"Johnny, outside of the Secret Service guys—and you gotta

figure from the way that honcho reacted, they knew what was going on—I'm the only person there who saw what happened, who ain't dead right now. I figure I got two chances of living to see my boy in the Little League. One, those guys figure that I'm scared shitless right now. Two, they figure I told them the truth, and until they find out otherwise, I don't have any tape of them." Coombs slid the videotape across the table, and it fell off into Harland's lap. "Hoss, they're right both times."

Harland sat in first class on the three-in-the-morning flight back to New York and told himself, again, that there was no reason to believe Coombs. The man was fifty percent drunk and one hundred percent scared.

It didn't happen the way Coombs said it had because it was insane. There was no reason for the people in the vans to do what they did; it had no logical objective or advantage, although Harland was prepared to believe the more-or-less official Secret Service account was a lie, to cover a botch-up. Maybe a Serviceman had panicked and started firing.

The videotape, now in Harland's coat pocket, proved only that some more people arrived, and that the Servicemen at the scene deferred to them. Superiors in the Service. There might have been no second videotape at all, or if there was, it showed —if it showed anything at all; the first was all but illegible—an approximation of the Secret Service version, not of Billy Coombs's sweaty paranoia. But: Had Harland witnessed the deaths of nineteen people within thirty seconds by machine-gun fire, his perceptions too would have been addled.

Except.

After a while, the stewardess finally stopped asking if he wanted anything, because he was staring at the back of the seat in front of him too intently to hear her.

Except.

The instant Harland first saw the carriage of the man who walked across the freeway toward the Secret Service leader, he was forty percent sure; when he heard his voice, especially the way its timbre became gentler as the Secret Service leader's became more hysterical, he became eighty-five percent sure; and he was confident that when he got back to New York and looked at Coombs's tape again, he'd be one hundred percent sure that he knew the man who had identified them as Copper Creek.

10

HARLAND HAD PERSUADED GEORGE, THE NIGHT SHIFT TECHIE, TO set up the tapes and the equipment for him in one of the editing rooms and then to go wherever it was that CBS techies go to sleep on company time, leaving Harland to play with the control board himself. The unions didn't much care if the CBS News staffers operated the board to look at old newsfilm, as long as it wasn't being edited for airplay.

There were two newstapes, taken from the CBS library, and Harland had them displayed on separate screens. He was working with the second now, raw, unedited tape shot at the site where a 747 passenger plane had crashed in North Carolina. Two hundred and twenty killed. Four or five months ago, it had been the top story for days.

He thought he'd seen something three viewings ago, when he'd played the tape at double speed, and now he was creeping the tape, and searching for it. The camera cut from shot to shot of metal twisted into amorphic shapes, something smoldering that was still recognizable as a seat or a suitcase, the inevitable heartbreaker shot of a child's toy. What he thought he was looking for was to come up next, after CBS correspondent Charlie Fryar's stand-up among the ruins, past which Harland fast-forwarded.

The cameraman was shooting the airplane's logo, half-visible on the crumpled tail. Harland froze the image; by some sort of unimaginable occult microprocessor technology, he was able electronically to zoom in and enlarge a portion of the video image. The resolution suffered, but Harland was getting a better look at what he wanted to see. As the original cameraman had zoomed in on the tail section, the longer focal length of the lens also brought closer to the camera the figure of a man standing, arms folded and watching, from a rise of land at the edge of the splatter of wreckage. Harland enlarged the image as much as he could, until the picture threatened to break up into a dance of phosphenes.

He had three images frozen and enlarged on three screens now. On the left, a moment slivered from Billy Coombs's Houston videotape. The face was illegible, but Harland had chosen to freeze the image while the man was making a gesture he remembered from long ago. On the middle screen, also frozen and enlarged from file newstape, an image of what was certainly the same person. He stood with his arms folded the same way, leaning slightly to his right to hear what the person standing next to him was saying as he reserved half his attention for something going on ahead of him. Before Harland had enlarged the image, the whole video frame showed that the men were standing beside a twisted undulation of metal with SUNDOWN written upon it.

"Sam Painter," said Harland quietly to the three images, "what in the shit are you doing?"

In hopes of getting Rennie to slow down the vehicle and to turn down the Led Zeppelin eight-track tape that was buffeting her from any number of speakers inside Rennie's speeding, shag-walled, mirror-ceilinged van, Molly tried to restart the conversation.

"You don't look a lot like what I thought a computer whiz should."

Rennie Knowles was at the moment wearing a three-piece doubleknit off-the-rack-from-Sears suit with filthy jogging shoes and no tie. No shirt; Molly could see Mickey Mouse's ear on Rennie's T-shirt sticking up from the cleft of the double-knit vest. It probably wasn't the first time he'd been told that.

"You mean because I don't have eighteen mechanical pencils and ball-point pens that write in five different colors sticking out of my shirt pocket?" said Rennie. His corona of startling red hair still bounced in response to Led Zep although compassionately he turned it down. "That's because I write software. It's the hardware techies, the main-frame guys who design, they're the ones who all look like Beaver Cleaver's father. Just about all the young software writers are freaks. It really chaps these big companies when they have to hire us."

"You didn't get dressed up just for me, did you?" said Molly, casting a worried glance at the speedometer.

"But they really do have to hire us. Like, General Steel, they knew I was radical, man. Fuck, when they tried to recruit on campus at Ann Arbor in sixty-nine, like I helped trash the placement center." Rennie snorted, explored the van's ashtray for serviceable roaches, found none.

"Fact of life, man. The really good software writers, the ones that are gonna end up saving them a lotta money, they're all freaks. In fact, I don't think anybody straight could write good software." He made an exhilarating left turn.

"Shit, man, if you had told me five years ago I'd be writing programs for General Steel . . . But, man, the fuckin' Movement is fuckin' *dead*, man, and the money they pay is fan-tastic. This business shit is just another game anyway. And I get unlimited time to freak with a machine that's got one hundred twenty-eight-fuckin'-thousand-K's of memory."

"Look," said Molly, "I think I ought to tell you: Even if I don't use your name, they could still find out who gave me this information—"

"And fire me? Shit, man, I gotta get outa this town anyway. Gotta get to Oregon, see? So I'm ready for them." He giggled. "I got into the railroads' routing computers, fuck, two days after I went to work here, and wrote a little program. You know, like just to keep my hand in, trashing the imperialists.

"You know how many freight cars there are in the United States, man? There's gotta be six jillion of them, and they're all computer-routed. Well, there are sixty-seven sealed freight cars out there filled with the most expensive alloy General Steel makes, man, and for the last two years they ain't had any destinations, man, just routes. I've sent those fuckers back and forth across the country at least fifty times by now. Two and a half million bucks' worth when they were loaded, and shit, by now they're worth another million seven, million eight. More. I figure for severance pay of, oh, three hundred thousand, I'll load up the program that will tell General Steel where those fuckers are."

With a fingernail Molly riffled the edge of the stack of computer printout—Rennie called it hardcopy—Knowles had just given her. The columns of alphanumerics flickered past like the jerky frames of an old silent movie. The explanations and annotations Rennie had just spent six hours supplying started slipping from her memory.

"And you're sure it's forty percent. They produce forty percent more rolled steel than they report to the government? And have for the last *two years?*"

"Look, man; any data that is inaccessed as tight as the company locks . . . shit, man, it has to be right. I thought I could break the access codes in a couple of hours and call that stuff out, but it took me twelve fuckin' *hours*, man. Just about *ripped* me. I had Kiss tickets and had to miss it."

"*Someone* would notice overruns."

"Sure, man, but only at the top and bottom—the big ass executives, and the hardhats down on the milling line. Now your hardhat might think, 'Well, shit, they're making a piss lot of this fuckin' steel.' But after the whistle blows and he starts sucking down Schlitz, you think he's gonna think to ask why? Once it gets off the mills, nobody but the computer really knows how much there is, and where it's going."

"But the railroads. This much overrun, there'd be nothing but steel on the line between Pittsburgh and—"

"The cars are sent out from Pittsburgh in different directions, man. But it all ends up in the same place. Look, *our* computer talks to the railroad's computers. I can access out the routings if you want to see them, but you don't *need* to, man. It's *gotta* end up in Detroit. Figure it out. There's only one thing rolled steel that thick and that hard and that wide is used for—on machines that stamp out car bodies."

"Rennie, beginning May one, there are going to be mandatory federal controls on weight and engine displacement of new cars, and a year after that there are going to be limits on the number they can make. Because there's not going to be enough gas to *run* them. Detroit needs less steel, not forty percent more."

Rennie smiled. "Absolutely true. Unless."

"Unless what?"

The van rolled to a stop in front of the passenger-loading area for United flights leaving Pittsburgh's airport. Rennie leaned on the steering wheel and popped the Led Zep tape out of the deck. "Unless Detroit is going to build bigger cars and build more cars, and just tell the feds to go fuck themselves."

Molly had a few minutes before her plane, so she used them to check in at the *Times* with Len Gass. "I saw a copy of the *Times* with today's date on it in the Pittsburgh airport, and I'm taking it as a good sign that we might publish again tomorrow. Who's buying us today?"

"I've heard the *National Enquirer*."

"Jesus, who's your source?"

"The boy who delivers from the deli."

"I wouldn't mind that," said Molly. "I'll put in for the UFOs-menace-Jackie-O beat." She scrunched around in the phone cubicle to get a look at the clock. No problem. "Did you have a chance to get those aircraft registrations checked out?"

"Yep."

"Hmmn," said Molly, as she wrote down the names of the corporations.

"Does the 'hmmn' mean anything, or are you treading water?"

"It means I'm not surprised. Lennie, I'm going to have to call you back. I have to catch a plane. On second thought, tell the *Enquirer* I'd prefer the cure-cancer-diet beat."

Molly didn't have to run for a plane; but she was treading water, and she didn't particularly want Gass to realize it. She sat in one of the departure lounge seats, Rennie Knowles's hardcopy printout poking out of her purse, and tried to make what she'd been picking up come together.

The more she thought about it, Rennie sounded plausible; it did look as though General Steel—and some corporate buddies—were planning to tell the feds to go fuck themselves. But Molly, even offhand, could think of eight ways the steel overrun violated the Federal Omnibus Resources and Manufacturing Act; and, if Federal Motors was to put the steel to the use for which it was manufactured, eight ways FedMo would break the same law.

The large corporations had shown no quarter in fighting the Omni Act. They had screamed that it violated several laws of nature, God, and man, that of supply and demand among them, and that it would mean the end of the sacred American free marketplace. They retaliated by literally jamming the courts. Eight *billion* documents had been produced in one case alone. But even with Congress as badly spooked by the energy situation as it was, it was not immune to the lobbyists; the Fortune 500 had been provided with ample places to end-run the Omni Act. There were plenty of ways for Federal Steel and FedMo to do this less bluntly. Justice was counting on a quick test case against a very big defendant as a demonstration of the need for the Omni, and of the government's will to enforce it. A forty percent steel overrun seemed to be indefensible. It was frightening; the calmness in Rennie's hardcopy suggested the will of the Congress was simply to be ignored.

Something was blocking Molly's vision. Two men, standing in front of her. They were vaguely fortyish, vaguely handsome, expensively but unremarkably dressed.

"Molly Rice," said one of them, smiling.

Molly knew what they wanted in an instant, even before they

sat down in the seats on either side of her. Knew not who they were, but what they were; the meaning and consequence of their presence. She felt the first surge of fear as an acidic churning in her stomach.

"Miss Rice," said the one who spoke, who took the seat to her left. "We know you have a plane to catch, but we'll be very brief. Very emphatic." He spoke quietly, pleasantly. And smiled.

"You have gathered information which, were it widely known, would inconvenience a great number of people. We represent those interests. They would deeply appreciate it if you were to stop this right now. Destroy your notes. Report back to the *Times* that your leads have run out, that there is no story." He folded his hands in his lap.

"But we come to the problem of inducement, don't we? You are a highly principled journalist. Strongly motivated. Our principals are willing to give you money, but we aren't even going to bother to offer it. Bribery would only offend you, and you'd certainly redouble your efforts, to punish us for the attempt."

He leaned closer to her. Molly could feel the fear churning up out of her stomach, starting to make her dizzy.

"So let's make it clear. I'll spell it out. I am making a threat of physical harm . . . no, I *promise* you physical harm if you continue with this. Permanent harm, Molly. Pain beyond your comprehension, given by people who know what they're doing, who've had lots of practice at it, and who enjoy it very, very much."

Something exploded at the side of Molly's face. She sucked in her breath and mewled and threw up her hand to her cheek. The other man had lightly touched her hair. And smiled.

The first man was standing. "Have a nice flight." Then they were gone.

Molly was able to make it into the women's john—thank God, empty—before she vomited. She locked the door to the stall and sat there, dabbing at her lips with a Kleenex, waiting to stop trembling. *It's not like you weren't expecting it, honey.* She'd been expecting it since she saw the airplanes shoved into the hangars up in Michigan. She was making people hide who weren't used to hiding, and it angered them. It was only a question of when she'd get close enough to make them feel threatened. What did surprise her was how frightened she'd been. *I thought they'd do it over the phone.* She half-laughed. *They had you barfing in the john, kid. Thought you had bigger balls than that.*

She heard her flight being called, and took a moment to blot a wet paper towel over her forehead. Molly looked at her drained face in the mirror. *Get used to the fear, honey. You're going to have to learn to live with it.*

Harland didn't know what to expect when he sat down with the telephone to try to find Sam Painter. Did someone who was in the business of visiting sites of mass death have an office?

He certainly didn't expect to find out with just the second phone call.

"Painter?" said a freelance writer who had also known Painter when the three of them were in Vietnam. Harland covered for CBS; Painter was a colonel in the Special Forces. "Sure, I know how you can reach Sam Painter. You got a Pentagon phone directory?"

Harland didn't, but the CBS Washington bureau did. And there he was: Painter, Sam. Then some meaningless military acronym and an extension number. Nothing to lose, thought Harland. He called it and got a secretary type. Painter wasn't there. Harland IDed himself and asked the secretary to tell Painter that John Harland, CBS News, would like to talk with him in Washington, tomorrow if possible, and could he call back? Harland realized that there was a very low probability that Sam Painter would return the call because there was a very high probability that, whatever he was doing in that office in the Pentagon, he didn't want to talk to CBS News about it. But he might return the call because it was Harland who placed it, and because probabilities weren't of much use in anticipating Sam Painter.

A photograph of Harland shoving a microphone into Sam Painter's face while a Vietnamese village burned in the background accompanied the first *TV Guide* piece on Harland, the one officially designating him as someone to watch. That had been when? Seventy-two? Early seventy-three? Harland spent but three or four months in Vietnam. For one of them he traveled with Painter's command, doing an in-depth, war-as-microcosm piece.

When he left the office that Saturday afternoon—Painter hadn't returned his call—he found a print of that picture. He studied it, retrieving what he knew—or thought he knew—about Painter. He had hardly become friends with the man. Harland couldn't imagine Painter being friends with anybody. But they had come at least to respect each other for being professionals. Sam Painter was a brilliant soldier: totally dispassionate, intelligent, precisely articulate. He functioned better under extreme stress than anyone Harland had ever known. His men obeyed him absolutely. For no logical reason, he scared Harland shitless.

Harland was about to go to bed when the phone rang. Molly. He picked it up and held the mouthpiece so that it would sound as though he were calling off to someone in the next room. "That's okay, Trish, I got it." Then into the mouthpiece: "Hello?" But it wasn't Molly.

"Mr. Harland?" Male. Unfamiliar. Harland frowned. His unlisted phone number was one of his most precious possessions, fiercely guarded. He'd talk to anyone who called him at his office, but he tried to keep the world from chasing him into the apartment. Less than ten people in the world, only two at CBS, knew how to get him at home. They knew they could get him there to invite him to dinner, or to talk about the Knicks' season, or to ask how to unplug a toilet because Harland was good at such handyman things. But if it was about business, it had better be about nothing less heavyweight than a presidential assassination or World War III.

"This is six-six-four-one," said Harland.

"I'm calling for Sam Painter," said the voice. "He will be in his office in Washington all day tomorrow, and will be pleased to see you again. At your convenience." Then Harland was listening to a dial tone.

He had not given Painter's office the unlisted number.

On the way down to Washington, Harland marshaled what little post-Vietnam data he had on Painter, which was very little. His contact knew only that Painter had resigned his commission and was working in the office of the Joint Chiefs of Staff as a civilian consultant. Harland formulated something like a strategy. It would hardly do any good to run into Painter's office waving Billy Coombs's videotape and start demanding explanations. Were he to repeat Coombs's accusations, Painter would never tell him the reasons that brought him to Sundown, to the 747 crashsite, to Houston. Harland needed to find out as much as he could without driving Painter into deeper cover. Painter obviously knew Harland was onto something, and he was going to try to shortstop him. He was willing to talk to Harland in hopes that he could give Harland a little truth, and Harland might mistake it for the big truth.

So Harland decided to try this: to let Painter believe he'd discovered the nature of Painter's ostensible job with the Joint Chiefs—on the assumption that it was classified enough and sinister enough to make a good news piece—he'd pretend to ferret out of Painter only what Painter was pretending to be doing. Mutual sandbagging. It was the sort of game that amused Painter; he might enjoy it enough to tell Harland more than he really needed to.

Painter's section was not in a deeply secure part of the Pentagon. All he needed to get there was a visitor's pass, which was waiting for him at a checkpoint. Harland was expecting something more dramatic than an ordinary door to an ordinary office with another acronym on it: JCS SCENREALT.

There was a man at the desk in the outer office of Painter's suite. He smiled politely and totally without warmth when Harland came in. He greeted him by name before Harland introduced himself. He had a hard body, short hair, a small moustache, cold green eyes. Harland decided that there was something wrong with the way he dressed. It was not what he was wearing—a bland, doubleknit brown suit—but what he wasn't wearing. He should be wearing weapons, thought Harland: sidearms, knives, grenades, a piano-wire garrote.

Harland was told he could go right in, and he did, through a door in a wall hung with decorations remarkable only for their absence of military reference.

Painter didn't hear Harland when he walked in. He was at a desk, writing on a legal pad, a yellow island in a tumble of books and looseleaf notebooks. The last time Harland had seen him he was wearing fatigues, and now Painter was wearing a rugby shirt. But that was all that had changed.

Painter looked up, recognized Harland, and smiled.

"Hello, John." He stood up and shook hands with Harland across his desk.

Harland nodded at Painter's shirt. "I hate guys my own age who can still look good in shirts like that. If I tried to wear something with stripes I'd look like a contour map of Tibet."

"You look fine, John. That's a handsome suit. You wear your success very well."

"Cunningly tailored to hide a spare tire." Harland tilted his head to look at the books on Painter's desk. "Jesus, you must be worried about me seeing classified documents. That's Hebrew, isn't it? I've heard it was difficult to learn."

"Relatively. Chinese was harder." Painter leaned back in his chair, rubbed the eraser of his pencil across his lip. He would look at Harland with an unvarying small smile. "John, I've been pleased by your success. I admired your work in Vietnam, and

I admire it more today." He said it without a trace of effusion, as if it weren't praise, but simply observed data.

"Thank you very much. I guess I should reciprocate here, and I would. Praise you for your success." Harland crossed his legs. "If I knew what it was you were doing."

Painter's smile spread to his eyes. Good, thought Harland. He *is* enjoying this. Harland smiled back at him. "Sorry. Am I rushing it? Should we continue with banalities for a while longer before I casually ask the first obliquely probing question?"

"John, did you check with the JCS press office about my section?" Harland shook his head. "Good. It would have wasted your time. They lie so clumsily. It would have been no challenge for you." He looked at Harland a moment, tapping the pencil eraser against his chin. "John, this section is not classified as such. But it is sensitive. I shall be very careful what I tell you, but what I tell you will be true. Let's start over again, back with the banalities."

"Okay, how about: 'Gee, Sam, how are the wife and kids?' "

"Fine, except that I don't have any."

"I know you don't. I'm vamping. How about: 'Gee, Sam, I didn't know you weren't in the Army anymore. When did you resign your commission?' "

"Three years ago."

"I thought you'd be a lifer. You sounded like it over there. You'd be a general by now, wouldn't you, if you'd stayed in?"

Painter shook his head. "I was passed over for general. Twice."

"Passed over? Big mistake. You're brilliant."

"I chap asses."

"Ah yes. I remember. You chapped one too many?"

"I chapped several too many."

"So you told them to stuff their Army where the sun don't shine?"

"Not really. I stayed in until this job with JCS came along."

"So the section is 'sensitive' in the sense that the Army wants it staffed by civilians. Well. That's revelatory." Harland re-crossed his legs. "Here's where you're supposed to volunteer what it is this section does. Otherwise, the conversation comes to a dead stop."

"You aren't showing me any leverage, John. I have a posi-tion to hold here, and you aren't showing me enough strength to make me regroup."

"Okay, you got it. Sam, how come you keep showing up in our newsfilm?"

The eraser missed its cadence by a millisecond.

"We got you at the plane crash in North Carolina, we got you at the train wreck in Kansas, lots of other places. We got you showing up wherever there's been big trouble." A lie; only at two places beside Billy Coombs's videotape; but it was a reasonable extrapolation, and an immediately undetectable lie. "Unless you at least make a shot at giving me a plausibly dull explanation, the kind that convinces a reporter he's got no story here, I'm going to have to go on the air with half a story. You know. The old 'what's the military doing involved in patently nonmilitary affairs?' Sinister number. It could cause you piles of grief. . . . How's that?"

Painter nodded his head. "Damn good, John. Really well-played point." He tore the top page off the legal pad and tossed the pad to Harland along with a pencil. "You may want to take notes. The section is designated SCENREALT. Scenarios for Reaction Alternatives."

"Well, that speaks volumes. How big is it?"

"We've had as many as twelve, as few as three. Seven now. All civilians, although several are *former* military. We're a study group, John. Emphasize *study*. We deal with research and theory. The section devises scenarios under which a military reaction to an act of civilian or foreign terrorism might be desirable."

"Like what happens if it's an American airplane at Entebbe?"

"That was one of our scenarios."

"Like what happens if terrorists get a nuclear device?"

"That was another one. Terrorism is a growth industry, John. It's way beyond aging Weathermen and Puerto Rican nationalists making pipe bombs. There are going to be situations where civilian response will not be adequate. The military has technology and ubiquity. It could be helpful."

"But there are . . . sensitivities."

"There are sensitivities."

"Like the possibility of the military preempting civilian authority."

"We have scenarios where that occurs, but the circumstances would be extreme."

"And a military participation in civil intelligence?"

"Considered only in theory and speculation."

Harland nodded at the Hebrew literature on Painter's desk. "The Israelis take it a good way past theory."

"We aren't modeling on Israel."

"So then you were in Kansas . . . researching."

"I visit the sites of terrorist incidents. Incidentally, according to our scenarios, a military response there would not have been appropriate."

"And the plane crash? Do you think the plane was sabotaged by terrorists?"

"We will study the FAA report. My feeling is that the plane did not crash as a result of terrorism."

"Could I see some of your scenarios and your recommended responses?"

"Of course, John. Not to take with you, but to read here. They're interesting." He leaned back in his chair. "Read all you want. You won't use them, John. You know it would be irresponsible, that what the section does is eighty percent imagination anyway. You're too much of a professional to make up a story when there's no story."

Harland put the legal pad back on Painter's desk. "Damn good, Sam. You played that point very well." He stood, felt exhausted. "Just about wore me out. I gotta get back to New York. Am I going to see you any more in our newsfilm?"

"I'll make sure that you don't."

"Then if I want to see you again, I'll have to take you to lunch sometime. Look me up." They shook hands. "Enjoyed it, Sam."

After Harland left, the man from the outer office came in and sat down in the chair across from Painter's desk. "Will he drop it?"

"Jesus no," said Painter. "Careers are made on stories like this."

"Then is he going to go on television and tell the whole fucking country about the section?"

"No, because he knows SCENREALT is a cover. He's not going to break half a story, and let all the other media in the country in on it. He's not going to share it with anybody until he gets it all."

The other man looked out the window behind Painter. "So. When and how?"

Painter looked at him. "No. Nobody touches him."

After no small amount of complaining, Harland finally had his time alone with a typewriter and his notes on Martin Vandellen. He was spending it—had spent the last couple of hours—twirling with a pencil eraser the one sheet of paper that contained a few vague sentences about Vandellen, staring off through the glass of his cubbyhole into the middle distance of the newsroom, and thinking about Sam Painter. And what to do about Sam Painter, if to do anything about Sam Painter. He would soon be at the point where he would have to Get on the Story in the formal sense: go to his producer, get a camera crew, tell them where to go and what to shoot. To do that, he would have to submit himself to a classic journalistic process; it cast reporters as assistant district attorneys seeking search warrants and their editors as judges with short attention spans and tight budgets. Harland would have to show probable cause why the story would be interesting. But at the moment all he had was bits of newsfilm that showed a man present in the aftermath of several news events—and his perfectly reasonable explanation for being there.

The trouble with reasonable explanations is that they make the kind of newstape that never makes it to air.

The reasonable explanations had made Harland unreasonably frightened. He was chasing the story principally so that his unease could be found either justifiable or dismissable. He was going to have to put together more evidence before he went to his producer, more justification than the fact that Sam Painter's smile scared him shitless.

"You wanna see something weird?" It was Jerry Lee, leaning against the door of Harland's office. He was holding up several videocassettes. "Commercials."

"Most commercials are weird," said Harland.

"How many are classified?"

As they walked down to the editing room, Lee told Harland how the cassettes has been slipped to him by a zealous young man in the Program Practices department.

"All commercials go through Program Practices, right?" said Lee. "Make sure the vaginal deodorant spots don't gross everybody out, that there's a reasonable chance the FTC won't file suit over the claims for vitamins. These things are all screened first by the peons in Program Practices, and if there's any problems, they bump them upstairs. Apparently these got routed to this kid, but before he got around to looking at them, somebody found out that somebody screwed up, because they got taken off his desk overnight. And when he asked, he was told to forget about them."

"And being young and single and able to afford principles, he somehow got the tapes—"

"Don't ask him how."

"—and gave them to you."

"Third choice after Woodward or Bernstein." Lee had dropped the cassette into the player and thumbed it on.

There were three spots. As they played, Harland tried to see how they were weird, and he couldn't. They were normal specimens of commercials: improbably beautiful people being made improbably happy by use of a product or service. The first was for an airline. A husband arrives home through a blizzard to be met by wifey at the door. Thoughts of Miami Beach are on both minds. Wishing and the airline make it so; a splice of the film and they're sitting on the Sunliner, headed south, care visibly lifting from their brows. The second equated the purchase of a gas furnace with making the family circle more cohesive. The third was an archetype, shot with a very long lens to emphasize the selling point: While his family cringed in fear, a man nervously tried to maneuver his car from the on ramp of a freeway into a stream of traffic growling with omnivorous trucks. A voice reminded him that for the safety of his loved ones, he should be driving a big car. Cut to the car the voice would recommend.

"The last one is the work of geniuses," said Harland. "I haven't seen guilt used to sell something that effectively since life insurance. So what's weird? They're commercials, just like commercials have always been."

"Some star newsman," said Lee. "Think about it. In the first one, they're selling air travel, right? To the sunny south? Well, if you called *now* you *might* be able to get a seat from the Northeast *anywhere* south by the end of March. The second one sells gas furnaces. Gas furnaces? When there's five hours of gas available to burn a day in the Midwest? Maybe twelve hours a day even in the gas-producing states? And Johnny, did you see how the people in that snug little house were dressed? Shirtsleeves. And did you see the closeup of the hand coming into the shot and turning the thermostat *up*? To *eighty*?"

And the new big car, thought Harland. *After the first of the fiscal year, a car that big would be illegal to manufacture.*

"Agency people are not dumb," said Lee. "How come they're working so hard at creating consumer needs their accounts will have no opportunity to fulfill?" Lee thumbed another button and the cassette popped out of the machine.

"Did the kid from Program Practices say a schedule has been bought for these spots?" said Harland.

"A big schedule, starting in about three weeks, and building to a monster schedule by the end of the contract. They've probably bought the same schedule on the other networks. By mid-February those three spots are just about all America is going to be seeing on television."

11

MOLLY GRIMACED BOTH AT THE NOISE THE 747 WAS MAKING AS it began its takeoff roll and at the idea that she would soon have to be mingling with its turbojet brethren on the ramps and runways of New Orleans International. She hated following those things around in Cessnas, both in the air and on the ground. Every light-plane pilot's favorite hangar horror story was being brushed by the invisible horizontal tornado of those monsters' wingtip vortex. Whenever she could, she rented from a field that didn't serve the heavy jets, but there was no reasonable alternative here. Hundreds of light plane pilots follow the heavies every day, she told herself. Just fly above them when you're behind them on a final approach and land down the runway beyond where they touch down. The aviation catechism on vortex avoidance gave her no comfort. *If you could only see the damn things.*

The FBO she'd phoned from Houston was a pretty good choice for one made essentially at random. He'd even had someone meet her airline flight and drive her across the airport to the general-aviation section.

The 172 was waiting for her in the tiedowns, freshly washed. She filled out the rental agreement, noted her destination and planned stops. The FBO handed her a key and a checklist and told her that the 172 was topped off with gas and filled with oil. There was another point in the catechism for that: Don't believe anybody. She opened the left door and pulled from the glove box the engine-maintenance logbook. She checked them against the Hobbs meter, which indicated the number of hours the engine had been operating. An FAA-required overhaul had been performed on schedule, twelve hours ago.

She preflighted the plane in exactly the same sequence she had preflighted Cessnas since she took her first flying lesson. Left side of the plane first. Flaps set properly into their tracks; an acceptable one-eighth rotation in tie rod to ailerons; Pitot tube clear; stall warning port clear. Undo tiedown chain. Step on the strut, elbows up on the leading edge of the wing, fuel tank cap off, visual check of fuel level. It was indeed gassed up. Static air intake clear. Engine air intakes clear. No more than routine nicks in the propeller. Open the port and check the oil level. It was indeed oiled up. Pull the lever and bleed some avgas out of the sump; no bubbles in the puddle means no water in the line. Right side of airplane. Leading edge, flap tracks, aileron tie rod, tiedown chain. Cargo hatch closed. Bolts connecting the rudder. Still there. Bolts connecting the elevator. Still there. Tail tiedown.

That was no guarantee that the engine would not fail in its thirteenth hour after overhaul, nor that any or all of the components she had just inspected would not come apart; but Molly could take some comfort, as the plane stalled and spun in, that at least she had been conscientious.

She got into the left front seat, finished the cabin checklist, turned on the radios, and called clearance delivery. Five minutes later—miraculous: no heavy jets ahead of her in the queue of aircraft that ground control had assembled at the base of the runway—Molly had received clearance for takeoff. In the cool air, the 172 was ready to lift off of its own accord at sixty knots. She climbed over Lake Pontchartrain and came west to a heading of two-six-nine.

*　　*　　*

Harland had heard about the tape, knew that it was being passed around the office. It hadn't gotten to him yet, and he hadn't asked to listen to it. He didn't think he would like to hear it. Someone had once offered to play for him tapes of the noises Grissom, White, and Chaffee made inside the Apollo capsule as it burned atop the launch tower at Cape Kennedy in 1967. He passed. But the *60 Minutes* producer who had the 747 tapes didn't put it in the form of a question. He was passing Harland's office, saw that he was still staring off into the middle distance, and just put the audio cassette player down on Harland's desk.

"Got a second, John?" said the producer. "I'd like you to listen to this. Been playing it for everybody around here. See if you can figure out what these people are saying." He handed Harland a Xerox copy of a tentative transcript. He rewound the tape, watching for the footage counter to roll up a location.

"Are these the flight recorder tapes from the 747 crash?"

"Yeah. The parts the FAA isn't releasing. They say it's unintelligible. Which it almost is. Almost."

Good, thought Harland. Since he couldn't refuse to listen—he's supposed to be a tough newsman, after all, and there was the matter of a colleague's request—maybe he'd be lucky and not be able to understand anything.

"We bought these things?"

"From a *very* nervous FAA employee. It's a dub, obviously, of the pilots' conversation, and not a very good one. The FAA guy had to sneak out the original and dub it off in a closet somewhere so he could put the original tape back." He found the spot for which he was searching and stopped the tape. "Here's the last transmission the National Transportation Safety Board transcribed in the prelim accident report. The pilot is responding to an air-traffic controller who's advising him of traffic. Unknown aircraft, northeast of his position, two thousand feet above him."

The captain's voice was clear, firm, bass; a pro. It was the kind of voice that made the passengers feel secure when it came from the cabin speakers to announce the cruising altitude and weather at the destination city.

"*Thank you sir, I have him in sight.*"

"And this is what they say is unintelligible . . ."

"*—fucking Christ—*" "That's the copilot," said the producer. Then a blast of white noise. "*—son of bitch crazy, he's going—*" "*—oh God, oh Jesus—*" More white noise, garbles. "This is ATC again," said the producer. The ground controller was asking the 747 the nature of his difficulty, and repeating that his transmissions were breaking up. "The radios have to be kept keyed on by a finger," said the producer. "The pilots were getting pushed around so much, the G forces . . ."

"*—pull up, he's breaking down—*" Garbles. A final spray of white noise. The *60 Minutes* producer turned off the cassette.

Harland said that no, he didn't understand any more of the garbles than anyone else. But he asked if he could keep the Xerox copy of the NTSB transcript. And for a dub of the cassette. He opened his lower left desk drawer and slid the transcript into a large brown envelope. He'd written "Sam" on it, in grease pencil.

Things had gone very well for Molly, in Bay St. Louis, in Morgan City, in De Quincy. Her nervous sources had all been willing to meet her at the local airports with their Xeroxes of Xeroxes of Xeroxes. Blurry, but useful. Molly had suffered excessive social cups of airport coffee; her landing to refuel in Lafayette was more critical in terms of a ladies' room than gasoline. The *Times* was going to screech a little when she presented them the bill for the Cessna. But they were in a hurry for the story; travel among the three meetings would have taken two days in a car.

New Orleans was a hundred and two nautical miles away— less than an hour. She asked a line boy to top off the Cessna's tanks and walked into the Lafayette flight service station to close her flight plan from De Quincy and file a new one to New Orleans; she'd open it by radio once she was in the air.

The weather briefer said there'd be no problems into NO; cold, but clear and dry.

The line boy had parked the Texaco truck and was rolling Molly's credit card through the imprinter. So far in allocating fuel the feds had been reasonably kind to operators of light planes. It was still relatively easy to get aviation gas in areas of thin population where there was no scheduled air-taxi service. But it was still wise to call ahead to make sure there was fuel available at one's scheduled fuel stops, and to stick to one's flight plan.

There was a man peering through the right-side window into the Cessna when Molly walked out of the FBO's office toward the ramp. He was looking at the panel, the universal obsession of light-plane aviation; every light-plane owner was constantly thinking of moving up or over to a new plane. Every refueling ramp at every airfield was a showroom.

"Nice panel," the man said. "You like that DME?"

"So far," said Molly. "It's rented."

"Nice plane. The FBO keeps it in good shape." Molly had unlocked the door. "You're heading for Morgan City?"

"Already been there."

"I was going to say, if you're headed for Morgan City, don't worry about fuel. There's always plenty. Lot of aviation there. That's where they do all the flying out to the offshore rigs."

"Right."

"Have a good flight. Weather's good everywhere."

"Right," said Molly, and closed the door. Molly was never comfortable with the practice and seldom peered through parked planes' windows at someone else's avionics. Felt like looking through someone's living room window to her.

Molly taxied to the end of the active runway, did her engine run-up, checked the control surfaces. She switched to the tower frequency and told the controller she was ready for takeoff.

She had the Cessna climbing toward eight thousand five hundred feet. It's an efficient cruising altitude, and it's better to fly high for best use of the radio navigation aids. It's not very good for sightseeing, but there was little to see in this treeless Louisiana delta land besides fields. She hoped she might come over an oil refinery. She still had the low-time pilot's fascination with how human enterprise looked from the air.

She had reached eight thousand five hundred and had the plane trimmed out for cruise. The needle of the VOR was centered; she was on victor twenty, the airway to New Orleans. The wind was almost dead on her nose, so there wasn't that much correction to be made for drift. She was going to have little to do for the next half hour.

She felt a sudden urge for country and western, and looked on the sectional map for a radio station she might be able to pick up on the ADF radio. No, not country and western. Cajun music. There had to be a French-speaking station in Lafayette. It had been years since she'd heard Cajun music.

She'd found a station noted on the sectional and was tuning toward its frequency when the engine cut out.

In the time it took for her mind to register that the warm vibration of the engine was gone, the engine came back on again. Her fingers were still on the dial of the ADF. The engine cut out again, stayed off for half a second, caught with a chug that yawed the plane the slightest bit with its torque.

For the time it took for Molly to bring her hand back to the throttle, the engine ran smoothly. Then it cut out again and began to chatter. Even before the earliest expedition of fear entered her stomach and her mind began shifting from Cajun music to the possibility that the Cessna's engine might be failing, Molly had already pulled out the lever that directed heat from the exhaust into the carburetor. That, she had been drilled over and over when she was in flight school, was the first thing to do if the engine started running rough, in case the cause was ice in the carburetor.

The engine rattled for five more seconds, then stopped. In its place Molly heard the slipstream—the noise of the air coursing by the surface of the airplane. She reached down to the floor and felt for the fuel-tank selector valve, looked down at it. It was set to "both." Fuel was flowing to the engine from both tanks. Molly realized that she was feeling for the fuel valve not because it was the next proper step in the emergency procedure, but because once her flight instructor had sneaked the valve to "off" with his foot to make a simulated emergency landing seem more authentic. It was a dream reaction; feeling for the valve proved that she was alert, that she was a good girl. Doing the right thing would cause her CFI to be there in the right seat, to approve, to tell her it was just a drill and allow her to turn the engine on again.

Molly looked at the instruments. Nothing was telling her anything was wrong. The radios were on, the gyrocompass was functioning. There was no electrical failure. The oil pressure had not yet fallen out of the green-for-good sector on its dial. The oil temperature was normal. *There is no reason for this. If there is no reason, there's no remedy, and therefore no hope.*

She felt white noise turning the corners of her consciousness uselessly crystalline. "Straighten up," she shouted at herself. She had not drilled in emergency landings since her biennial flight review a year and a half ago. The emergency-landing procedures were on the cabin checklist. She could not remember where she had put the checklist.

"Fuck the checklist, honey, you know what the emergency procedures are." *Conserve altitude. You're still at eight thousand five hundred*—she looked at the altimeter—*eight thousand two hundred feet, and that's money in the bank.* She trimmed the plane for the speed that would allow it to glide the farthest.

Choose a landing site, and do not change it. At least she wasn't over the Rockies. The land was dead flat and mostly agricultural. She could put down in a field. *Choose one that's brown, not green.* Green meant it was probably under irrigation. The wheels would touch down in water and she'd nose the plane over, at seventy miles per hour. In a dry plowed field, land with the furrows; she might trash the landing gear, might even bend the prop. But she'd walk away. *And you know what they say in aviation, any landing you can walk away from is a good landing . . .*

Seven thousand six hundred.

Aviate.

Better was a road. She was paralleling one to her left. But it took frequent right-angle turns, following fence lines, and there was bright vegetation on either side of it. Probably narrow, and with ditches. And almost certainly utility poles on one side or the other. Another road on her nose, perpendicular to this one. Too far away to tell what it was like. *Head for it, and if it doesn't look right, settle for a field beyond it.*

Five thousand four hundred.

Communicate.

Molly turned the second radio to 121.5, the emergency frequency. Do it now, when the transmission would carry further at altitude. Somebody somewhere, surely the FSS back in Lafayette, was listening to 121.5. If—*don't say if, honey, say when*—when she got the plane down, help would be sent. She'd run through this dozens of time in practice. This time she really turned on the microphone. But she didn't say anything. *I haven't tried to restart this thing yet. What if the fucker starts and I fly on?* Molly thought of how embarrassing that would be. The FAA would send out the highway patrol, the sheriffs, maybe the Civil Air Patrol. She thought that maybe she should try to restart . . .

Four thousand seven hundred.

"Mayday, mayday. Skyhawk four six seven kilo Quebec. Lost my engine, I'm thirty-two miles DME east of Lafayette on victor twenty, landing it on a road."

Fuck pride.

Three thousand one hundred.

No one had answered on 121.5. FSS in Lafayette must be on a coffee break. *Well, fuck 'em. They can't help me land this thing anyway.*

Two thousand seven hundred.

At two thousand, she tried the restart procedure. Fuel mixture. Cycle master switch. Starter. It didn't start, but Molly didn't expect it to. She was going through the steps impatiently, as a formality. Landing her airplane was the business at hand. She was going through the formalities for Don, her flight instructor, to whom she now spoke as though he were in the right seat.

The intersecting road coming up wasn't looking good. It didn't look any wider. By now she was under a layer of clouds at twelve thousand feet, and even though it was getting on to late afternoon, there were no shadows to help her tell if there were utility poles parallel to it.

One thousand seven hundred.

"I'm doing a pretty good job, huh, Don?" *I haven't shit my pants. Whataya think? Think I'll pass my check ride? I'm remembering my procedures. I'm getting all the glide out this thing I'm going to get. I did all the things you told me to do. I looked all through all one hundred and eighty degrees for the best landing site, I . . .*

I looked everywhere but right under me. Molly put the plane in a tight left bank. The universe turned from half blue to all green and brown. Rice fields. A tight right bank. She leaned over to look out the right door. She was able to see almost straight down. More rice fields. *Well. A good idea.*

Something at the edge of her vision. Just about to slide behind out of sight beyond the rear right window was an airstrip.

"Don! All right!" she screamed. She tightened the right bank. Okay, so she was changing the landing site. Don would forgive her, trading a narrow road for a crop duster's strip. She studied it as the Cessna completed its turn. Gray. Good. That meant it was used enough to be dusty. Beyond it, an irrigation canal with raised banks. No problem. The strip is long enough to stop. She was going to make it. She thought briefly about getting back on 121.5 and canceling the emergency. No. Too busy.

One thousand. The strip was coming up fast. She could see the tanks used for refueling the agplanes. Molly needed to bleed off some of the altitude and airspeed she husbanded, so she put on ten degrees of flaps.

She was not slowing to her satisfaction. She looked down, saw from the movement in the fields of—what? Dried sugarcane stalks?—that she was landing downwind, being blown past the point on the runway where she'd want to touch down. Dumb, dumb not turning downwind when the engine first failed. But not fatal, and nothing to do about it, except put on more flaps to bring down the airspeed.

Seven hundred. She was aligned with the duster strip now. Five hundred. Something bright beyond the near end of the runway. Round, yellow.

The signals used to mark electric transmission lines.

A rush of panic, worse than the one when the engine first failed, made Molly grunt. She did not fear the power lines. She had the altitude and airspeed to clear them. And clearing them meant that the tailwind would blow her—how far? Two-thirds of the way?—down the duster strip. Two-thirds of the way, she might make it; there was a strip of sugarcane between the end of the strip and the irrigation canal. But no further.

Land short of the lines? Nothing but rice fields below. The plane would nose over, and she'd have the engine in her chest. *Go under the lines.* No. Only if she could add power to drag in to the end of the strip. There was one glide slope, the steepest angle through the closest point she could come to the lines, that would put her on the ground with the most room for rollout. She had to dissipate the precise amount of the plane's kinetic energy.

Molly realized she was panting. She took several deep breaths. *The rest of the flaps . . . now.* She felt the Cessna slow. And sink. *Too soon.* It fell toward the power lines. Instinctively she pulled the nose up, to stretch the glide over the lines. Illusionary: The airspeed indicator dropped out of the green, into the white arc where only the extra lift provided by the flaps kept it from stalling in the sky. The stall warning cleared its throat, then became a bleat. She felt a bump, then several; lift was trying to peel away from the surface of the wings.

"Nose *down*, asshole." *This is going to take balls, honey.* She would have to keep the nose down, aiming directly into the wires, to gain enough airspeed so that she could trade it for lift, pulling up the nose at the last instant to clear the wires. And so she dove the plane directly at them. She saw two birds, frightened by her approach, clamber off the lines. She saw how the wires were encrusted with droppings. When she could bear the proximity to the wires no longer, she pulled up the nose.

She did not know if she would clear the wires; but if she hit them, it would be the furthest ones, the last ones she had to clear. She thought that was pretty good.

Then the wires were going past the wingtip. She arched her back, but she did not hit them, although she felt their static electricity in her hair.

From a height of sixty feet she dove the plane toward the ground, in search of friction. Now earth rushed at her. At the last possible instant, when the Cessna would have made contact with the front wheel of the tricycle landing gear and turned itself into a ball, she pulled up the nose.

The plane hit evenly on all three wheels at once. The windmilling prop bit into the dust, momentarily grayed out the windshield. The suspension bounced the plane into the air again, and it glided further down the strip, sideways. Molly's hand was jerked off the control yoke. She kicked hard on the right rudder, to straighten the plane, but there was nothing she could do to get it down on the land again. She was now at least three-quarters of the way down the strip.

The plane touched down again, bounced a little. Molly slapped up the lever and the flaps began retracting, putting more weight on the tires. It stuck to the earth this time, but at a speed where Molly could barely control the rollout. She could see the top of the irrigation canal above the dead stalks of sugarcane. She stood on the brakes. She saw that she would not be able to stop the plane before it crossed the end of the strip.

When it entered the dead cane, Molly threw her arms over her face. In darkness, the cane chattering against the plane, she was thrown right, the shoulder harness biting into her, then left. Her head banged against the window. She awaited the embankment.

Finally, deceleration, a force pushing her forward in the harness. The plane tilted forward, and settled back. And then it was motionless.

She opened her eyes and saw the wall of hard dirt seven feet ahead of her.

A smell: Sharp. Dried cane rammed into the cowling, against the hot engine. There were at least thirty-five gallons of gasoline still in the tanks. The door opened easily. She fell out, landing on her hands and knees. She pushed through the dried cane. When she looked back, she was perhaps a hundred feet from the plane. She sat down then, because she couldn't stand, and then lay back, because she couldn't sit. The cane was an iris, and a bank of clouds lidded the blue at zenith behind them.

Molly sat cross-legged in the middle of a bed in a medium-dreary dreary room of a no-more-dreary-than-any-other hotel chain. She was surrounded by the aftermath of a room-service meal, several notebooks, and the boxes, Styrofoam packing forms, plastic wrappers, instruction books, and warranty cards that had come around and with an expensive 35mm camera and a cheap cassette tape recorder.

She had put the cassette on Record and propped it up so that its built-in microphone was pointing to her. She stared at the perforated black disc, sniffed the Japanese-electronics smell, heard the recorder make dutiful sibilant sounds as its capstan turned. But she had nothing to say to it. She turned it off, re-wound it past the thirty seconds of silence. *Oh for three. This is getting dumb. Turn it on and say anything.*

The tape stopped at its beginning. Molly stabbed it to Record and blurted out what first came to the front of her brain, which for some reason was:

"A wop bop a loo bop a wop bam boom. That's Little Richard. But are you old enough to remember Little Richard?

I keep forgetting. You're a baby." A running private joke with Harland; she was eight months older than he. But he was more than old enough to remember Little Richard.

You've stopped. Keep going.

"This is my fourth try at this. Turn on tape recorder, get embarrassed, not say anything, turn off tape recorder, rewind tape recorder, turn on tape recorder, get embarrassed . . . I hate tape recorders, that might have something to do with it. But I don't have time to write it down, and . . . This is just so fucking *paranoid*. I feel like such an ass, and the thought of you actually listening to this . . . these . . ."

You're not making any sense. But don't stop and go back. You might not start again.

"Okay. Today I went out and bought this handy-dandy nineteen-ninety-nine-plus-Louisiana-sales-tax tape recorder and a Nikon FM, which did not cost nineteen ninety-nine, because . . ." She laughed. "Because some people are trying to kill me." *Paaaaar-a-noid.* "That's not exactly right. There are people who *can* kill me anytime they want to, and they want me to know it. Does that sound less paranoid? The reason I know this is that I was in the airport in Pittsburgh and these charmers came up and told me. That they can kill me anytime they want to.

"And I was flying around in a Cessna today, and I got about twenty miles away from the airport, on a full tank of gas, and the engine quit on me. I made a very interesting landing in some sugarcane, and when I was able to see, think, feel, and walk again, I found that somebody—I assume a guy who was lounging around the plane in Lafayette, maybe not one of the Pittsburgh charmers but probably one of their many pals—had gone to the trouble of sticking an earplug, one of the things you wear around airports to cut down on the noise, up the vent on the fuel tanks. The effect is really neat-o. The tanks feed fuel by gravity; the plane doesn't have a fuel pump. You fly just long enough to get unsafely away from the airfield, and it's like keeping your finger over the end of a straw. The tanks are full to the top, a vacuum forms. No fuel gets to the engine.

---
148 ---

"You know what's really darling about this? If they wanted to take me out—and can there be *any* doubt that the charmers know their shit about taking people out?—there are three thousand ways they could have dicked up that airplane so that I don't make any landing at all. But they wanted to give me a shot at living. The land was flat. The way they worked it, if I was flying the plane right, and I was, I'd have altitude, control of the plane, and a very good chance of landing the mother and walking away. And as it was, I flew away. The plane wasn't even scratched. A crop-duster pilot came by in his pickup where I put the plane down and towed me back on the strip. We found the earplug. Off I went on my merry way. I got a mouse on my forehead, and that's it.

"If I'm reading this right, I think they prefer scaring me into calling off the dogs than creating some sort of dead-cookie media martyr. Plus I think they get more of their sweet little rocks off from the thought of me alive and shitless and doing what they want me to do." She stopped. *Keep going.*

"Well, I've given it some heavy thought, ace. Calling off the dogs. I *am* shitless. I'm pretty sure yesterday was my last free ticket from the Pittsburgh charmers. Which is why you're going to find these little cassettes and little boxes of slides here. If all this is indeed paranoia, I'll snatch them up and burn them. You'll see or hear them just if—am I saying this?—I buy the farm. 'Buy the farm.' *Shit.*

"Look, Harland. I just don't want the charmers to get the notes and the stuff if they get me. You know? Grab the flag before it falls. Win the Pulitzer for the Gipper." *Twerp, he'll know you're starting to cry.* "Look, it's a real motherfucker of a story, and you're lucky I'm giving it to you, and not some real reporter who's not in show business."

She turned off the recorder. She'd start back with Michigan after she washed her face.

12

A SIREN WENT BY SEVEN FLOORS BELOW AND IT WOKE HARLAND up. It could have been pigeons, or someone slamming a door two apartments away. Harland was a light sleeper, and Molly could sleep through the demolition of the building.

He knew that he wouldn't be able to go back to sleep right away, but he went through the procedures anyway. He got up and took a leak and lay back down. When he sensed that his eyes were growing more open with every blink, he gave up and got up. He went into the bathroom, where he'd put a dimmer in the light switch for times such as these, so he could dose himself with small increments of light; turning them on at once made his stomach pump acid.

He went into the living room. There were shelves, stacks, and piles of books, but none he wanted to read. The idea of watching television depressed him. Insomniacs watched TV at two in the morning. He was *not* an insomniac. He was just a light sleeper.

He saw the three days' unsorted mail on the counter. He decided to open it and put it in proper piles. Useful work, and it seemed lulling.

He discarded without opening the free offers from the resort communities and solicitations from the save-the-whatever committees, pleased that he was able to sneak them into the garbage past Molly, even though it was no challenge when she wasn't here to frisk him when he came upstairs with the mail. The next two letters were obviously magazine-subscription renewal notices. The thought of having to deal with those depressed him, and he decided to open only letters that were not addressed by computers. The next envelope was face down in the pile, and had a postmark on its back. When Harland turned it over, he saw that its first cancellation was nine days earlier, in New York. Misrouted to Cincinnati, where it was noticed and sent back. The cancellation on the back was as much explanation and apology as the Postal Service ever offered.

Inside the envelope was a three-by-five white index card. Typed upon it was: PHOTO OPPORTUNITY. Peachtree Mall. Atlanta. January 23.

Harland felt his cheeks flush. There was a sour churning in his stomach. He got up and walked quickly around the living room, rubbing the stubble on his chin with the back of his hand. He threw the card away from him. "Son of a *bitch*. Why are you telling *me*?" He sat on the couch, hunched forward, and stared at the index card where it had fluttered to the carpet.

Clearly, he would have to act upon this. Extrapolating from the events that followed the arrival of the last three-by-five white index card, it was probable that sometime tomorrow— Jesus, maybe already—they will blow up a place called Peachtree Mall. Or burn it down. Or just walk in with machine guns and start tearing people apart.

Options. Options. He could call the Atlanta police, who might be persuaded that he is indeed John Harland of CBS News, calling at two a.m. to tell them that he's been contacted by maniacs who intend to waste Peachtree Mall, whatever that is, sometime tomorrow. A fat chance. He might call the New York police—he knew a couple of names in press relations— and they might be persuaded to call the Atlanta police and have a little cop-to-cop talk.

Or he could call a number in his notebook. That suddenly

made the most sense. It rang only once, and the person answered it by repeating the last four digits of the number.

"I want Painter."

"Leave your number," said the voice.

"Get him on the phone, ace. Don't tell me you can't reach him. You can get him in two seconds, I know you can. The son of a bitch is probably wired twenty-four hours a day like the fucking RCA Building."

"I happen to know he's asleep."

Harland took a breath. "Some king-sized shit is about to hit the king-sized fan, and after it's over I will tell Painter that an asshole operator sat there with his finger up it while there was still time to do something. Ace, you probably know a lot better than me just how thoroughly he would break your balls."

"Je-suss," sighed the voice. But Harland heard the line start to gargle beeps. In a moment, he heard: "Painter."

Harland said: "There's a photo opportunity." And then he listened, more carefully than he ever had for any sound, to the duration and the quality of the silence before Painter's reply, and for how he said what he said.

After a moment of only ozone breathing over the microwave dishes, Painter said: "What . . . ?" in a voice still caked with sleep. Harland knew it was a feeble proof of the argument that Painter truly did not realize what "Photo Opportunity" meant. That the phrase did not strip sleep from him would have to do for snap-decision purposes.

"Sam, this is John Harland. I believe that I've been contacted by terrorists who were involved in that Kansas thing. I think that they are telling me that tomorrow—shit, *today*—they are going to do something in a place called Peachtree Mall, in Atlanta."

Harland heard Painter exhale into the phone. After a moment: "It's crazies, John. Haven't you had to deal with nutcases before?"

"This has a high probability of being legit."

"Terrorists don't call up CBS News and tell them what they're going to do before they do it."

"They do if they want network coverage."

"They get their network coverage anyway. Call the cops in Atlanta if it'll make you feel any better."

"I called you."

"I'm in Washington, but you don't need to call anybody, John, because it's just a nutcase—"

"Because it was the right call. Wasn't it? I'm right, aren't I, Sam? If you know anything about this, you better the fuck tell me, and tell me what I'm supposed to do about it, because this is scaring the living shit out of me."

"John, you're not making any sense. What, do you want *me* to call the Atlanta—?"

"God *damn*." Harland slammed down the phone. He glared out the window for a moment, then back at the three-by-five index card. Then he picked up the phone and dialed Eastern Airlines. Busy. Then Delta Airlines. Busy. Then Eastern and Delta in Atlanta. Both busy. Then Houston. Both busy. Molly kept an Official Airline Guide in her study.

There was an Eastern flight from LaGuardia to Atlanta that left in a few hours, an awful stop-everywhere milk run, but it was the quickest way he could get to Atlanta. He'd have to hope he could get a seat. He called the doorman and asked him to get a cab. He pulled some clothes on. He took time to call the service and to write a note for Molly in case she was on her way home now:

Had to leave town. Will call. Not to worry.
Dan Deadline.

Molly had weighed her present need to hear his voice against simple courtesy. It was nearly three-thirty in the morning in New York and Harland was certainly asleep. Harland, and courtesy, lost. But the phone rang four times, and she knew it was the service even before she heard the lobster-shift operator's voice; the whisper of electricity entering the instrument would have awakened Harland before the first strike of Western Electric's clapper against Western Electric's bell. Harland's message said only that he was leaving town, very quickly, and would check in after he got where he was going.

"It's that TV slut, I know it is," said Molly. The same operator had been on the lobster shift for more than a year, and sometimes assisted Molly in needling Harland. "They've checked out for grimy sex in Newark. Tell him I've got a private dick on his ass with an Instamatic, so whatever that turkey puts out had better be worth it." She hung up and thought about whether or not to be concerned.

She had bought four Heath Bars before the hotel newsstand had closed. The one she began unwrapping was the last. *Terrific. A pound of carbohydrates and no sexual release. I'll come home to him one big zit.* The sugar high was deserting her, and she was starting to feel dingy-tired. There were just a few minutes of tape left on this cassette. She decided to fill it up and go to sleep.

She thumbed the recorder to Record. Talking was easier now. "Plus. Over the last five or six weeks, the top management of the Fortune Five Hundred companies has been out to lunch. I mean *gone*. But not that you'd notice it unless you happened to be working a story that would take you from one company to another. You'd find that one chief executive officer is on vacation. Backpacking, no can reach. Your next CEO is on sabbatical. And the next one is on retreat, whatever that is. Or resting after minor surgery. It got to where I started calling their houses, and after a while I could tell that when their wives said they didn't know where they were, they weren't lying. They really didn't, and some of them were about to freak.

"And I keep picking up a date. Different contexts. A wife will say 'Try reaching him after . . .' 'He says he'll be back after . . .' Some of my contacts have noticed it with their bosses. They'll get instructions to pay for something through . . . Move up termination dates to . . . Say that something will be negotiated only through . . . Jesus, is there something about February fifteenth I don't know about? A holiday I haven't noticed? It's not Elvis's birthday, is it?"

The tape pulled up taut against the end of the reel and Molly turned off the recorder. This was the time when, if she was working this late at home and Harland was asleep, she would put on headphones and albums of Vivaldi and Jerry Jeff Walker, stacked alternately on the turntable.

She put the recorder on the stand between the beds and slid down under the covers, which she had half-pulled up around her. She was still dressed, and she didn't move the notebooks and Heath Bar wrappers covering the bedspread.

Harland was the last to be seated on the Eastern Atlanta flight. He knew that he looked nervous enough, and disheveled enough, to make any hijacker-personality-profile go tilt three different ways. The LaGuardia ticket-counter personnel had called to verify his American Express card, which they never do. The drones at the security gate pretended the magnetometer had broken down so they would have an excuse to take him aside for a body search.

"I don't blame you," Harland told the guard.

"Pardon me?"

"Nothing."

He was the only person in first who did not fold up the arm rests to sleep across two seats. He would read two words of a magazine and put it down, and he drank so much coffee he had to take a leak every fifteen minutes. Whenever he got up, the poor stewardesses thought this, surely, was the time he was going to come up with the knife and put it at one of their throats.

The stews still did not look entirely comfortable, even after the jetway had been pushed up to the door in Atlanta, as they lined up to wish him his ritual Nice Day as he deplaned. Harland had slowed, for just an instant, and tried to think of something amusing to say in apology or explanation. But the poor stews, smiling their surgically affixed stew-smiles even though they were clearly terrified, almost visibly shrank from him. He feared that if he said anything they would start stabbing hidden alarm buttons, so he just left.

He asked the cabdriver to take him to Peachtree Mall. Harland then hoped for the driver to turn around and say, "Where, buddy?" Harland would then know that he had spent the night terrifying stewardesses for absolutely nothing. He would have been enormously relieved to have heard that; enough that Harland would have smiled as he gave the middle-aged black man ten dollars, whistled as he walked back into the terminal, and sung himself to sleep on a bench as he waited however long it took to get the next plane back to New York.

But the driver said, "Yes, suh, Peachtree Mall," and dropped the flag. "Fabulous place, that Peachtree Mall. You stayin' at the ho-tel there?"

"Uh, yeah," said Harland. "What's there, at the mall? Besides the hotel?"

"Man, just about anythin' you want. All kinda stores, and a movin' picture house, and an ice-skatin' rink. Fabulous place."

"Is there anything going on there now?"

"Goin' on?"

"Like, uh . . ."

"Like what?"

Yeah, John, like what? "Like a convention, or a political rally?"

"Nothin' that I know 'bout. About lebenteen million people shoppin's all."

Harland spent the rest of the fifteen-odd minutes it took to reach the mall looking out the window. Fatigue and tension were at a standoff inside him: the former too unrelenting to allow his mind to work efficiently, the latter refusing to let him sleep.

Peachtree Mall was typical shopping-center-Oz architecture floating in an asphalt gulf of parking space, most of which was full. It took the driver almost as long to beat his way down the service road to the mall entrance as it did to get from the airport. Harland finally asked the driver just to let him out. He struck out on foot for the central core of glitter and acute angles, breasting through the parked cars.

There were three levels of shops, all facing in to common balconies on each level. The ice rink was at ground level. Harland stopped, looked around, a stump in the stream of people flowing around him. *What? Where? When?* "Why and how," Harland said aloud. The five questions one learned in high-school journalism every news story needs to answer. *Will the terrorists in the mall please hold up their hands?*

Harland saw the mall entrance to the hotel and made for it. The functions board in the hotel lobby was totally benign. It logged sales meetings for a paper-products company and a sewing-machine company at noon. A wedding reception and dinner in the afternoon. No government holding press conferences, no subcommittee holding hearings in the ballroom, no defense contractors holding seminars.

He went back outside into the mall and circumnavigated all three levels. Nothing. Not a ticket office of a foreign-flag airline. No convenient and vulnerable symbol of imperialism; no local offices of a stockbroker, no energy-company display booths. There was a branch office of a Georgia savings-and-loan association; he didn't see what interest terrorists would have in that.

Harland sat down upon a bench a level above the ice rink and pressed a hand against his acidic stomach. He was starting to feel, along with tired, painfully dumb. *What are they going to do, asshole? Hijack Wicks 'n Sticks?* To be feeling at that moment something very much like a sucker, he felt something very much like relief; he thought an exchange of anxiety for sheepishness was more than a fair trade.

He went to a pay phone and found that he would not be able to get a plane back to New York before the next morning. Fine with him. He felt as though he could sleep until then. He went to one of the men's stores and bought a change of clothes and underwear, to a drugstore for toothpaste and a toothbrush. He checked into the hotel and called his producer in New York. The truth would have been an entirely acceptable reason to explain his being in Atlanta; he would not have been the first journalist to chase spuriousness a great distance to an empty nest. But Harland was too embarrassed to speak it. He said that he had to run there overnight because he had a lead on the Vandellen piece. There was a chance he might warm a source with cold feet about talking on camera; but hope had been false. He wouldn't. There was commiseration from the other end about the waste of his time. Harland hung up, and awaited the sleep of the untroubled, which he told himself was by logic his. It came, but not quickly.

Whatever it was that wanted to wake Harland, ahead of the full ration of sleep his body demanded, wanted to wake him badly; it had to burrow through several insulating layers of fatigue. Harland came conscious leaning up on an elbow. He reflexively picked up the phone. It wasn't ringing, and he knew it hadn't; he had awoken with a message already received: *Get dressed. Get downstairs.* The acidic anxiety he thought he'd gotten behind him that morning was back, at double strength.

He turned on the television before he reached for his pants. It warmed up as he pulled the pants on and reached for his shoes, then showed him *Leave It to Beaver.* Clicked channels, through an old movie, through *The Six Million Dollar Man.* Then a woman sitting in a newsroom set, saying ". . . we have no more details than that. We have an Action Live News unit on its way to Peachtree Mall at the moment . . ." Harland buttoned his shirt as he pulled the door shut.

The lobby was full of cops. "What's going on?" he asked the first at hand.

"There's a little trouble in the mall," said the policeman, who showed no inclination to move from the path Harland intended to make toward the mall entrance. "Sir, are you a guest in the hotel?"

"Right."

"We're asking everybody to stay in the hotel, please, and not go into the mall."

"Yeah, but what—"

"Just some trouble. If you go back to your room, sir, you'll be able to see it on television." The officer pushed the elevator call button.

"Right," said Harland. "Good idea." He got back on the elevator and pushed the button that would take him to the underground parking garage. This mall was not designed to be made secure, Harland told himself. Too many stores, too many doors. They don't have that many cops. He got off in the garage, found a stairway, walked up one flight.

He pushed through the door that put him on the ice-rink level and into a mass of people, all craning to see what was in an expanding pool of light at one end of the mall. Right again. They don't have that many cops. They weren't going to have much luck keeping rubberneckers out.

"What's going on?" Harland asked a kid standing at the back of the crush.

"Radio said that there's a bunch of dudes with guns, man. They're standing at the doors and won't let nobody out."

"Out of where?"

"Out of the movie theater, man."

Harland leaned his face against the window of a bookstore. *Oh Jesus. People are going to die. I could have done more. I should have done more. But I didn't, and people are going to die.*

Painter. Harland knew that Painter was here, close, and had answers. Harland raged at Painter for things he hadn't told Harland, things that might lift the guilt shrilling inside Harland's skull.

Harland found a pay phone and called the number in Washington he'd called the night before. A different voice, but with the same inflections, answered with the same four digits. "Tell Painter this is John Harland, and—"

"Painter is not here."

"That's right, he's not there, he's in Peachtree Mall in Atlanta, which is where I am, and I want to see him."

"Can't be reached."

"He can be reached. What kind of an idiot asshole do you think I am? In five minutes, in the Mexican restaurant on the third level."

"Or?"

"Or? Painter knows what the fuck 'or.' *Or* I send up as big a shitstorm around him as CBS News is capable of raising. He'd love *that*, wouldn't he, the covert-freak. *Tell him.*"

Harland half-ran up the three flights of stairs to the top level. He pushed through the gawkers, eight-deep around the balcony, who were leaning in to see the roped-off area in front of the theater. He shoved his way in through the entrance to the restaurant. Two waitresses were standing in the door, trying to get a look. "Sir, uh . . . I don't know if we're open. Hey, Julie, are we open?"

"I just want a place to sit down for a minute," said Harland. He slid into a booth. "Can I just sit down for a minute? I don't need anything."

"Yeah, sure, I guess so," said the waitress, just as happy to get back to spectating. Harland leaned his head back against the vinyl banquette. There was a painting of a bullfighter, on black velvet, hung on the wall opposite him.

He had beaten Painter there by about forty-five seconds.

Painter was dressed in jeans and the rugby shirt. Harland recognized, from the Pentagon office, the man who walked in with him and then took up a station at the entrance.

"The man who took your call said you sounded a combination of scared to death and pissed off enough to kill me. He appears to have put it mildly."

"It was real, wasn't it, Sam? The 'photo opportunity' shit."

"Yes."

"You never thought it was nutcases, did you?"

"No."

"How long have you been here?"

"Since a little before you."

"You probably don't have to worry about plane connections when you travel, huh?"

"No."

Harland reached for a salt shaker. "Are people going to get killed here?"

Painter shrugged.

"Oh shit, they *are*, aren't they?" said Harland. He ran his hands through his hair. "And I could have called somebody. I could have tried. You son of a bitch, you—"

"We wanted you only not to call the police. They would have thrashed around here, and whoever sent you the note would have called today off. We were looking forward to their introducing themselves."

Harland kneaded his eyes with the heels of his hands. "How many people? In the movie."

"It's a Clint Eastwood movie. It's doing pretty close to capacity business. About seven hundred. They say there are six of them. One on each exit from the auditorium. We can see two of them. They stay in the lobby to do the communicating."

"With you?"

"With the Atlanta police. We are interested observers."

"So far."

"So far."

"What do they want?"

"So far, not a thing. They just list things the police are not supposed to try, like cut off the electricity or the water. Nobody's been hurt. Their positions are dirt simple to hold. There they sit, here we sit."

Harland was looking down at the table. "They can't fly that movie theater to Libya, can they?"

"They cannot."

"They don't expect to get away."

"No."

"They don't expect to live."

"No."

"Maybe all they want to do is get into the *Guinness Book of World Records* for most hostages killed. Sam, you've *made* me help them!" Harland slapped the salt shaker off the table.

"You're being a bit hard on yourself, John. Lighten up on the guilt. They would have just done what they were planning to do today sometime later, someplace else. We couldn't stop them. And you might call us professionals at that kind of thing. Don't expect more of yourself."

Harland found himself in an unseemly rush to believe him. Painter sensed that, and smiled. "I have just what you need to forget that guilt, get it behind you in a good old-fashioned surge of moral outrage. Let me be of help. I'd like to tell you about us now, my men and I, but not because of the shitstorm you said you were going to raise about us on CBS. We could deal with that, well before it happened."

Harland supposed he knew how Painter would deal with it.

"This is going to surprise you. I hope it will. Surprise is part of this tactic. I am, always have been, despite the stereotype you have of me, a person of childlike faiths. I have faith that, after I tell you about me and my men and what we do—and I'm going to tell you everything you want to hear—after you are repelled and outraged, I believe that you will think about it; and sort it out; and decide not to raise an alarm. Because you will have run into the crunch of every moral man, which is pragmatism and deep concern for his own sweet ass." Painter looked at the tabletop.

"Talk," said Harland. "You think I've got a Panasonic stuck up my ass? I won't be able to substantiate any of what you say anyhow, will I?"

"We know you aren't wired. You have been scanned. No, you won't be able to substantiate. This is mostly for your benefit, John. And mine. Your reaction could be instructive. I don't need approval. I don't expect approval, but I can reasonably expect pragmatis—"

"What's Copper Creek?" Harland realized he had said it too loud and suddenly: uncool.

"Just what you suspect. It's where we took our first casualties. Let me talk, John. I think I can anticipate most of your questions. Listen. This country is going to get skinny, John. It's been living high on the hog, and it's just about out of hog. Americans are way out of practice at being deprived. They never were very good at it to begin with. They're going to freeze the rest of this winter, and the next one is going to be worse. They're going to start sweating this summer, in those office buildings whose windows don't even open. There are people in the South—you're probably one of them—who haven't slept without air conditioning in their lives. They're going to get mad because they can't get what they want, and then they're going to get scared. There are groups that are going to exacerbate it. Weaken things. It works, you know. Not some shithead anti-nukers, or righties, or Middle East crazies with machine guns, or Weathermen with a plutonium satchel charge they put together from stolen power-plant fuel . . . none of them can bring down the government. They're not able to. They *can* do the job for somebody else. If they try hard enough and long enough . . ." Harland knew from the quick glance Painter took at Harland's face that Sam wanted approval more than he might think. Shifting a little in his seat, Sam went on.

"A well-thought-out act of terrorism is extraordinarily debilitating. It's arrogant, infuriating. There are no acceptable resolutions. It offends the John Wayne in Americans to give in to any punk terrorist's demands; and human sacrifice is generally unappealing. Contempt generally ends up focused upon the authority figures who must deal with the terrorists for failure to find the unfindable solution."

Harland felt as though he had been given a prompt; but he said nothing.

"John, think. Get us tired and whining and petulant enough, and we'll turn the country over to the businessmen and politicians—you know who they are—who say, 'Look, we can take care of these nasty people. Just don't ask us how, and by the way, we'll need to repeal the first ten amendments to the Constitution.' "

"This is moderately grotesque. A left-wing spook."

Painter leaned forward a little. "Terrorists have one liability. Their acts are meaningless unless they're public. Money or arms might be part of the demands, but what they need is the ink—media. Give them that, and even if they don't get to Algeria, or the half-billion in bullion, or the release of their buddies from jail, they'll know they've jerked some people around. Maybe a governor. Maybe even the President if they work it right; they've made all our stomachs burn. They'll die happy.

"But there's always a time when it's . . . containable. Before it's public, before there are spectators and reporters from *The Washington Post* and John Harland and the cameras. Stop them then . . . stop it then, and there is no terrorism. There are no terrorists. No hostages. That's what we do, with Copper Creek. We come, and contain, and . . . erase."

As Harland had come to understand, he had reflexively pushed against the edge of the table in front of him. Now his elbows were locked straight, and his arms trembled.

"Sam, no."

"John . . ."

"*You kill the hostages too.*"

"Yes."

"In the plane crash in North Carolina . . ."

"Yes."

"The dam accident in West Virginia."

"Everyone in Copper Creek was dead anyway. The good guys, the bad guys, our guys, the innocent bystanders. There was steam, from stolen radioactive waste."

"And you make them look like accidents."

"They *were* accidents. Misfortune. In a world full of free will, you got nobody to blame but yourself. One chooses flight A instead of flight B and flight A falls out of the sky. You take the fork of the road that leads to the drunken driver instead of the fork that doesn't. The President and the joint chiefs, when they created us, decided with regret that to be taken by a terrorist is now . . . fatal, a new environmental poison. Think of it as the carcinogen of the week."

"More? Besides the airplanes, and . . . More times when you killed . . ."

"They never happened. There was no trauma, no acquiescence, no crazy-making, no impossible decisions about pride and the value of life. *Nothing* happened."

Harland felt packed in excelsior, synapses blocked, capable only of echoic reactions.

"John. You do understand why you cannot tell anyone about Copper Creek?"

"Yes." His eyes on the tabletop. His voice had no breath behind it.

"Why it would be dangerous."

"Yes."

"Tell me why."

"Because you . . ." Harland looked up at him. ". . . are attractive."

"Yes," said Painter, with something at the periphery of his eyes, which Harland thought was regret.

"This is getting easier," said Molly, the tape recorder propped up on the bed where she sat crosslegged. "I can both talk and address Kodak film mailers at the same time, which is what I'm doing now. This is tape number five, and will go with slides number five. Most people would have figured that out by now, since tape one went with the first bunch of slides and so forth. But Harland is a little slow. You have to do see-Spot-run for little Johnny . . .

"I am in another Holiday Inn. Or is it a Ramada Inn, or is it a TraveLodge. I'd reach over and look at the book of matches, but I'm too tired. I have spent all day running around and peeking through the windows of warehouses, which have not been washed since 1946, with a source who was so scared he about shit his pants every time a stoplight turned red and another car pulled up beside us. That's what the first half dozen, if I can read my notes, I say again, the first half dozen pictures on this roll should be—insides of warehouses taken through dirty windows. You won't be able to see anything, but it's the thought that counts.

"My source was able to get us inside two. The next pictures should show the outside of them. Inside, some pictures of what's being stored in those warehouses. There was zip light inside. If the automatic exposure on the camera worked all right and I didn't move too much, you should see beer cans. My source says there are about two million in the places he showed me, and he figures he knows where there may be two hundred million more. Beer cans, Coke cans, apple-juice cans, bloody-Mary-mix cans. Yes, they are illegal under the Omni. Yes, all beverages must be sold in glass deposit containers. My source thinks they're coming from overseas, but you can't smuggle in that many. They rattle, for openers. I think there are factories here in the states that still make them. They're piling up, Harland, millions of illegal empty beer cans. There they sit. And what in the fuck for? Millions upon millions. . . ."

Harland had gone back to his room and called New York to volunteer to cover the theater situation. He was thanked and, as he had anticipated, was declined. ABC had been headhunting the woman in the CBS Atlanta bureau. He knew CBS wanted to keep her; bump her off a story like this for a New York guy and she'd be gone by Monday.

He had realized when he got back to his room that he'd forgotten to ask Painter the question he most needed answered. He dialed the number in Washington, and was put through to Painter with no resistance.

"What're you going to do, Sam?" Harland had said. "There are seven hundred people. It should be a lot of fun."

"You miss the point, John. This went public before we could get here. We do nothing. My recommendation has been turned down."

"Which was?"

"That we go in there and make the people with the guns dead."

"And how many Clint Eastwood fans go with them?"

"As few as possible. As many as it takes. That's more up to them than it is to us. The answer to your question is: We do nothing until they make demands. We react as determined by the acceptability of the demands."

"What's an unacceptable demand?"

"Anything. I can't take your calls any more on this channel," said Painter. "We need it. I will have someone call you and keep you briefed." He was gone.

Harland sat in the room and watched the local TV coverage. The same picture of the front of the theater reappeared as the stations cut back live upon rumors, movement in the lobby, anything. Five minutes after Painter hung up, the phone rang. "Sam wanted you to know what it's like inside. There are four exits from the auditorium, two to the mall's exterior, two into the theater lobby, which opens into the mall plaza. We assume there's a machine gun at each door. One of them comes out to the doors to the mall to talk, or uses the phone. They're feeding the people junk from the concession stand. They say they are not ready to discuss demands."

Harland fell asleep with the television showing him pictures of the agonized relatives of those inside the theater pushing at the police barricades. They were sick, angry. Petulant.

The phone woke him at ten the next morning. "Hold the line for Painter," said the voice. Then: "They're brilliant, John."

"Sam?"

"They just issued their demand. They want the NFL playoff game today canceled."

"*What?*"

"They want to see the teams leave the dressing rooms and get on planes and leave Cincinnati. Live. On TV. The President is going to have less than a half hour to act. As if he had any choice. Jesus Christ, is that *brilliant*." Genuine admiration in his voice.

"It's crazy. What possible good—"

"Possible good? First, it's too trivial a demand to risk calling a bluff. A football game versus loss of life? No contest. Second, it's going to affect thirty million people who might think, for just a fraction of a second, 'So what if a few people get killed; the government's taking away my game that I've been looking forward to for a week.' Third, it's going to give the President of the United States some practice at saying yes to tiny shitheads. This is the most brilliant and damaging act of terrorism ever committed in this country, and we should have killed them when we had a chance."

They said the government had two hours to show them what they wanted. They got it: The images of the confused and un-smiling football players leaving their dressing rooms, still taped up. The Miami players getting off the buses at the Cincinnati airport, almost shoved into the charter by the police and federal marshals. The charter taking off.

The NFL commissioner had appeared on television, saying that on the advice of the FBI, he would have no comment on rescheduling the game. The people inside the theater had not communicated since the Dolphins' charter landed in Miami. A little before seven, Harland's phone rang again.

"Sam says to tell you they're moving. Someone will meet you in the lobby. We'll get you a good seat."

There was a guy in a rugby shirt waiting for Harland at the base of the elevators. He headed for the entrance to the mall. Harland fell in beside him.

"They've got cans of spray paint," said rugby shirt. "They're blacking out the inside of the glass lobby doors." Rugby shirt pushed through a door into a stairwell, headed down. "How close do you want to get?"

"How close do you mean by close?"

"Close as in close enough to get your ass shot off."

"Almost that close," said Harland.

For the two days inside the theater, they had worn the same blue mechanic's coveralls, the same ski masks, the same surgeon's gloves. There were seven of them. One at each door, two for relief, one negotiator. The negotiator had been the only one to speak to the captive audience. When the terrorists were ready to leave, the negotiator, speaking through the bullhorn that distorted his voice, told the audience that the lights would go out for a few moments, and not to panic. There was, of course, instant panic the moment it became dark; in the last few seconds, as the lights dimmed, everyone could see that from the satchels that the terrorists carried, each was taking a gas mask.

Fifteen seconds later, from the front of the theater, came the muzzle flashes from the machine gun, strobing in the total darkness.

A screaming avalanche burst through the two outside exits, filled the lobby, and then pushed through the spray-painted doors, which had been unlocked. As the police, uselessly, tried to contain it, it was joined by a reciprocal surge of those who were outside. They pushed through police lines, arms outstretched to those for whom they had waited fearfully.

Harland watched with Painter as, with screams of reunion and relief, the people ran, past the police, through the spectators, scattering into the sea of vehicles in the parking lot, beyond the lights, away.

Inside, amid the drifts of candy wrappers and popcorn boxes, in piles near the exits, Harland saw the seven blue mechanic's overalls, seven ski masks; seven gas masks whose use had been ceremonial, simply to compound the fear of those who saw them being put on. Seven machine guns. An eighth had been weighted down and pointed at the screen, into which, after a simple time-delay device attached to the trigger housing had triggered it, it had innocently spent its clip. Medical personnel were treating the fractures and cuts of those who had stumbled. One—a five year old—was dead.

Harland looked at the coveralls the terrorists had shed in the dark and thought of the faces of the people as they came out of the theater, of those waiting outside, of the unbearable mewling noises they made when the unmistakable sound of the machine guns was heard through the walls. *The indecency,* Harland thought, *is that they got away by pretending to be their own victims. It was too easy. They should have paid more dues. They are owed pain.*

He saw that Painter was looking at him. He wondered if that last thought was on his face. From Painter's answering smile he knew that it was.

13

WHEN HARLAND OPENED THE MAILBOX AND SAW THAT THERE
was no mail in it, he thought: *Molly.* She was back, and had
emptied it; that was not only the happier alternative to no mail
being delivered but, considering the number of periodicals to
which she subscribed, the likelier one. Opening his door confirmed it; her coat was thrown on a sofa, and the mail abandoned beside it, the postman's rubberband still around it. Harland knew that Molly would have to be very tired not at least
to glance at what she'd been sent.

Harland saw her bags dropped in the bedroom door, un-
opened, and Molly asleep, in a fresh nightgown but on top of
the covers. Harland weighed his urge to touch her and talk
with her against letting her sleep. *A tale I could tell you, kid.*
But he couldn't. He needed someone to talk to about Copper
Creek, but not Molly. Anyone but Molly, and not because of
their rivalry. Because Molly would see Copper Creek as the
unspeakable he had been telling himself it was, and Molly
would rage, as he had told himself he should. But he had not
raged. If he told Molly about Copper Creek, she would ask
why he did not. He would have no answer for her because
he had none for himself, and that frightened him.

He was on his way, quietly, to the bathroom when she said, between coughs: "Don't do that."

"What?"

"Try to sneak through the room without waking me." Harland sat beside her on the bed. She spooned herself around his back and scrunched her face against his thigh. She was still three-quarters asleep. "I have my needs, you know. It's hell out there, kid. Days and days without a man. I'll get zits." Harland was scratching her back. Her voice began to clabber: "I've dreamed about this moment. If you put me to sleep, you'll just have to do it twice in the morning. Wings, wings. Up on the wings." Harland scratched around her shoulder blades. She told him that she loved him, and then she was asleep.

When Harland woke up, he was late for work and she was gone. He called her desk at the *Times*. After the third call and the city-room operator's saying that she was not at her desk, Harland decided that Molly wasn't picking up. She usually didn't when she was deep into work. If it had been important, he could have asked for the extension of the guy at the desk next to hers and asked him to ask her to pick up. But he didn't want to interrupt her.

He was at CBS late. When he got home, there was a puddle of blood on the kitchen floor, leaked from a piece of roast still sitting on butcher paper on the drainboard. He cleaned up the puddle, dealt with the roast, and followed the sound of the typewriter to Molly's study.

He leaned against the doorjamb, which, by unspoken protocols, was as close as he could come to her notes and typewriter when she was working. "Earth to Molly, Earth to Molly, the roast has defrosted nicely and is now decomposing."

Molly clicked off the typewriter and said, as Harland anticipated, "Shit." Harland put his arm around her as she walked past. "Sit in the living room and I'll bring you a beer. I've put in the roast."

"I put the oven on Preheat and went in here to do a little

work and . . . Goddamn it. We won't be able to eat until midnight."

"Not to worry. I put it in the microwave."

"It won't brown. It'll come out looking like leprosy." She sat on the sofa and leaned her head back on the cushion. "So much for domesticity. I'm sorry. I'll do the veggies."

"It'll be all right, I'll take care of it," said Harland. He handed her the beer. "How's it going? The big story."

"It's going."

"When do you finish?"

"Maybe Wednesday. Probably Thursday."

"Would it make any difference if I told you that if you don't get a little rest, it'll be published posthumously?"

Say "Funny you should say that" and tell him about the Cessna. Tell him you're tired and dingy and spooked and the story scares you. Crawl into his arms and cry. He'll love it. Be helpless. It's easy.

"I'll quit after we eat," she said, and immediately wished she could take it back. There was an edge to it she had not intended to apply, but she was not equipped at the moment to make explanations. She got up and headed back toward her study and said, "How much longer until we eat?"

"Maybe twenty minutes."

"I need to make some phone calls."

"Baby." She stopped, but didn't turn around. "Can I ask what's wrong?"

"It's work."

"If it's work, then I won't ask." She went on into the study. "But it is just work?"

"Just work."

"Vermont. This weekend."

"Yes." She closed the door.

Molly finished the story on Thursday and spent most of Friday with Len Gass. They went from the office of *Times* executive to the office of higher *Times* executive to the office of *Times* libel lawyers answering essentially the same question: *You're sure about this*. She said yes, in tones that to her sounded as though they carried conviction. When asked, she named the sources who would allow her to reveal them just to her editors, not for print. She would not name the sources who would not allow her to reveal them to anyone. Gass would stay behind and fight the nervous executives as she waited in outer offices.

She and Gass expected to lose a little. There was in her story some pinching in the dark; one simply listened carefully to see who said ouch, and how it was said. For what the executives decided was lack of substantiation, the names of a couple of companies were changed to "a large East Coast corporation"; the libel lawyers prevailed in a few places. But she lost less than she'd anticipated, and the piece would not be cautiously buried. The story was being saved for Sunday, and it would go page one.

There was a message waiting for her when she finally got back to her desk: A name, a phone number, and "He wants to meet you Sat. nite."

And so much, thought Molly, *for "this weekend for sure."* On Sunday morning Harland would have made breakfast while she went down to the village for the *Times*. They would have read while they ate, she taking the magazine and pretending not to be watching him while he read her story . . .

She put down the phone message, which she had folded into accordion pleats, and picked up the phone. To her disappointment, she got lucky, first call, with plane reservations.

She beat Harland home, and the phone was ringing as she walked in the door. It was Nona, her actress friend.

"I am calling to get you and Harland over here Saturday for dinner, but the second you picked up the phone I remembered that this is the big Vermont weekend."

"The big Vermont weekend is off."

Nona sighed. "Dear heart, are you running away for that darn newspaper again?"

"Nona, can I take off my coat before you start reading *Cosmo* to me?"

"I mean, there's a limit."

"I'm on a story, Nona."

"I thought you'd *finished* the goddamn story."

"It's a running story. There are follow-ups, new developments. After we break it, everybody else will get on it and I'm going to have to hump it to stay ahead. He's in the business too. He's done this to me as often as I've done it to him."

"Was he pissed?"

"He was pissed. He never says he's pissed, but I know he was. He was disappointed. Jesus, hon, you think I'm not? It's *work*."

"At least he's pissed off. There is always the chance, dear heart, that if you keep jerking him around he'll stop getting pissed, or giving a fart in general about what you do."

"Yes, yes, Nona, and who else will put up with me? I know, I know. He's a fucking treasure. What can I say? I'm counting on staying lucky."

"How long are you going to be gone?"

"I don't know."

"Jerk."

"Yeah."

Molly gave the top drawer of her file cabinet too hard a push, and it shut with a noise that, while hardly a thud, was nearly loud enough to wake Harland, even through two closed doors. She grimaced, heard no stirrings from the bedroom, and then flicked off the Pause button on the cassette recorder.

". . . and the original of my story, the one without the chickenshit changes the *Times* made, is in the top drawer of my file cabinet. You'll see that I didn't use some of the stuff I've been talking about on the tapes because I haven't been able to see what they have to do with anything else. The beer cans, for example. The reason the stuff about the salt domes isn't there—remember Molly Goes to Louisiana from tape two or three or thereabouts?—is that I just don't have the goods. The energy companies have ten thousand ways to juggle figures to prove that they *have* reported the oil in those salt domes to the feds. But now I got a lead that, if it works out, should let me get them by the nuts."

She watched the tape reels go round. *Don't go. It's easy not to go.* "I can't put off going, fatso. Not even for a day, sincerely true, so I could go to Vermont with you, which is something I want/wanted to do so badly I can't . . . I'm getting my tenses confused. I'll cover the waterfront: I love you, I have loved you, I will love you . . ."

Molly turned off the cassette. She was not prepared to cover the contingency for which she made the tape: *I did love you.*

Harland knew Molly did not casually cancel their plans to go to Vermont, but he was not able to make himself acknowledge the circumstance as extenuating; he felt cheated.

Harland did a bad job of getting angry. Molly called him names and slammed doors and usually finished feeling spent and refreshed. Harland punished by withdrawing; he was polite and understanding. He knew he was being insufferable as he smiled and said he understood, all the way down the elevator as he walked Molly out front and waited for a cab. He wished he could have stopped being the way he was; and he was disturbed by Molly's attitude. She failed to challenge him for it, and as the cab waited she held on to him longer than she usually did. He was grateful for it, but the abnormality disturbed him.

Jerry Lee called.

"Molly there?"

"Just left."

"You've seen the *Times*?"

"Not yet. Molly's story in it?"

"She didn't tell you anything about it?"

"You kidding?"

"You've been sleeping next to *that* story, and all you know is what you read in the papers, huh? I love it. Just love it."

"What? What?"

"It's in the fan, buddy. Buy a copy."

"Read me the lead."

Harland heard newsprint rustle. "Her story is page one, above the fold, under a three-column head. Are you sitting down? 'The *Times* has learned that as many as fifteen major corporations have been engaged in secret negotiations to consolidate managements and pool earnings, and are now amassing stockpiles of consumer goods and critical raw materials.' "

"My *God*, Molly," said Harland.

" 'The participants apparently have as final objective merger into one entity, under the name of American Basic Industries, whose assets would total as much as eleven percent of the gross national product.

" 'Many of these activities are illegal under provisions of the Federal Omnibus Energy Act. The proposed merger, which would create the largest and most powerful non-governmental entity in American history, would clearly violate federal anti-trust law. Part of the corporations' objective in forming it would seem to be testing the federal government's will—or capacity—to oppose it . . .' The story goes on for half a page inside."

"My *God*."

"An eye-opener, wouldn't you say?" said Lee.

"Jesus, no wonder she looked wiped out all the time. What's the reaction?"

"Icy, to put it gently. Encon and pals will have no comment until Monday. We called Justice, and whatever janitor answers the phone on Saturday afternoons said they have no evidence, no ongoing investigations . . . waffle waffle waffle. Smart of the *Times* to break this in a Sunday edition. They get a whole weekend of 'no comments' to make it look more like the truth. Oh, this is fun. Everybody else gets to run with the story and attribute the *Times*, and the *Times* gets to sweat the libel suits. If you don't have a separate bank account from Molly, you'd better get one."

"Molly's no kid, Jerry. She makes things stick."

"Come on, Johnny. She's a pro at digging up the dirties, but you know she's in love with conspiracy. Her story reads like a masochistic fantasy for liberals."

True, thought Harland.

"There's a lot of Exhibit A and Exhibit B in this piece, but some of the conclusions are circumstantial and wishful thinking. You wanna bet the *Times* ends up making retractions?"

"Twenty bucks."

"Twenty bucks? I wouldn't want to be you if Molly finds out that you risked a big twenty on her professional rep. By the way, you can count on me to tell her."

"I know you will. Fifty."

"Ten," said Lee. "She could fool me . . ."

Harland made himself some coffee. The phone rang.

"Molly Rice, please." Harland stiffened at the sound of an unfamilar voice calling on the unlisted phone.

"Who's calling, please?"

"Ah." The voice was male, very pleasant. "Oh, I don't think she would remember my name. I ran into her once, and she said I should look her up if I was ever in New York."

"If you could give me your name, I—"

"Can you give her a message? Would you tell her please that the fellow from the Pittsburgh airport would like to get together with her?"

Molly went two days on the road without calling in. Then, after the one brief call where she strained to crack wise while evading his questions about where she was, she went three.

On that third day Harland finally called up Len Gass at the *Times*. Gass heard panic at the edges of Harland's voice. Prefacing it with assurances that Molly wouldn't want him to do this, he gave a number where he expected her to be.

For one of the few times he could remember, Harland shouted at her: That they loved each other, and that meant responsibility, and that not calling in for three days was irresponsible. Fuck the job, *The New York Times*, and the Pulitzer prize if she won it.

There was no fight in her. In a flat and diminished voice she apologized, over and over. Finally she did ask: "Make some allowances, baby. Just a few more days." And then: "I'm so sick of being scared."

She hung up. When he called back, the line was busy; was for an hour. Finally the desk clerk said she'd checked out.

Harland looked up the area code. Arizona.

It was only natural for the *Times* to want the break for itself. For that, and to allow a full trading day on the stock exchange for those favored enough to have been told the day before, the press conference was called at a time thirty minutes past the *Post*'s last deadline.

The *Times* had been sold. For nine hundred million dollars cash, effective immediately, to Panex Communications.

The general counsels of both companies nonanswered questions; the principals were not present. Sellers of newspapers generally don't show up at the sale. The chairman of the board of Panex did not like to be interviewed or photographed and generally didn't show up anywhere unless he was subpoenaed.

All the New York stations covered the announcement live. The people in the CBS newsroom watched the WCBS reporter doing his stand-up, listing Panex's broadcast and newspaper holdings, its extensive acquisitions in the last six months, the corporation's battles against Justice antitrust and divestiture suits. Jerry Lee looked genuinely depressed; it was one of the few times Harland saw his friend fail to camouflage his feelings with antic dour.

"Panex doesn't have the cash, Johnny," said Lee, still looking at the screen. "Not nine hundred. They're fronting for somebody who does."

"Hey. Now who's the conspiracy freak?"

"*The New York Times*," said Lee. "Sold to a fucking Swiss bank account."

An hour after the *Times* announcement was out on the wires, Molly called.

"Now if the *Times* were a TV station," said Harland, "you'd be out on your ass. In broadcasting, management fires everybody at a new acquisition. It's instinct. They can't help themselves."

Molly's voice was flat, featureless. "Harland, I'm changing planes in Chicago, on my way home. Two hours before the announcement, they called me in. They took me off my story, Harland."

"Off your story? Why?"

"I have to decide what to do, and I have to talk. Can you come with me to Vermont this afternoon?"

Harland had to do the newscast from Washington that evening. But Molly's plane was due at LaGuardia a little before Harland had to catch the Washington shuttle. He would meet her there, give her the car. She'd drive on to Vermont and he'd meet her there the next day, taking a commuter plane to the field nearest the village.

She said nothing when she saw him standing outside the security gate. Just held him. Her plane had been late. They had time for half a drink.

"Okay," said Harland, "so why are you off your story?"

"They're making Len an assistant managing editor. They're offering me his job."

"Son of a bitch, Molly, that's sensational."

"Uh huh," she said. "I'm off my *story*, Harland. They pulled me off."

"Because they're promoting you. Won't you be management now?"

"They're killing the story and trying to buy me off."

"Nobody can kill that story."

"The paper might run some more words, but they are not going to *work* it anymore. I know this. As of two hours ago, the story is dead in the *Times*."

"Molly, do you think someone paid nine hundred million dollars for *The New York Times* to get you off your story?" He said it as softly as he could.

Her face grew taut. Harland saw that it said *Be on my side*, and he started to speak up, to say that he was. Then she softened. She took his hand, and to his relief he saw something recognizable as a smile. "Harland, if getting me off this story is a conspiracy or isn't a conspiracy, I don't fucking care right now. Not a rat's ass. I'm giving it a rest, baby. It can all go to hell on a Honda. I gotta lie down with you for a few days, or I'm gonna go tilt."

The news budgets contained only the bleakness that was the lot of the weekend journalist. To make the situation more arid, both AP's and UPI's broadcast wire machines in the CBS Washington newsroom had been down two hours. Harland resolved to use the outage to his advantage. Since all that the national wires were surely transmitting was bad weather news and bad economic news, he argued a case with the producer to lead with anything but weather or economic news; not to avoid bad news, but simply in the interest of offering the viewer a greater variety of bad news. He proposed a Mexico train crash, twenty-three dead, and pretty good film from the Mexican TV network. He prevailed, and a little too easily. Tolliver was behaving oddly; he didn't quite look at Harland. By the third or fourth time, Harland had about decided to ask what was wrong.

Two hours before airtime Harland was writing lead-ins. He suddenly sensed something and looked up. He saw Jerry Lee walking across the room toward his office.

"Jerry, what are you . . ."

When Lee established eye contact with Harland, he did not lose it, not as he walked through the open door, walked without greeting around Harland's desk.

Harland saw Lee's eyes and knew that he was bringing him pain.

Lee knelt beside where Harland sat, put his hand on Harland's wrist, and squeezed it. "Johnny, Molly went off a thruway interchange . . ."

He heard the rest of Lee's words but his brain put a filter on them. *I will not hear "dead."*

Cautiously his brain began to process words, then phrases: ". . . intensive care . . ." ". . . they just don't know . . ."

"They sent a Gulfstream for you and I came with it," said Lee. "There's no quicker way you could get to her, and . . . I didn't want you to read it on the wire, Johnny."

"You asked Pete to turn off the national wire."

"They put it on the wire, because her story is still hot."

"So you could come here to tell me first."

"We go back a ways, Johnny. Bad shit like this comes with the territory. You want to take anything?"

"If she dies . . . If she . . ."

Lee told Harland what he knew on the way back.

"She and another car went off the interchange and twenty feet down to another ramp. The other driver is DOA. People on the ramp where she landed stopped to help, but nobody on the ramp from where she fell stopped to say what happened. There was ice, and—"

"She's a good driver. She started driving when she was fourteen, in Arkansas. Her grandfather taught her."

There was a limo waiting for them at Teterboro.

"You haven't been to the hospital?" said Harland.

"Nona went there. I went for you."

"I appreciate it. No, I wouldn't want to read it on the wire."

There was a clot of reporters in the intensive-care waiting room. Harland knew a few of them. He had stood himself in hospital waiting rooms. They felt enough like buzzards, waiting to see if some stranger died, without having the job to do on one of their own. He managed something like a smile for them as he walked by.

* * *

The resident trauma surgeon was in his early thirties, with a beard. "Are you her husband?"

"Essentially," said Harland. "We live together."

The doctor glared at the reporters and pulled Harland by the arm into a stairwell. "Mr. Harland, this is as straight as I can say it. She has had massive trauma. What we have repaired so far have been the life-threatening injuries. She has lost her spleen and a kidney. She almost got a rib fragment in her heart, but our thoracic man did a brilliant job removing it. She has a broken jaw and pelvis and femur."

"Is there brain damage? I don't think . . . no, I *know* she wouldn't want . . . machines . . ." The image was too evil for Harland to harbor it.

"Her EEG is normal. There won't be any decisions like that to make. She has had a very large amount of intestinal bleeding and her blood pressure will not stabilize. She could fibrilate. If she doesn't, and if she stabilizes in the next four or five hours. . . ." He shrugged. "It's going to be very tough."

"Conscious?"

"Marginally."

"I want to . . ."

"You could go in for three or four minutes. I don't suppose I could talk you out of it. For your sake."

For three minutes at a time, once an hour, the doctor let him sit and hold her hand. He did not flinch at the tubes and wires and sallow skin and blue lips when he saw her the first time, because he did not allow himself to see them. He saw only what he recognized as familiar components of Molly: The spread of hair on the pillow was Molly. A thin gold chain he had given her was Molly. He did not allow himself to cry or tremble because he saw that she would sometimes turn her head and almost open her eyes. He wanted to make sure that if she should see him, she would see him smiling.

In the fourth hour, just as his time was up, her head rolled to the left, away from him, and when it rolled back her eyes were open. They focused on his face, and Harland saw recognition form behind them. He saw that her jaw moved as far as pain and the apparatus immobilizing it would allow. Harland smiled. Slowly, she discovered that she could smile, a quarter of an inch, with the right side of her face. Harland wiggled his eyebrows. And she wiggled her eyebrows. Then her eyes lidded again, and her head rolled again to the left.

As Harland neared the door, his three minutes up, he heard a beeping sound. He knew it came from the monitors wired to Molly. He did not look around, but from the corner of his vision he saw a nurse run to a cart parked against the wall and begin pushing it toward Molly's bed.

"Please, Mr. Harland." The doctor's voice, behind him. "Go on out."

He walked out, past Jerry Lee and Nona, and into the stairwell. He sat down on the landing. Jerry Lee did not follow.

Harland was incapable of moving even his eyes. The composition of descending concrete steps, parallel handrails, the sign saying OXYGEN IN USE THIS FLOOR, burned into his retinas.

He eventually became aware of movement to the side. The doctor sat on his haunches next to him. Harland heard, a floor below, someone enter the stairwell and start down.

After a few moments, Harland pulled himself up by the handrail and said: "I thank you for trying."

14

He thought he would walk past the reporters and photographers who had been waiting hours for him to leave. But he
stopped and let one of them ask him if he had a statement. He
smiled and said that Molly would not have approved of this;
that she was really an old-fashioned newspaper type who hated
the journalist as celebrity; that she would want her obit to be
no longer than four or five paragraphs and run on page twenty-
three.

Harland stood with Lee under the portico of the hospital entrance, realizing that now he should go home, and that he was
not capable of doing that. Lee asked Harland to spend the night
at his place, and Harland said yes.

He performed, for the next three days, immaculately. He
called Molly's mother and father in Little Rock, who kindly
allowed him the responsibilities of a husband. He arranged that
the hospital take the parts of Molly that were transplantable,
and for the rest of her to be cremated. He claimed Molly's
purse.

The Rices wanted to have a memorial service for their
daughter in Little Rock, and they asked Harland to sit with
them and Molly's younger sister. Harland and Molly had no
feeling about religion one way or another, so Harland went,

feeling that Molly would find no hypocrisy in holding a small ceremony for the benefit of her parents, who were routinely religious.

The *Times* sent a corporate plane full of Molly's editors and fellow reporters; CBS sent Lee and the president of News to go with Harland. There were network and national press at the church, but they just photographed from a quiet distance.

There was food assembled by the Rices' friends and neighbors at their house. Harland shook hands like a son-in-law with aunts he'd met before and cousins he hadn't, and the publisher of Molly's first paper, and Molly's high-school classmates.

Harland told the Rices he had to go. Molly's mother took Harland into a pantry and said that although she and her daughters loved each other, they were not intimate; but she knew that Molly was happier while she was living with Harland than at any time in her life, and that she and her husband were grateful to him, and loved him. He squeezed her hand and kissed her and left.

Harland and Jerry sat in the rental car. CBS's Gulfstream was waiting on the ramp.

"Jerry, I can't get on the plane. I've got things to do I haven't been able to do since she died. I don't figure that anybody will want to watch me do them, so I'll need to be by myself."

"I figured that."

"I might as well do it here."

Jerry let Harland off at the cab stand. "Are you going to be all right?"

"I'll let you know. Give me three or four days."

Harland asked the driver to stop at the first motel he saw. He paid for a room, locked the door behind him. He made it to the bed just as his knees were pulled up by a vacuum, forming in his gut, which threatened to implode him. He cried until his eyes were swelled shut, until his head throbbed; the muscles of his face cramped, mucus dripped off his lips. Finally he retched into the bathtub. He slept there, on the bathroom floor. When he awoke, he washed his face and went back into the bedroom. He turned on the television, turned off the sound. He lay down. The set was showing Huckleberry Hound cartoons. Without moving except to void himself, without making sound, he looked at them, and the *Six Million Dollar Man* reruns, and at the newscasts and the late show, whatever that channel was broadcasting into the silent object and the white noise when it was broadcasting nothing, for thirty-seven hours.

Then he washed his face again and went home.

CBS had told Harland to take as much time off as he needed, but when he got back to New York, he went to the office instead of the apartment. He sat in his office, spread his Vandellen file over his desk, and stared at it for half an hour. He finally told Jerry Lee: "This is stupid. I have to go there. It's where I live."

"Want company?"

"No. It was my place before it was our place. I'll just have to make it my place again."

Harland got condolences from the doorman, the accumulated mail and condolences from the building manager's office. His throat tightened when he saw the pile of magazines with Molly's name on the mailing labels. *Get used to that.*

It required a force of will to turn his key in the door and push it. It opened a foot and a half and stopped. Harland looked down. The bottom of the door was wedged against a throw pillow from the couch. Through the slice of open door he saw the record albums pulled off onto the floor, the drawers on the end tables emptied, debris from the kitchen, chaos.

Harland reflexively pulled back. *They might still be in there.* Then feelings of territory, images of strangers in his space, touching his things, Molly's things, replaced fear in his backbrain. He pushed open the door with his shoulder. *I hope the cocksuckers still are.*

Harland ran through the kitchen, the bedroom. Empty. Into the bathroom. Something was written on the glass of the shower stall, with something red. Maybe a grease pencil. *GO TO.* More below it, but it had been rubbed out. Then he noticed the televisions were still there, the stereo, the microwave, the cameras and lenses.

Harland's study was rifled, but Molly's was dissected. Every drawer in her desk and two file cabinets had been emptied. What they had not wanted they had left on the floor. Harland took a step on the pile of paper and felt something crunch underneath it. He moved the papers aside with a toe and saw pieces of Molly's treasured JFK-and-Jackie souvenir-of-Washington-D.C. plastic ashtray in which she'd kept paperclips.

Harland picked up Molly's overturned desk chair and sat in it. To know what was missing from Molly's study, Harland would have to know what had been there. And he had no idea.

If there was nothing missing, there was no point in calling the police. He knelt and began gathering Molly's albums.

It took him almost four hours to straighten up the apartment. He was almost grateful for the occupation. After he finished, he sat at the dining table and felt the needs that had sent him to the motel in Little Rock challenge him again. *No. Enough.* He would wash up. He would eat. He would minister to himself with routine. In the bathroom, before he washed his hands, he rubbed some more at the graffiti on the shower-stall glass. It was an effort to get the stuff off, and he wondered what was written that would make its author change his mind firmly enough to rub that hard that long.

Harland had no emotional interest in food, but he had barely eaten in days, and his stomach was knotting. Nothing in the refrigerator fulfilled his prerequisites of blandness and simplicity of preparation. He pulled at the freezer door, thinking of ice cream. He remembered as it opened that on his last night home, however many eternities ago that was, he'd eaten the last on hand.

There was a one-pound-eight-ounce Baskin-Robbins carton waiting for him. Harland closed his eyes and leaned his head against the freezer door. She must have bought it on her way in from the airport. Before.

He had been made newly incapable of eating anything, but he reached for the carton, to confirm that Molly had bought him burgundy cherry. He opened it.

She had. On top of the ice cream was a piece of paper. On it Molly had written: GO TO VERMONT ANYWAY.

Harland pretty well expected what he found when he slid the rented car down the indifferently plowed road and stopped it at the bank of snow that defined the cutoff to the cabin. It was nearly dark as he pushed through the snow beside the line of windbreak trees and bushes. It kept the snow only thigh-deep in what in summer were two tire ruts. Even before he mounted the steps onto the deck of the A-frame, he saw that the front door was open. They had no need to be subtle here; the doorframe was split apart by a crowbar. There was a drift of snow into the cabin, skinned with ice. Harland had to put his shoulder into the door to open it wide enough to pass in.

Chaos again. Less chaos, only because there were fewer objects inside to strew about than in the New York apartment. He and Molly agreed that work was forbidden there; they were not allowed even to write letters. There were perhaps a dozen paperback books, no papers, no notes.

Harland looked in the same places the visitors had looked: in the bathroom, the kitchen shelves, in the sleeping loft, in the shed outside where Harland kept a snow blower. They had either found what they had looked for; or Molly had hidden it well; or she had not hidden anything there. He saw no evidence of anything he did not know previously to exist there. *Baby, you're going to have to tell me what it is you want me to find.*

But he looked. He looked behind the refrigerator, because he had once happened upon a Christmas present Molly had hidden from him there. He thought of all the kinds of places he had hidden grass and looked there. He pursued hidden-behind-loose boards theories and hidden-in-plain-sight theories. In most places he found evidence that the visitors had looked there before him. He looked four hours and found nothing; he corrected himself: He had either found nothing, or found it and not yet recognized it.

He didn't build a fire; its warmth would be made cheerless by the memories it invoked. He slept in a sleeping bag on the sofa.

In the morning he looked in a few places he'd not thought of the day before, and found nothing. He realized there was nothing more to do. He looked around for something that needed taking back. There was nothing. He pulled the door shut, and walked back toward the road.

He sat in the front seat of the car, waiting for the windows to defog, and looked toward the A-frame. He knew he wouldn't want to come back.

Harland remembered that he had actually dropped the car into gear when he heard the tapping on the driver's side window. A man, made hostile and anonymous by being almost totally swathed against the cold, was walking around the front of Harland's car, staring in at him. Harland was instantly at the cusp between panic and the last sounds of reason, which told him there was no logical reason to panic. It was a paralytic moment, and accordingly Harland did nothing until the man had repeated the gesture: Harland was to roll down his window.

"You belong to this house?"

Harland was aware that the man was moving his hands at his waist, below the level of the car window.

"Snowplow's kept your box covered," he said. "We're not supposed to deliver to your box unless you keep a path shoveled." When the man's hands came back up, he had two small bright yellow packages in them. He handed them in through the window. As Harland took them, he saw the Postal Service patch on the shoulder of the man's parka. "If you want to see the rest of your pictures," said the postman, "you're going to have to come on into town and pick 'em up. And you got a bunch of cassette tape things too."

* * *

Harland, sitting at the kitchen table of the apartment in New York, put the cassette Molly had labeled "#1" into the tape recorder and put it on Play. There was a brief hiss of tape across playback head. Then:

"A wop bop a loo bop a wop bam boom . . ."

Harland turned it off and closed his eyes. *I can't do it, baby. Not eight of them. I could maybe manage to listen to a minute of you; maybe I could stand two minutes. Not eight whole tapes.*

But it was important to her, Harland told himself, *so I will do it. It will help if you don't think of the sound as Molly.* Just as data; the memory of chromium oxide. He turned the tape recorder back on and listened to the story of the Cessna and salt domes in Louisiana.

She filled more than half of the sixty-minute cassette, counting her mildly obscene closing, in which Harland perceived exactly the affection she had intended. He learned, in listening to her subsequent tapes, to stop before she began ending them. There was simply too much pain.

He got a beer, looked out the living room window. The flush of rage he had felt when Molly said she thought someone was trying to kill her had percolated down to something like an acid frustration. *Feeling protective, ace? A little late.*

He felt his loyalty compromised by hindsight. Molly was that particular kind of cynic produced from the raw stock of New Frontier college idealist when Kennedy was assassinated; and of an adversary journalist who expected her adversaries to fight back. She had told Harland—more with pride than anger —how her grandfather had been beaten and burned out for the stories he had run in his small-town Arkansas paper; how she had answered the phone when she was a girl and heard threats meant for her father, who had covered Little Rock politics; how she had been threatened—tires slashed, pets poisoned—in her small-paper and bureau days.

It was a kind of vanity to suspect, as she had, that, in retaliation to her investigative piece, New York Bell, under the screen of "construction problems," had deliberately degraded their phone service into a nightmare for more than a month. She recognized that and laughed at it—usually.

There was a bit of the flagellant in Molly. She had never before suggested anyone was trying to kill her; but her suspicion on the tapes was a reasonable extrapolation of her predispositions. Molly felt that the venal instincts of a government or corporate entity darkened in exponential proportion to its size. Now she had concluded that she had finally happened upon an adversary with enough at stake to include, among its ripostes, killing.

Until the moment Molly voiced it on the tape, Harland had never even thought of Molly's being murdered. The police had never spoken of anything but an accident. He could not, from that or the subsequent tapes he began playing, reasonably expect that deliberation could be proved in Molly's death. Or logically suspected.

He did know, by the time he had played the fourth and fifth tapes, that she had been very efficiently frightened. It had robbed her of rest and perspective. Pops and sentence splices began appearing in Molly's monologues. She apologized for having forgotten to push the Record button, and having to go back and search for where she left off. Gaps of empty hiss appeared where she had forgotten to push the Record button as well as the Play button; she was simply unwilling to go back to record over the silence. Toward the final tapes, she grew too impatient—more likely, by the flatness of her voice, simply too weary—to rewind the tapes. She just put the recorded tapes in their mailing cartons with a slip of paper on which "rewind" had been scribbled.

The tape marked "#8," played in both directions, was entirely blank. She just didn't notice that the Record button was not depressed, and she didn't rewind and play back to check that a recording had been made.

Harland set up the screen and slide projector and arranged the slides in the holder in the order of the numbers stamped on the corner of each—the same order they had been exposed in the camera. He fast-forwarded the tape to the point on the footage counter where, as he had noted down when he first listened to the tapes, Molly's narration began.

"Okay. Roll number one, slide number one. Looks like an innocent swamp, huh? Assuming I got the exposure right. With a few oil wells in it? But you see the wells? Go on to number two for a closer look at the wells. They're not taking oil out of the ground. They're putting it into the ground. Big salt domes under there . . ."

The fast film, automatic exposure control, and reflex focusing made most of the pictures legible; but Molly was an indifferent photographer and she knew it. There were none that were by themselves revelatory enough to warrant publication. There were photographs of rolls of sheet steel on a rail siding. In her cassette narration, Molly said they were illegally manufactured; but there was nothing about the photograph that distinguished the rolls of metal Molly photographed from rolls of legally manufactured sheet steel. She took a photograph of the outside of the warehouses where the illicit soft-drink cans were stored. But there had been too little light to shoot inside; her attempt was underexposed and blurry from her trying to hand-hold the camera at a slow shutter speed. The photographs did little more than to confirm that Molly had physically visited the places she wrote about in her *Times* story. She must have sensed the uselessness of them, for in the later rolls she exposed only half the usable frames before dropping them into mailboxes.

The same fatigue that caused her to become careless with the mechanics of the tape recorder affected her bookkeeping with the photographs. Molly was having to narrate a slide show of unprocessed film, working from notes and, in the final rolls, tattered memory. Her narration did not always match the order of numbered slides, or she would forget she had taken one, leaving Harland with an image he could not put in context: the exterior of an unknown building, in an unknown city; a ship moored in an anonymous harbor. The narration for the seventh box of slides was apparently on the blank eighth cassette tape. Harland looked at the thirteen slides. All were photographs of the exterior of a building with large pipes running into it and, apparently inside the same building, of a complicated control panel. Some of the closeups of the panel were shaky and canted, fuzzily focused, as if they were taken quickly. Harland was confident that the installation had something to do with oil. He was confident of nothing else.

Harland saw a reporter who was at first exhilarated, then frightened, by what she was discovering; then she was verbally mugged and began listening to a paranoia at which she normally would have laughed.

He owed someone for that.

For all the pain of listening to Molly's voice, Harland felt there was little he could do to keep her story alive. There was almost nothing in her notes that had not been absorbed into her *Times* story. She herself said that she had about decided that the soft-drink-can-stockpile lead, in which she had become lost in a Chinese puzzle box of dummy corporations, wasn't worth the time of pursuit.

She had asked him to finish her business; he wanted to, desperately, but she had left him no enigmas.

No. One.

Harland racked the slide tray back to the beginning and put the image of the building with the pipes on the screen. There was a chain-link fence around it, nothing very formidable. No signs to denote its location or function. Wait. In the corner of the screen, the *edge* of a sign. She must have composed the picture to include the sign, then moved the camera just a bit as she took the exposure. He advanced the tray to the next slide: Another exterior, from a different position. The sign was in the frame again, but this time at too oblique an angle to the camera to read its writing. *Come on, baby, take a picture of the sign.* But the next was virtually the same angle as the slide preceding it, and there were no more exteriors. The pictures of the control panels were too poor to make out much detail; when the labels on the dials were legible, they said amorphic things like *Flow* and *Pressure.*

He went back to the beginning, to the first photograph of the outside of the building. The fan in the slide projector was the only sound in the room. *Okay, kid, I'll find out about the fucking building for you. Then you can give it a rest. I can give it a rest.*

At his desk in the CBS newsroom the next morning, Harland slid the box of slides back and forth across the desk top and thought about Larry Amble.

Molly thinks he is In on It, but not a big enough honcho to include in the partial list of participants in the Fourteenmile Point meeting she printed in the *Times.* Molly's assignment of sinister objective to Fourteenmile Point was the most harshly attacked of her allegations—probably because, as even Harland had to concede, it was the most conjectural. Most of those accused of being there denied it. Some agreed that they were in Michigan, but they were there to dispense wisdom in the spirit of the seminar. The secrecy was primarily to allow the executives to concentrate, out of reach of subordinates' phone calls.

If one has a question about oil patch machinery, an oil company flack is the logical first place to take it; that's why they're there. But if Molly's instincts were correct, if he was In on It, Amble should be the last person to see the slides. Harland had met Larry Amble, routinely, before. They had done business more frequently back in Harland's bureau days, when Amble was playing in Encon's PR minor leagues. He seemed to Harland no more or less suspicious than any other corporate mouthpiece; he had no strong feelings about him. He decided that he should test Molly, Amble, and himself: Encounter Amble across his desk and see if it caused Harland any disquietude. Harland, as much as Molly, trusted subjectives when it came time to judge whether somebody was a Good Guy or a Bad Guy.

He called up Amble's secretary and left word he'd like to drop by. He got a callback fifteen minutes later, saying that Amble was in the CBS neighborhood and would be glad to come by Harland's office. Harland didn't want that, so a compromise was reached: the lunchroom of the Museum of Modern Art.

The lunchroom had just opened, and the crowd was still thin. Amble was waiting for him with two cups of coffee and a PR smile that he allowed to decay, smoothly, into concern.

"John, I can't tell you how sorry—"

Harland smiled. "Larry, Molly would think that grief is a totally bullshit emotion . . ."

Amble smiled and nodded. "Yes, she would."

". . . and she would say I've done enough feeling sorry for myself already, and don't need anybody else chipping in. But thanks for saying it."

"I just want you to know that our denials of her story . . . they were tough, but I don't want you to think they were attacks on her, personally. She was always fair with us, but . . . Jesus, John, we just had to come out hard on this. What really threw us was how someone like Molly could be so far . . . well, so far off base, John."

"Larry . . ." Harland held up his hands. "We've all got jobs. If you've still got any guilt about yours, I can give you a chance to work it off." Harland reached into his shirt pocket and brought out one of the slides.

"Molly was sort of a half-ass photographer. I was going through her stuff, found a bunch of slides she must have taken before I knew her. This is one, from a vacation, I guess. It looks like an oil-field installation or something. I'm going to send the slides to her folks, and I think they might like to know what it is. Where it is, if that's possible."

Harland handed the slide to Amble and watched him very carefully as he held it up to the light. First subjective: The way he closed his hand around the slide after he finished looking at it. "You got me," he said. Very levelly. Second subjective: "But I'll sure try to find out." He slid the slide into a pocket.

"Are there any more of the same place?" said Amble. He looked past Harland as he said it, into the sculpture garden.

Third subjective. "Because it would be . . . you know, it would help my people pin it down."

"I'm not sure," said Harland. "I'd have to look some more."

"I could send a messenger home with you. So they'd get right back to me . . ."

Harland told Amble he'd call for the messenger if he found anything else. He went back to the office, picked up the slides and cassettes, walked to the Chase Manhattan Bank, and rented a safe-deposit box.

15

HARLAND ANSWERED HIS OFFICE PHONE.

"Mr. Harland?"

"Yes."

"This is Martin Vandellen."

Jesus. Vandellen. Harland had all but forgotten he was due to have another interview session with him. It had been agreed upon another life ago.

"I was saddened by the loss of Molly Rice. She covered one of my campaigns for a while. I was rather disappointed when the paper assigned her elsewhere. I had come to depend upon her at press conferences. She asked the kind of questions that make me think, and I appreciated it. She was scrupulous. I think she deeply loved being a journalist."

"Molly . . . yes. She did."

"I will avoid the rest of the well-meaning platitudes. I am confident that no one knows how you feel."

"Thanks for that."

"Would you like to finish our conversation?"

"Very much."

"So would I. Would sometime next week be convenient? After that would be very difficult, I'm afraid."

"Fine."

"A full day be enough?"

"Fine."

"And can you stay with us overnight at Sandstone?"

"Yes. Thank you."

"Please hold on, and someone will work out arrangements. Thank you, Mr. Harland. Mend quickly. Hurt is rewarding if one learns from it. Grief is useless."

As Harland waited on hold, he suddenly remembered Jerry Lee's instant analysis after Vandellen's final primary loss: *Americans don't want a president who doesn't cry at weddings . . .*

Harland met with his producer and the production manager. Arrangements were made for Harland to go to Colorado as soon as flights could be booked. United, upon being presented its latest fuel allocation, had just dropped another westbound. Even for a business-priority reservation—they would have to fly out of their destination city within three days of arrival—the soonest the film crew could get out was two days away.

When he got back to his desk, his mail had been delivered. Among it was a yellow box from the Kodak Processing Laboratory, sent on to the forwarding address Harland had given to the village post office in Vermont.

He had torn open the mailing sleeve and had held up the first slide to the light—it looked like a roadsign—when his phone rang.

"John? Hoss, how you doin'?" Red Kuntz, calling from Houston. You don't forget voices like that.

"Red? Doin' fine. How's the pipeline bidniss?" Harland had spent his college years grimly beating back his Texas accent so he could speak without trace of regionalism; he enjoyed the infrequent opportunities to rediscover it talking with people from back home.

"Shit, I'm retired. I'm supposed to be a consultant, but I must be retired because nobody consults with me. They give me an office about half the size of the Astrodome and I'm in it about one day a week. Rest of the time I go out duck huntin' and that's fine with them."

"You should have known that would happen before you sold your company."

"Aw, piss on 'em, I don't care. Pipelinin' ain't no fun anymore. Texas Eastern can have it. I got tired of havin' to fill out forty-four hunnerd EPA forms ever time I had to take a leak. Hey. When you gonna come see an old man? I think of you and that program you did on me and the other ol' timey oil-patch farts ever time I see you on the TV. You still the only goddamn news reporter who can talk about the oil bidniss without the corner of your mouth turnin' down."

"Well, when you grow up in Angleton . . . I had folks who worked in the fields."

"I thought dang, I just oughta fly on up there and see ol' John and bring the pictures with me. But my pilot says I'm just about run through my goddam fuel allocation, and I'm gonna have to save it to get to the NCAA finals. Ain't that sorry shit? I bet I pumped more light crude up north than anybody in the oil patch, and here for love or money I can't get enough to keep a little pissant Lear in the air."

"So you got the slides?"

"Yeah, and I seen right off what they was of. I been there. It's Caroline Junction."

"Caroline Junction."

"Up in Alberta, deep into Canada. You heard of that, ain't you?"

" 'Fraid not."

"Hoss, it's the main control station of the Alaska natural-gas pipeline. Two lines come from Alaska and they join up there and go into the south forty-eight as one humongous forty-eight-incher. Like I said, I seen right away that it was Caroline Junction, but there was something funny about something and I just couldn't put my finger on it. I looked at them things and I *looked* at 'em, and then I looked at that second one of the control room—"

"Which one, Red? Which number? I have the originals here; you've got duplicates."

"Well, these pictures ain't so sharp, but you can see it good and clear in number eight. Funniest damn thing I ever saw. Course, you'd have to be in the gas-transmission bidniss to see it . . ."

"What, Red?"

"Well, they must have pulled them monitors out for maintenance or something, and the ol' boy who put 'em back in, put 'em in backasswards. Most hilarious thing I ever saw. Jesus Christ knows how many cubic feet a second is going through that thing, and the instruments show it's going the *wrong way*. North."

Harland borrowed a projector from the art department and went into a conference room with the new batch of slides. They were numbered "#9"; Molly's annotations were probably on the blank cassette. The first slide was indeed of a road sign: HIGH POINT 12 ROCKDALE 25. On the second frame, Molly had walked down the highway and shot back in the opposite direction to show the writing on the other side of the sign, which gave the mileage to two other towns: NEW ELM 8 EMMET 14.

The sequence and composition of the photographs were of no apparent significance. She took a picture in the direction of a range of low mountains in the distance. Then she walked off into the low scrub vegetation, toward a thirsty-looking tree, and took another frame. In the next one, the same tree was in the foreground. In the next frame, Harland noticed that she had walked toward a dry wash that was in the middle background in the preceding picture. In the next, she was standing down inside the wash.

A silver line appeared in the background in one frame. Molly was methodically snapping away as she approached it. The chain-link fence was at least six feet tall and endless: Molly photographed in both its directions to show that it marched over the horizon. In the foreground, a posted-no-trespassing sign had been attached to the chain link. It was the last slide.

Harland went back to the beginning and ran the slides again, but he had no idea what the series of pictures was intended to tell him, the function Molly meant for them to serve. He didn't know what he should look for; he saw roadsigns, arid land, and a very long fence. It could be anywhere. The land was characteristic of West Texas, half of New Mexico, almost all of Arizona, lots of California. He could look in road atlases for the names of the towns; but how many New Elms are there? High Points? How many—

Harland froze as he started to push the button that advanced the slide changer.

She's dropping breadcrumbs.

There may be lots of Rockdales, and lots of High Points, but there's probably only one pair exactly thirteen miles apart. And only one point on one road twelve miles from High Point and eight miles from New Elm.

He racked the slide holder back to the beginning and started clicking through the slides again. *Baby, I hear you talking.* And from that point you walk off the road toward the thirsty-looking tree, then look for the dry wash, walk down it until the fence, then . . .

Then what? Harland picked up the Kodak mailing sleeve and looked at the mailing label Molly had addressed. It was a thirty-six-exposure mailer, but there were only twenty slides in the box. Molly must have thought there was a thirty-six-exposure roll in the camera. She had not been able to show what was at the end of the path she was tracing because she had run out of film.

The camera crew went on from the airport to a hotel in Denver. A car and driver from Sandstone were waiting for Harland. He drove out to Sandstone as the light was failing, in a salmon world. There was almost no room left in his passport for visa stamps, but mountains and snow still turned him into a tourist. A Gulf Coast boy, he thought.

The driver apologized for his indirect route to Sandstone; as a result of the latest energy allocations, the city was unable to keep all its snowplows running. Only vital streets were kept open during the ceaseless blanketing of snow; one was no longer able to go the most direct route to one's destination.

The highway from Denver toward Sandstone was kept open, and the nearly three-mile-long private road from the highway cutoff to the main complex of buildings was plowed clean.

Harland slept in one of the apartments assigned to a scientist there for several months doing research; he was temporarily absent. A bedroom, living room, and efficiency kitchen, and a study equipped with a terminal to the central computer. All the researchers had access to it. He saw that the television supplied the Denver stations and a closed-circuit Sandstone channel. When he had it briefly on, a physicist was delivering a paper. Harland remembered from the previous visit that the researchers present were encouraged to take some time to see what those in other disciplines were doing.

Harland was told that Vandellen would like to have breakfast with him at eight, before the camera crew was due at ten. Before Harland turned out the light, he watched snow fall into the light spill from the huge window in the bedroom. He imagined that the view out that window tomorrow would be awesome.

It was. He had kept the shades open, and light woke him about six-thirty. The snow had stopped. Harland suddenly felt there was regeneration available outside—just by walking into that morning—and that he needed it.

The cold burned his lungs and easily invaded his coat, which was too thin to enable him to spend much time outside. Regeneration he felt. He finally had to close his eyes to the sky, the trees, the iron red of the mountainside the snow had yet to cover; close them not against a surfeit of light, but simply to the intensity of the colors, excited by the clarity of the air to a dizzying vibrancy.

The cold was about to drive him in, but he took a moment

to strip a few needles from a fir just off the path and crush them between his gloves. He drew in the smell of Christmas trees. As he turned to go back in, he saw that Martin Vandellen was standing near the entrance, smiling at him.

Harland walked up to him, feeling a little sheepish from having been observed behaving lyrically.

"I've lived around here off and on for twenty years and am unable myself to resist these mornings," said Vandellen. They shook hands.

Harland looked at Vandellen's arctic suit. "Please say you don't run twelve miles every morning."

"I don't. Running is physiologically useless unless one does it hard enough to make it painful, and then one can't think of anything but the pain. I don't find that at all spiritual. I find it boring. I do like to walk, because I can think when I walk. For exercise I play racquetball."

"Will you play today? I'd like to shoot you playing."

"Certainly. Can I trust you to splice out my poor shots?"

They walked on to Vandellen's quarters. Breakfast foods had been left for them in covered serving dishes. Harland never saw a servant attend Vandellen. They served their own plates.

Harland realized that Vandellen established control of the conversation, and that he wanted to talk about Harland. Harland found it curious at first, then voluptuous.

". . . Then reporters do have personal feelings about the subjects and the people they cover," said Vandellen.

"Just as anybody has feelings about anything. We're not supposed to let them get in the way, though. That's the phrase everybody uses when reporters talk about personal bias: 'Not get in the way.' "

"So they're suppressed."

"Basically."

"Ah, suppression."

"I know, I know. The shrinks' best friend. The bias is applied anyway; it just becomes subconscious."

"What are your feelings?"

"Irrelevant."

"How the people who see your program will perceive me is a function of your attitudes. It's not irrelevant to me. Don't you concede that viewers who watch you—and think enough to realize you have biases—have the privilege of knowing what your instincts are?"

"Truth in labeling?"

"Very good analogy."

"Journalists should register their biases with the government? List them at the beginning of their stories?"

"No, that's nonsensical. This is just informal curiosity, you understand. Don't you think reporters should make themselves available to the informal curiosity of others?" Vandellen smiled at him. Harland was not so big a media star not to get a rush from Martin Vandellen's showing interest in what John Harland thinks.

"I'm yours."

"What are your politics?"

"I can truthfully say that I'm virtually apolitical. I don't vote."

"But everybody has an idealized vision of himself having the right ideas. I would guess you visualize yourself as a liberal. Kennedy-era college student . . ."

"Lower-middle-class origins and white-Southerner guilt. Yes, sort of a liberal. That's not hard to guess." Harland smiled and worried at a few crumbs of toast on the tablecloth with a knife. "But I'm starting to surprise myself."

"With unexpected conversion to attitudes you previously thought of as conservative."

"I can't bring myself to use the word. I use euphemisims like 'practical' or 'productive.' I feel traitorous. JFK died for my sins, in advance."

Those often around him said that there was no casual conversation with Martin Vandellen; one felt that everything one said to him was weighed and measured. Harland felt that almost immediately, that his replies were being listened to carefully. He found himself working at making them precise and efficient. At first he thought he was just trying to be accommodating;

then he realized he was working to please this man, and he had no idea why.

"Do you ever dislike people on whom you report?"

"Some. About in the same proportion as I like and dislike persons on whom I don't report."

"Do you report on people whom you envy?"

Harland cut his eyes to meet Vandellen's. "That's what is known in the trade as a very direct question."

Vandellen was smiling, to preserve the understanding that this interviewer-interviewee role-reversal was supposed to be a novelty act.

"Just a bit of your own. I've been asked even more direct ones even more directly."

"I—" Harland stopped, laughed very gently. "I am imagining your asking that of Molly. She would say 'no,' add 'you asshole,' and maybe have put the bowl of oatmeal on your head. Because she wasn't envious. She believed she had the best job in the world. Molly thought the presidents and the senators and the board chairmen should be envious of her.

"Look, sorry, but I've still got all the petty vices of everybody else. I envy. Who doesn't? Anybody envies. I envy people who can eat anything they want and not put on weight. I might envy somebody I'm covering because of something he has: money, sometimes. A perk. Most of the time I envy a skill. It's just a matter of degree. I think about it, then I stop thinking about it. But nothing's ever caused me to eat my heart out. If I turned green, it would show on camera."

"Do you envy power? But then you have your own not-inconsiderable power."

Harland waved away his words. "We don't have power. The people who say journalists have too much power think influence is the same thing as power, and it's not. We have influence, and a lot of it. But we don't have power. Power is when you say something and people are supposed to do it. I don't have the ability to order anybody to do anything. Well, one secretary."

"Yet it's available. You are approached to run for office, are you not? The senate, if I remember the *Newsweek* article. Sixty percent recognition factor."

"Jesus. Name recognition. The reasons people will vote for somebody: just because they recognize his name. Basketball players as senators. It doesn't flatter me; it scares me."

"And you never considered taking advantage of this . . . availability?"

"I have fantasies. Very small ones, very brief ones. Daydreams. Everybody has the one where you're . . . in charge, and very good at it. Wise and just. Having the power intrigues me; what you have to go through to get it appalls me."

"Campaigns."

"I could never do it. Absolutely sordid. No reflection."

A phone buzzed on a table behind Vandellen, and he reached for it. "I found no pleasure in them at all. And in no way are they an accurate expression of the will of the people." The phone call was to tell Vandellen that Harland's film crew had arrived. They got up to walk to the main reception area to meet them.

Harland stopped as Vandellen held the door for him. He suddenly found himself needing to say this: "I really don't, you know. Have any itches."

Vandellen smiled. "Everyone, John, has itches."

It hadn't been that hard to find. There were at most seven states with that kind of topography and vegetation. It took him less time than he'd anticipated to find which one.

He thought the towns might be too small to be indexed on the fairly cursory road atlases available in the library, so he worked from the U.S. Postal Service Zip Code Directory. He tried California first. There was an Emmet and a Rockdale, but they were more than two hundred miles apart. Nevada had a High Point, but it was in the northern part of the state; there wasn't that much green in Molly's pictures. None of the four names in New Mexico. Texas was out; he knew where the Rockdale was, and the topography didn't fit.

Arizona.

He waited until about an hour before he and the film crew were supposed to head on out to Stapleton Airport for the plane back to New York. Then he sent them on, saying he had decided to stay and do some more backgrounding. He spent the night at the Stapleton airport hotel and got up at six the next morning to catch the flight he'd reserved before he left New York.

The walk from the Phoenix airport passenger terminal to where he claimed his rental car—with gas enough for three hundred miles—convinced him that he had been cold long enough. He was going to gain a couple of thousand feet of altitude between Phoenix and the roadsigns shown in the first slide from box eight. There hadn't been any drifts of snow in the slides, just a light dusting. But there had been no sun. Harland had felt cold just looking at them.

He stopped at a shopping mall, and in an outdoors store bought a quilted coat with a hood and insulated snow pants big enough to fit over his trousers. Also gloves and boots. Then he drove northeast out of town.

The road climbed to a plateau and then leveled out again. Despite the late-morning sun, Harland could feel the temperature drop once he left the desert floor of Phoenix.

He stole a few quick glances at the Arizona roadmap on the seat beside him. He'd gotten it from a woman in the Arizona tourism booth at the airport. She had smiled and urged him to take five or six of them, since the state was so starved for tourists her booth was being shut down the end of the week, and she was out of a job.

It was more detailed than the road atlas he had available in New York; it supplied missing data. Three of the four towns had shown up in the Zip Code Directory, but only New Elm and Rockdale were on the atlas, which showed them to be, to the best of his estimation on the rather coarse scale of the map, about thirty miles apart. The slides of the roadsigns showed them to be eight miles from New Elm and twenty-five miles from Rockdale. That New Elm and that Rockdale. Had to be. A call to the cartography division of the Arizona Highway Department confirmed it.

Emmet came up. Harland saw why it didn't appear in the Zip Code Directory: It was three gas pumps, and a tilted grocery store with a CLOSED sign on it.

The road was tending northward from northeastward. The vegetation was changing into the kind shown in Molly's slides; it was less severe and defensive than the desert plants: an occasional cactus, but mostly low bushes, and occasional stumpy, bristly trees with pinched, thin leaves.

Harland felt a small zap of tension when he saw the sign for New Elm. The town was a substantially bigger deal than Emmet. Three gas stations—two of them newly opened—at the crossroad between the highway and a gravel road that extended for a hundred or so yards east and west until it succumbed to the scrub trees. The grocery store looked equally brand-new; it was a prefab metal building. So was the Laundromat. Harland pulled off the road and looked around the crossroads. Along the gravel crossroads were exactly similar trailer houses, big double-wides—maybe three dozen of them. *This whole place looks as though it was delivered by United Parcel*, thought Harland. *Yesterday.* And he smiled ". . . *arrived by United Parcel.*" Molly's line.

He didn't remember driving past anything but brush and cactus since he'd left the suburbs of Phoenix. He didn't see any livestock, nor mining operations, nor public-work projects under construction. Whatever brought people out here to live in their mobile homes, thought Harland, must be on the north side of town.

He drove on through New Elm; just outside of town he saw a roadsign that placed High Point twenty miles away and Rockdale thirty-three. The scrub trees and dry washes reclaimed the land. No agriculture, no construction. *Why do those people live back there?*

Then, off to the east side of the highway, a silver line at

the base of the far-distant mountains. It was no heat shimmer. It grew firmer and better defined as he approached it. The fence. The chain-link fence from slide box eight.

It paralleled the highway and headed off east, over a low hill. No sign to indicate its intention, or who its builder was. It continued over the rise in the road ahead, around a curve. "Jesus," said Harland, and noted the mileage on the odometer. It had rolled over almost one and a quarter miles before Harland noted something ahead: an indentation in the fence, a cutoff from the highway; and, Harland saw as he slowed, a guard station. He checked the odometer; still almost a mile and a half from the roadsigns.

A small sign, about eye level, attached to the chain-link gate: AVALON RESORT PROPERTIES. *Whatever Molly wanted me to know about*, Harland thought, *is inside there.* He now realized that the breadcrumbs would lead to a way through the fence; she wouldn't have left them if she had been able to get in routinely, through this gate.

As Harland slowed the car to a creep on the shoulder of the road, he noted that the guard was looking through the window at him. *What could it hurt? Play innocent and see what he smiles and says.*

He did not smile. The guard, dressed in a rent-a-cop uniform with a conspicuously large pistol, leaned on the car door after Harland had stopped at the barrier. He said, "Can I help you?" in a tone that clearly indicated he hoped he couldn't.

"Yeah," said Harland. "Sorry to bother you. Am I on the right road for Rockdale?"

"That way," said the guard, nodding his head north. "Twenty-six miles."

"That's good to know," said Harland. He dropped the car in reverse, then called out to the guard as he was turning around. "Uh, what kind of a resort can you build out here in these boonies? I mean, why would anybody come here?"

The guard took off his sunglasses and polished them, not looking at Harland. "There's a river back there. Government's building a dam, and there'll be a big lake in a couple of years."

"No kidding? Hey, I've been thinking of buying lake property. Can you drive back there and see where everything is going to be?"

" 'Fraid not. Not yet. Nothing much to see, and there's construction. Blasting. A little too dangerous."

"Yeah. Well, thanks for the directions." But the guard had already turned to go back to his station. Harland backed out and headed north. The fence stopped paralleling the road about half a mile past the guard station. It headed northeast, and disappeared over a low ridge. Harland watched the odometer, counted down the tenths. He saw vertical lines rise from the shimmer on both sides of the pavement.

The roadsigns. Harland pulled over and parked. HIGH POINT 12 ROCKDALE 25. He walked onto the middle of the pavement and looked back south. NEW ELM 8 EMMET 14.

She had stood exactly here. He drew a soft semicircle in the pavement with the toe of his shoe. *Dumb.* He scrubbed his numb face with his hands. *And I'm freezing. Get on with it.*

He looked south as he went back to the car to put on the cold-weather gear and wondered if the car could be seen from the guard station. Unlikely. It was more than a mile, and there was sort of a hill between them. A fail-safe: Harland raised the hood of the car. *If they come by, they'll think the car broke down and I got a ride into Rockdale.*

But they probably patrol. And there are probably God knows what kind of detection devices outside the fence and inside the fence. And I'm probably going to get caught.

"Just so they lock me up in some place that's warm," he said as he picked up a hand slide viewer and box eight. He walked a little way due east, away from the road, looking for the thirsty-looking tree in Molly's slide. The terrain was gravelly, and everything green was defended with thorns. About two hundred yards off the road he was able to distinguish the tree. He put in the next slide and turned slowly to the south until he got a match in his own field of vision with the composition of the slide. And there was the dry wash.

It was at most three feet deep, but that and the vegetation

on its banks broke the wind a little. Some feeling started to return to Harland's face. He walked, he thought, perhaps a quarter of a mile down the wash until he saw the fence reappear above the bushes. He climbed the bank and, anticipating sensing devices, stopped a few feet short of the fence.

He looked at the last slide. *The breadcrumbs stop here.* There was nothing in Molly's photograph that would distinguish the section of fence from any two hundred feet of what had to be tens of miles of fence. Harland assumed that Molly's way in was near here. *Okay, ace. Which direction down the fence?*

The same way he'd been walking, he decided. And a hundred yards down the fence, he saw what Molly had wanted him to see: where the dry wash had cut a gully under the fence more than big enough to crawl through. Which he did, after taking two very deep breaths. And making sure that it really was he who was squirming under a fence in the cold in Arizona, and not a John Harland impersonator.

Again, a decision about direction. The terrain on the inside of the fence was no different from the terrain on the outside of the fence. Since following the wash had turned out pretty well so far, Harland decided to follow the wash a little further.

Another hundred yards down it, another shape appeared above the top of the brush. Harland climbed up the bank of the wash and walked, lightly, toward the metal building. It was maybe ten feet square and seven feet tall. He saw an aging wooden sign, about to lose its perch on the side of the building: ARIZONA CINNABAR INC. Mercury ore. Mining. Too small to be an entrance. He heard a whine from it and, as he got closer, felt a breeze—warmer than the ambient air—from the louvers in the building's side. Ventilator shaft.

Harland walked up to it, expecting at any moment to set off whatever had been installed to detect his presence. The building was old; its metal exterior was pitted and rusting. But its fortifications were new. Cages had been built over the outside of the louvers to prevent their being pried apart. The door was new: metal, with a padlock. He looked through the louvers, squinting his eyes against the breeze, and saw only the blades, belt, and drive shaft of the slowly turning fan.

If what Molly wanted him to see was inside this building, this would be the end of the line: He didn't happen to have any acetylene torches, bolt-cutters, or plastic explosives on him.

But neither had Molly. She had almost certainly been guided here, by one of her sources. And the source either had a key to the padlock—in which case Harland was still at the end of the line—or a way in had been left for them.

Harland walked once around the building, saw nothing. There was no reason to believe that the way in was still available. He had no idea how long ago Molly had been here; it could have been as much as a month. The breach in security could have been discovered by now and closed. Or it could be hidden, at least enough to survive a cursory inspection.

Harland looked closely at the padlock, gave it a tentative tug. It held. But the hasp moved. The screws were both large and vandal-proof—slotted so that a screwdriver could only screw them in. But just from Harland's tug they had perceptibly backed out of their holes. He pushed the hasp flush with the surface of the door. There was enough room between the hasp and the back of the screwhead for him to insert the car key. The screw popped out easily. Its threads had been hacksawed off.

Harland popped out the rest of the screwheads, catching them and putting them in his pocket, and opened the door. He slipped in, and pushed the door closed except for a crack—enough to allow in a little light. In addition to the fan motors, the building housed only a three-foot-wide shaft with a metal ladder. *Down there. I'm supposed to go down there.* Harland was not pathologically claustrophobic; but he was a little—enough to become a little uncomfortable in an especially crowded elevator.

He closed the door to acclimate his eyes to the dark, then after a moment leaned over the shaft. To his relief, he saw faint light at the bottom, perhaps fifty feet down; he didn't think he would have been able to go into that hole in dead darkness.

He took the first step down to the descending rung, thinking again about detection devices. Whoever took care of the screws probably took care of them too. *But basically, ace, you're going to have to count on staying lucky.*

The walls of the shaft were smooth limestone and the ladder was firmly anchored, for which Harland was grateful. As he got toward the point where the ventilation shaft opened into the main mining shaft, he craned to see as much as he could of what he was getting into.

The light was very dim. He could see that the floor of the mine had been poured with concrete to level it. He could see the edge of a plastic drop cloth that had been used to cover something. That was all. He took another deep breath and descended to the bottom of the ladder.

He felt he should hide behind something. There were plenty of the waist-high objects covered with drop cloths behind which to duck—hundreds of them in this chamber. But a quick look around showed him nothing from which hiding was necessary. Or, as far as that goes, from which hiding was possible.

Harland picked up the corner of the drop cloth nearest him. Saw as he lifted it the wooden skid on which the objects rested, so that they could be transported by fork lift. Molly must have done the same thing, held her breath as Harland was doing . . .

Packages, each maybe a foot square, wrapped in brown paper. He took out his car key again and used it to peel up an edge of the tape used to seal one of them. And he tore off the end of the package.

Thomas Alva Edison stared at him. From bits of paper the size of a dollar bill, lightly yellow, with "1 KwH" printed in each corner.

A Xerox of a Xerox of a Xerox. Of these.

Harland stood unmoving for a moment, caught up in a reality splice between then/there and the lobby of a hotel, weeks ago in Houston. He saw the same image of Edison in his hand, just out of the envelope left for him with the room clerk, its resolution degraded by the cheap photocopy paper and by going through several generations of duplication; and he saw the same image crisp on the thick, rich paper. Saw the same image crumpled and discarded in the ashtrays by the elevators.

Harland pulled back another drop cloth, tore off the end of another package: "20 KwH" was printed in the corners of these. He didn't recognize the portrait. He leaned in to read the caption. Enrico Fermi. He reached to pull one of the bills from the stack, then recoiled—there was a metallic clang from the end of the chamber. Harland jerked his head in the direction of its origin and saw the cylinder of light from a flashlight. He reached again for the bill. *No. I won't get away if I take the time.* He took the three seconds needed to fold the corners of the plastic drop cloths back down, then headed back up the ladder.

He must have made a small sound, for just as he pulled his trailing leg up into the ventilator shaft, he looked down to see the cylinder of light cut through the space he had just left. He kept still and heard footsteps go past, then more clangs; the guard was likely passing into another chamber.

It took him about fifteen minutes to make his way to the wash and follow it back—running when he had the breath—to the thirsty-looking tree, then back to the road and the car. He did not take the time to replace the screwheads in the hasp. He fell once, and the hand viewer and some of Molly's slides spilled out of his pocket. He didn't take the time to pick them up. With every step he felt imminent discovery like a pressure on the back of his neck. He expected to see them standing there beside the car when he got to it, even expected to see them in the backseat when he opened the door.

But there was no one. He fell in behind the steering wheel and lay his forehead upon it, heaving clouds of condensed breath into the windshield. He held up his trembling hand and worked a small piece of rock from under the flesh of his palm, jammed there when he broke his fall. He felt in the pocket of the coat. *Oh shit, did the keys fall out too?* He found them, started the car, had to get out and slam the hood. Then he drove on north.

How many of those things in a package? How many packages to a skid? How many skids in that room? How many rooms?

I know where there are 500,000,000 of these . . .

It took Harland an extra seventy miles to get back to Phoenix. He did not go back along the same road, past the guard station and through New Elm, and its exactly uniform mobile homes.

16

HE HAD THROWN IT AWAY.

Harland knew that, even as he was climbing the ventilator shaft from the mine. On the plane from Phoenix he thought it through and reconfirmed it. When he got back to the apartment he opened the desk drawer into which he had first tossed the Xerox copy of the 1 KwH bill and demonstrated it: It was not there.

He had intended to give it to Molly. And had forgotten about it. He had come upon it straightening up the apartment after it had been ransacked. He remembered looking at it no more than a second and deciding he had to be rid of it. It reminded him of the gift night they had had together in Houston; Harland was then, was now, unable to deal with that.

Had there been a phone number written on the photocopied bill? Or was it on the piece of paper stapled to it? The number might have been that of the same person who had led Molly down the wash to the ventilator shaft.

Moot question. It was gone.

Molly was gone.

Harland sat in his office and stared at the bookcase. *Okay, kid. I got it for you. What do I do with it?* A couple of phone calls while he was waiting for the plane in Phoenix had established that there was an Avalon Development—it was a subsidiary of a huge energy company. That there was a federal dam project in the works; that there was a resort under development. No secret: The *Arizona Republic* had reported on it.

He was prepared in Molly's memory to call down what lightning he could onto what he had discovered: A subsidiary of a huge energy company was hiding millions of something that looked like money in an abandoned mine in Arizona.

So what?

The bills were yellow; not even the most zealous Secret Service agent could be persuadèd the cache was counterfeit U.S. currency. It was no more illegal than Monopoly money.

The connective tissues were still missing. Maybe Molly knew, or had strong suspicions, of the reasons for the bills' existence. But there seemed little point in Harland's revealing their presence and demanding an explanation; since Harland had no idea what sort of sinister value to assign to the ersatz money, any benign purpose its manufacturers might claim for it would be believable by default.

For his effort in Molly's behalf, he had data that might turn evidence if one knew of the existence of a crime. Mostly he had enigmas, and an occasional ambiguity that would support Molly's printed conclusions only if one was already disposed to share her suspicions. And prejudices.

As Molly had predicted, the *Times*'s followup—the Panex *Times*'s followup—on her story had been all diminuendo. The unbylined pieces crept deeper into the first section of the paper and slipped lower on the pages. They contained mostly denials by the companies Molly accused and statements by Justice Department officials that investigations were being made, but that no violation of federal law had been detected. That no other news organization had gotten on the story once it started shrinking in the *Times* was being interpreted as evidence that the paper had been infected by a reporter's subjectivities. It had acted hastily—stupidly, some were saying—and was now trying to slide out with a minimum of embarrassment.

"Johnny," Jerry Lee had said, as gently as he could, "when Molly was finishing up her story, they were all spooked at the *Times*. They knew the paper was about to be sold. They didn't know to who. I think they knew that the percentages on a story like this being accurate were lower than the *Times*'s standard. But what Molly said was going down was *scary*— scary enough that even the *suspicions* of a reporter with a rep like Molly's justified going with it.

"It was hard to believe, yeah. It still is, Johnny. But the people at the paper believed it should be on the street. And if it was said in *The New York Times*—the *Times*, after all, is the *Times*—there was a better chance of it getting followed up if the new owners were to kill it. It could have been the last days of the *Times*." Jerry Lee sighed.

"And it turns out they were the last days."

The Vandellen film the crew had brought back from Sandstone was better than Harland had hoped. It impressed the people upstairs at CBS News so much that they went even further upstairs, into network programming, to ask for another hour. It was proposed that the program be broadcast in two parts, on consecutive nights. There was whining and more than a little resistance from sales, and a compromise was reached: The program could go at two hours, but only if it was delayed so that it would be broadcast out of the critical ratings period in which it was originally set at one hour. Fine with Harland; from a network career spent entirely in news, he was used to being involved with loss-leader prestige programming. He would have another week to fiddle around with it.

He had had the unedited film of the Vandellen interview transferred to half-inch videotape so he could take it home and run it on his Betamax. He couldn't do any editing—a union editor would have to do that—but he could make notes, and work away from the reach of the CBS switchboard operator.

But the moment he had arranged his paraphernalia, including

a beer, on the table and slid the first cassette into the VTR, a phone buzzed—the house phone from the security desk in the lobby.

"John Harland, you have very loyal friends. I called everybody at CBS I knew, and nobody would give me your phone number. So finally I said to one of those assholes, Jesus, does he have an unlisted building? Okay if I send him a letter? I'm in the business too, you know. I'm not going to try to sell him something, goddamn it; I just haven't seen him and I've been thinking about him and I want to see how he is. This is Trish Denning."

"I figured that. Hello, Trish."

"So how is he?"

"He's fine."

"I just happened to be in the neighborhood. Do you believe that?"

"I—" Harland felt annoyed. Invaded. *What the shit do I say?*

"I don't think I can get past Punjab here without a body search, so could I talk you into coming down? Like for maybe a drink?" Harland heard the snap suddenly go out of Trish's patter. "John, I really feel shitty. I really did mean to send a note, because I haven't seen you to say anything. About Molly."

He closed his eyes. *She wants to be nice. She just wants to be nice. Be nice back. Make yourself. Show some vital signs.* "Come on up. I got beer."

"I'm sure you do. I've seen you drink it at fucking Elaine's. Jesus. What a hick. Bye."

Harland opened another beer and examined how he felt about a woman with known sexual interest in him rising in the elevator on the way to his apartment. What he felt was confusing and, finally, fatiguing. He decided—as he had tended to do, since Molly had died, with any situation that offered him the option—to waffle on feeling any way at all.

He opened the door and leaned against the jamb so he could wave down the hall at Trish as she got off the elevator.

"I just happened to be in the neighborhood because I changed to a later plane and took a cab from my office over to the front door of your building." She took the beer from Harland as she passed. "I don't know what *to* say, of course. I mean, Jesus, John. What *can* you say . . . "

"Trish, look, nobody knows what to say. I don't know what to say back. I never had anybody die on me before. People just want to make contact, and it's comforting. It truly is."

Trish walked over to Harland and squeezed his beerless hand gently with her beerless hand. Harland sensed a depth and directness of feeling that surprised and warmed him. "Good. Good. That makes me feel better. I thought people calling would just, you know, remind you."

"Trish, look. Right now the refrigerator reminds me. The carpet. Sixth Avenue and Fifty-first Street reminds me. Getting up. Going to bed. No. No damage. It has surprised me, how people just calling up and saying that they know it hurts . . . helps."

Trish looked at him. Then looked away. "Look, despite the fact that I've been rubbing up on you for God knows how long . . ."

"Very flattering."

". . . you think you could believe I didn't come over here to swoop, now that the coast is clear?"

"Sure. I can believe that."

"Because . . . when I heard about Molly, I cried on American Airlines, all the way across the country, for both of you." Trish smiled in a way Harland had never seen before. "John, I want to be nice people. Just audition as a friend. You know. Lend you books and borrow your albums and, when you go out of town, keep the cat . . ."

Harland smiled. "Don't have a cat."

". . . buy you a cat . . . All the boring routine bullshit." Trish turned and walked away, wrapping her arms around her head. "Son of a bitch, this has to be the worst timing in the history of human relations. Look, I'll give you my phone number. If Jerry Lee and his wife are out of town and nobody else answers the phone, call me. Screw screwing. We'll have lunch. We'll go to a Knicks game. We'll go to the library. . . . Please.

Don't be lonely. That's why I came. I put myself in your place, saw how I would act if I had a Molly and she . . . and . . . I got really scared, John."

Harland was moved. He reached out for her hands. He thought of kissing her—quickly, familiarly, confident that it would be more bonding than sexual. He said: "Hey. You passed the audition. You got the—"

His phone rang. He looked around at it, then back at Trish, who squeezed his hands and said: "Answer it. I'm going." She took a few steps toward the door, reaching into her purse for a pencil and one of her business cards.

"Can you stay?" said Harland, moving toward the phone.

She began writing on the back. "No quick decisions on whether or not I got the job." She opened the door. "Think about it. I don't return albums, I talk in libraries . . ."

Harland answered the phone: "Yeah."

Trish mouthed "Call me," put the card on the table beside the door.

"Trish . . ." said Harland, but she was gone.

"Mr. Harland?" Harland's divided attention was quickly focused by an unfamiliar voice on his unlisted phone.

"Who—"

"We're wondering if you'd be interested in another photo opportunity."

The sudden acid churning in his stomach. He dropped the receiver on his shoulder and said: "God *damn.*" Then into the phone: "Are you the fucking index-card people?"

"Yes."

"*I don't want this.*"

"Mr. Harland, we're not calling to tell you of our next action." The voice was male—calm and careful. Sounded to be in his mid-thirties. "We're wondering if you would like to meet with some of us. As a journalist. We would answer your questions and—"

And I'll break all your fucking skulls. But Harland didn't say that. "I'm afraid I couldn't be very detached, fella. You pretty much sent me through the mill over what I should do about those index cards. I've never been too sweet on terrorists in the first place."

"You're going to have some time to think about it. Our conversations will have to be no longer than thirty seconds at a time, so the calls can't be traced. We'll call back immediately. You are our first call, Mr. Harland. You should realize we will not hesitate to make our next call to NBC."

Harland hung up, stared at the tabletop. *A hell of a story.* The people who were calling him were reprehensible, and he, as a moral person, should want to have no truck with them. But a reporter has that small exception: He can *want* to have no truck with them, yet feel obliged to do it. For the sake of the public's right to know. *And because it's a hell of a story.*

The phone rang almost immediately after he had hung it up.

"Mr. Harland?" A female voice.

"Look," said Harland, "I don't know who you are or how you got my number, but please hang up. I'm expecting—"

"Have you decided to meet with us? I'm calling from a different phone, incidentally. You'll be talking with lots of different people calling from different places, but we'll be coordinated."

"If I agree, what's in it for me?"

"Interviews with the central committee of our organization. We provide cameras and tape. You take the videotape back with you."

"Unedited?"

"Of course. You may cut it any way you like. We have confidence in the common sense of what we're doing. No one will be able to edit the justification out of our actions nor the justice out of our convictions. Thirty seconds are up. Wait for the next call."

The next speaker was male. Midwestern accent. "Am I correct in assuming you are interested?"

"Maybe." Harland attempted reserve in saying that, but he doubted it was convincing. "How do we work it?"

"I'm afraid it will be complicated and, on your part, a little inconvenient. I'm sure you understand that before you meet anyone with our organization, we will have to satisfy ourselves that no one is following you to us. Please wait for the next caller."

Another woman. Different kind of static on the line. "You must tell no one of this, of course. It's in your interest, if you want the story. Someone could follow you without your knowledge or consent, and we intend to be very cautious. Assume that sometime between tomorrow and ten days from now you will be given a set of instructions that will result in the meeting. Do you have any questions? If so, someone will call you back to answer them."

"I . . . No."

"Then this is our last contact today. Thank you for your interest, Mr. Harland."

Harland hung up and began pacing his apartment, wired by the dizzying tension of the preceding twenty minutes. He was not sure what to do. *Probably because there's nothing to do . . .* He sat back down at the table, intending to go back to what he was doing before the house phone buzzed. His beer had turned warm. He stared for a moment at the silent screen of his television. When he turned off the VTR, the regular TV picture returned. There was a commercial on, of a happy family sitting in their toasty, gas-furnace-fired home. A hand reached into the picture, and turned the thermostat up to eighty . . .

He considered that he could get into more than a little trouble trucking with terrorists. *They could mail in those videotapes, ace.* But would CBS run the interviews if their reporter had been murdered by those who were interviewed?

Harland knew the answer. Of course they would; and he would hope that they would. But he finally decided it was unlikely they'd waste him after using him only once. Not when they could use him again.

Harland looked over his own shoulder. The angle on the screen of the KEM editing table was from a camera placed behind him. For that session, the first of three different interviews Harland and his crew had done that day at Sandstone, they had set up in Vandellen's quarters, right there at the table where Harland and Vandellen had just had breakfast. The dishes had been cleared away, and coffee left out for them. Vandellen wore a plaid flannel shirt. The plain stone walls made a terrific background; there was nothing on them to make the picture look busy.

He heard his voice from the speaker address Vandellen: "You have become somewhat of a recluse the past few—"

Vandellen smiled and looked down to stir his coffee. "John," he had said, "I have found that the media's definition of a 'recluse' is anyone who will not give them an interview upon demand. One of the greatest burdens off my shoulders since I left politics was not having to talk specifically to the objective of getting print and airtime. I have not given out interviews recently because I have little to say to anyone except to those who are involved in the work at Sandstone, and those elsewhere in the community of knowledge. There are more sensible ways to talk with them than in the general media. The issue is time. I rather suspect that my staff wishes I were a recluse. I would create—"

"Freeze that, please," said Harland to the film editor who was working with him.

He stared at the stilled image: Vandellen in the flannel shirt, sitting at a table in front of a wall. "What's up?" asked the editor.

"Something is wrong with that picture."

The editor looked at him, then at the frozen image. "What could be wrong with that picture? It's a guy sitting at a table. It's in focus, it's lit okay, it's—"

"No, it's not wrong, it's—"

"I'll play. Find Five Things Wrong with This Picture. Okay, is it the table, John? Does the table only have three legs?"

"It's something weird. Not just in this one. In all of the stuff we shot there."

"Want to give me a clue?"

"I don't have any, because I'm still waiting to find out what it is that I think is weird. Go ahead on."

The editor backed the film up a bit. ". . . wishes I were a recluse. I would create less work for them."

Harland's question: "But you are secretive about what goes on at Sandstone."

Vandellen answered, with no trace of annoyance: "Again, the media calls us secretive because we don't have a media-relations staff and don't call press conferences to announce our findings. But all our findings are published. Just look in the appropriate scholarly journals. You may recall at the beginning of Sandstone we did have press conferences. And you must concede that by the time our findings were interpreted on the spot by reporters unprepared in the first place to understand them, who ignored all our qualifications and cautions, the world was told we had made miracles. Found a cure for cancer—remember?— when we had done no such thing. It seems better simply to go about our business quietly and professionally, and not con-tinually—and cruelly—create false hopes."

"Why did you agree to be interviewed now?"

"We are aware that a supply of curiosity had been building up about Sandstone. It seemed time to bleed off the pressure of attention and satisfy it. And since I am neither reclusive nor secretive—"

The phone rang.

Photo opportunity, thought Harland, as he had every time a phone had rung near him that morning.

This was the editor's turf, and he reached for it, but Harland grabbed it from under his hand, saying: "I've had my calls for-warded back here, and . . ." He turned away from the editor. "Yeah? Harland."

The call was for the editor. Harland smiled a little sheepishly as he handed it to him. "Better get off the line," said the editor to whoever was calling, looking at Harland and smiling, "so John Harland can take the phone call he's expecting from God . . ." Harland took both their coffee cups out for refills.

He took the cups back to the newsroom pot; the coffee the techies made was villainous. He passed the editor on the way down the hall. He had to go deal with something, would be back in a minute. Harland nodded and went on back into the editing room.

The phone rang again.

"Mr. Harland?"

"Yeah."

"This is about the photo opportunity." A female voice. *"Immediately* go to Fifth Avenue and catch the first bus that passes heading downtown."

Harland stood with the cup at his lips, pinned to the moment. *Too quick. I'm not ready, I'm not prepared, I can't get my head . . . Okay, okay: I'm scared.* "Look, I'm in the middle of—"

"Immediately." Hung up.

Harland looked around, unsure of how quickly "immediately" was. Time-to-put-on-my-coat immediately? Time-to-write-a-note-for-the-editor immediately? He took the time to do both, writing out *Have to go. Get back with you later* in grease pencil and leaving it on the editing table.

He left the building on Fifty-first Street and immediately broke into a trot. The wind blew snowflakes down his neck. *Dumb. Walk. They said the first bus that passes, not any specific bus.* He leaned his head into the cold.

He got to Fifth Avenue and looked toward the park. A bus headed downtown was about three blocks away. Harland reasoned that unless the terrorists were riding to meet him on a Fifth Avenue bus, there had to be another step in making the connection beyond his getting on this bus and riding away on it. Why the first bus he saw? It was the same as saying *any* bus will do. So were there terrorists on every bus heading down Fifth Avenue?

He decided to let them worry about which bus he caught. The bus pulled up, he got on, put in the correct change, sat down. He looked at his fellow passengers. None was wearing a sign saying *I am a terrorist.* After the bus stopped at Forty-eighth Street, he was aware that one of the embarking passengers had sat down beside him. A middle-aged man, swathed in a scarf, with a Macy's shopping bag.

The bus stopped at Forty-fourth Street. Passengers got on. Passengers got off. The man next to Harland picked up his Macy's shopping bag and said, "Stand in the rear door before the bus stops at the next stop, Mr. Harland." He stepped off the bus as it pulled away. He was gone in the crowd on the sidewalk.

Harland was standing in the door as the bus stopped at Forty-second Street in front of the library. He opened it. Harland was ready, but he received no instructions from anyone getting on or off. People shoved around him until someone said, "What are you, crazy? Get out, go on, get outa da door." He was about to close the door when someone pushing past said, "Get in the cab parked at the corner." When Harland turned to look at the body belonging to the voice, all he saw was a red parka heading uptown, legs contained by denims below it.

The cab was a . . . cab. As Harland neared it, he saw that the Off-Duty light was on. *Waiting for me.* He opened the back door and got in.

The driver—Harland noticed from the posted license his name was Isaac Wein—turned and looked at Harland. "You new in town?" he said.

Harland looked back at him.

"Because if you're new in town, you might not know what the Off-Duty light means. It means I'm off duty, I don't take fares, the cab's not going anyplace, and you should get out."

"They told me . . ."

"Who told you what?" said Wein. Harland studied Wein's expression and was just about sure. But he said to confirm it, "You aren't waiting for me."

"Don't cause me no trouble," said Wein. "I'm waiting for three o'clock so I can go the fuck home. Are you not going to get out of my cab, and cause me trouble?"

Harland got out and looked around the intersection. It was the only parked cab around. After about two minutes, Isaac Wein drove away, fareless. Harland stood at the intersection, looking around hopelessly, bouncing up and down in the cold, for another twenty minutes. Then he got a cab back to Sixth Avenue and back up to Fifty-first Street to the CBS building.

The lobby security guard saw him coming and reached into his desk drawer. "You got lucky. Just missed the kid who left this for you." The guard was holding up a letter-sized envelope. "Looked to me like the pouncing type and I was about to run him off, but he just plopped this down and left." He held it over his wastebasket. "Want to eighty-six it?"

"What kind of kid?"

"Just a kid. Red parka."

Harland took the envelope, opened it. "How long ago?"

"Forty-five seconds, maximum."

Harland looked at the Fifty-first and Fiftieth Street entrances. "Did you see . . ." *Forget it. He's gone.*

The envelope contained a three-by-five index card. On it was typed: WE WERE TESTING. WE KNOW YOU WERE INCONVENIENCED, BUT WE ARE CONFIDENT YOU'LL UNDERSTAND. EXPECT ANOTHER CALL.

"Rat bastards," said Harland, who balled up the paper and threw it into the wastebasket.

He went back upstairs and fetched the editor from his office. "Had to go out," he said in explanation.

"Cold enough for you?" said the editor.

He felt frustrated enough to punch his fist through something. Instead, he tried to wrestle his attention back to Martin Vandellen:

". . . innovation is useless if no one implements it. Our countrymen, John, have the baffling tendency of listening to hysterics at precisely the worst times. Brilliant people present brilliant solutions to enormous problems. And the new Luddites take out their little hammers and start to smash the machines before they can be built. Good is not exclusively the prerogative of these shrill and stupid people to determine . . ."

The next call came thirty-six hours later, at home. It was the same procedure as before. This time he was handed off all the way to Washington Square before he was abandoned on a park bench.

The third call was eight hours after that. He was called back before he could get out the door and told to cancel. The next time he was called was at three in the morning, and he told them to go fuck themselves.

17

HARLAND'S ERRATIC APPEARANCES AND DISAPPEARANCES WERE NOT unnoticed at CBS. While he had a large reserve of scrupulously reliable past performance, he knew that standing up his producer and a technician for a narration session—twice—could no longer be explained away with an "I got tied up."

When he came in late the morning after the three a.m. phone call, his producer said, "My lord, John" upon seeing his face. Harland walked on past toward the editing rooms.

"I had a bad night. I'll get us back on schedule today."

He made a poor start at it. The editor was running the Vandellen interview footage from which Harland intended to assemble the last segment of the second program. But Harland was barely listening to the words. Concurrent rasping questions were playing on a loop, spliced head to tail, inside his brain. One segued to the other, the other segued to the first: *Am I over my head with the photo-opportunity people? . . . What is wrong with this footage?*

He'd been looking at the same images for a week: The camera panned across the room to establish Vandellen sitting at his breakfast table. Slowly it tightened to the classic talking-head shot—Vandellen answering Harland's question: "Did you once say that you felt you were born into the wrong time and place?"

"Wrong time, right place. This is a splendid country. What this country could achieve is . . . thrilling."

"When would you have preferred to live?"

"Late nineteenth century. There was one enormous technological discovery after another, but no one was frightened by them. There truly were giants in the land, and people realized that there was benefit in trusting them. The country was alive."

"And now it's not?"

"And now it operates on specious egalitarianism. We insure that our controlling class is not elitist by electing the most visibly incompetent."

"You speak as though you were an outsider. But you were in the controlling class. High in it, for years."

"Yes, I walked among them and I had a vote—and I was visibly incompetent. I accomplished nothing lasting, nor even significant. I mourn now, for the time I earnestly misspent. There are a few good minds among the controllers, but they're totally involved in the crushing task of dealing with the other controllers, who have no minds at all. Someone who has no skill other than to be stubborn is, in our system, a controller as powerful as someone with insight, reason, and prescience. It's mad, archaic, and exhausting. I got out."

"Mr. Harland . . ."

Harland realized he had answered the phone in his sleep. He swam up into consciousness standing beside his desk in his office, phone in hand, staring at the sofa, aware he must have fallen asleep there. It was eleven o'clock at night.

". . . we apologize for what we know has been a frustrating and exhausting—" Harland became conscious enough to recognize the voice.

"Look, I don't remember if it was you on the phone when I told you people to go fuck yourselves. If it wasn't, I'm pleased to repeat it: Go fuck yourselves."

"We hope you realize the need to give anyone who might

be monitoring you as little opportunity as possible to anticipate where you'll be next."

"You're a little slow, aren't you? I don't want to play anymore."

"We're confident now that the next time we contact you, our meeting will be completed, assuming you are as cooperative as you have been in the past."

"Don't. Fucking. Call." But she had hung up.

Harland believed her. He knew, as he was being jerked around, that he was being jerked around for a purpose. The first time he had told them off he had spoken from frustration and fatigue. He had repeated it just then, he had to admit, because being jerked around had depleted his ego; he was trying to restock it by talking tough. They knew that too. And would call again.

And Harland knew he would go. He knew that much about himself. He did not know enough about himself, not at that hour, not as numbed as he felt his brain becoming, to know if he would ask for help before he went.

He scrubbed his eyelids with the heels of his hands, picked up off his desk the notes he'd been working on—how long ago? —when he knew he had to lie down for just a little while. He walked off through the empty newsroom—the *Evening News* crew had left, the *Morning News* crew had yet to arrive—toward the editing rooms. He still had no idea how to end the first Vandellen program. Unless he came up with something by five-thirty in the morning, his producer was going to finish cutting it himself, and for good reason: Air date was two days away.

The editor had long since gone. Harland spooled up the rough assembly of interview footage they'd been working on that afternoon. Harland watched the Academy leader count down, the slate identifying the reel of film being held up in front of the camera . . .

"Sorry," said Harland's voice from the speaker. "Next time we'll be more careful of how much film we have left in the camera. You want me to repeat the question?"

"Not necessary," said Vandellen. "Shall I just go ahead?"

"Please . . ."

Do I do this alone? All his professional life Harland had practiced the reporter's detachment. He stood back. He watched.
He was neither advocate nor intermediary. He didn't hinder.
*And I don't help. I don't surrender my notes to the court, to
aid either the defense or the prosecution. I don't set up the
crooks for the cops. I don't help the crooks commit a crime.*

Entropy. No moral imbalance in this situation to lean him
toward a decision.

". . . There are economic Luddites as well, Mr. Harland. They
perceive this country as sliced up into obscene corporate
duchies, duchies to be tolerated, basically to be taxed, taxed for
the benefit of the political controlling class. And never allowed
to interact, even if the interaction is logical and extraordinarily
beneficial, because the new tradition holds any cooperation
among corporations as despotic . . ."

*Okay. How about this for a reason: simple fear. What if I
learn more than they want me to know? That next they're
going to murder half of Congress? Nuke New York? Press
cards aren't bulletproof. They could mail in those videotapes.
Worse: They'd lock you in a room with a television and you
could watch them do it, watch the people die, while you
scrupulously retained your reporter's detachment.*

". . . The corporations who fund Sandstone find in it one of
the few enterprises in which they can legally cooperate. There
is no parallel to Sandstone in the public sector, where it logically belongs . . ."

Molly.

Harland squeezed his eyes shut at the memory of the tapes
and how she tried to wisecrack away the fear. *Oh kid. Don't
you know? Fear is God telling you you're in over your head.*
If she had stopped being a scrupulous reporter and a fanatic
*Times*woman just a little sooner . . . *How much more would*

we know of what she had worked so hard to tell us? Would she be alive?

". . . I anticipate that the private sector will begin to provide where the public sector fails, to the limits they are permitted to act. The private sector will be forced into more conspicuous altruism, simply to hold the fabric of our society together. It will have no choice. Simple self-interest. The private sector is the only force left in the country where common sense and pragmatism are still operating practices . . ."

Molly. *Forgive me, kid. I'm not the Lone Ranger. I just don't have the guts.*

He stopped the film, picked up the phone, dialed. After one ring, it was answered by a man who repeated the last four digits of the number.

"This is John Harland. Get me Painter."

The connection was made within fifteen seconds. Harland could hear great distance sighing in the background behind Painter's voice, which dopplered up and down in pitch. "Hello, John. I'm afraid this is going to be a poor connection. There are a couple of radio patches in it."

"Sam, I've been in contact with the terrorists. They want me to interview them. They're going public."

"They've set up a meeting?"

"Yes."

"When and where?"

"I don't know. They feed my itinerary to me one step at a time, and they watch me."

"And?"

"And . . ." *Do it. It needs to be done.* ". . . I'll set them up for you."

Sam Painter didn't reply immediately. Then he said, "That would be very helpful."

"You're going to have to tail me. Very carefully. If they found out I was setting them up, I imagine they would kill me."

"Probably."

"So you'll be careful."

"We'll be loose. Lose you if we have to rather than put you in a corner."

"They could call any minute, Sam. The way they work it, I have to drop everything and go that second, or the deal's off. How long would it take to get someone watching the CBS Building?"

"I'm not sure. Soon, but not instantly."

"I'll go out the Fifty-first Street entrance. After that, I can't tell you anything about what to expect."

"John. I'll work hard on this. But no guarantees. Either way: Whether we're on you, if we've lost you . . . there'll be no way for you to know."

"Yeah."

"But you're still going."

"Yeah. You got a minute?"

"A few."

Harland had no intention of doing this until the moment he began: He told Painter about Molly's tapes, about Fourteen-mile Point, about Caroline Junction, about the packages in the mine in Arizona. Maybe he shouldn't have. He would know later; but at the moment he knew of no one else with the capability of acting on the information. And just releasing it, to anyone, made its presence inside him less uncomfortable by half.

"You've had the recorders on, I trust?"

"Oh sure," said Painter. "Is this free of charge, John? You want something back in exchange?"

"No. Yes. Tell me, straight: How much of this does the community of spooks already know?"

"Most of it, I'm afraid. The hoards of oil and gas are pretty standard rumors, John, and they generally prove to be rumors. Arizona is new, I think, at least to me. Very interesting. I'll get back to you on it."

If I can be got back to. Again, an empty moment.

"May I ask, John, what made you decide to trust me with this?"

"You can ask. I'm too tired right now to tell you."

Harland could see Painter's soft smile as he said it: "It'll be interesting, won't it? Seeing if you made the right decision."

Harland let himself doze. Two hours. Then his quartz-everything watch beeped. The sleep helped a little. He went back to the editing table and by force of will focused his attention on the remaining eleven minutes of airtime he had to put in order.

Harland sipped some cold coffee salvaged from the newsroom pot and listened to himself asking Vandellen: ". . . You talk as though you think the system will collapse."

"I'm more afraid that it won't . . ."

Harland was now capable of concentrating enough on the work at hand to feel the return of the old frustration—of sensing an anomaly in the interview footage and not knowing what it was. *Something he's saying now that doesn't match with what he said the visit before . . . No. You've checked that. Dead end.* He had had transcripts made of the two interview trips to Sandstone. Nothing. *It's not in what people say. It's in how the place looks . . .*

In the small, quiet room, he was so focused on the KEM table's screen and speaker that to his perception the phone didn't ring as much as explode. Harland snatched it up, flinching, just to quieten it. It took the space of time to raise it to his ear for him to realize who was calling him, and why. And that he was not ready to go.

"Mr. Harland, you will need to be standing at the northeast corner of Fiftieth and Fifth within nine mintues."

"Look. I just can't. Not this *instant*." Harland had left the KEM table running: ". . . *Collapse will be the only conclusive proof that the country will accept of the system's absurd obsolescence* . . ."

"Can't you put it off—"

"No."

"I have a *program* to get on the air in forty-eight hours. I need half a day."

". . . *I don't expect any changes. No natural changes. The system appears to be evolution-proof. It has enormous tenacity. The depressing, destructive endurance of the mediocre . . ."*

"We're not contacting you again."

"Jesus, then four *hours*. If you want me so goddamn bad, you can wait four goddamn *hours*."

". . . The system endures because its inventors were smart enough to give it its own built-in iconology. The system preserves itself by defining any nontraditional alternative to itself as treason . . ."

"And Mr. Harland; your leaving by either the Fiftieth or Fifty-first Street entrances is unacceptable. Use another way out of the building. You're due on the corner nine minutes from . . . now."

"Assholes, I can't go four blocks in—" The caller had hung up. Harland stood so quickly that his chair rolled almost out into the hall. Froze for a moment. There were at least two other ways out of the building that would get him outside so that he would not pass in view of anyone keeping watch on the public entrances.

Nine minutes.

He might be able to do it, if he didn't stop to . . . stop to think about what he was doing. About walking away from the program.

He turned toward the door, sensed motion behind him: The image of Vandellen, talking from the screen of the KEM table.

". . . The system is senile. But it's beloved. Irrationally beloved . . ."

Harland found himself taking two strides to the table, grabbing the moving ribbon of film, jerking it out of the sprockets, screaming loudly enough to hurt his throat: *"What is fucking wrong with this picture?"*

Harland got off the elevator on the third floor, ran to a stairwell at the west end of the building. At its base was a fire exit that Harland knew would put him out on a loading dock well back of the public entrances. A sign on the door told him that if he pushed it open after six p.m., an alarm would sound. He did, it did.

He hadn't taken the time to button his coat, but the cold on Fifty-first Street forced him to, his rapidly numbing fingers struggling to fasten the buttons as he broke into a trot. It was lightly snowing. It was three o'clock.

When he turned south, he all but had Fifth Avenue to himself. Halfway down the block, he had to stop for a moment, not because he was winded, but to take a scarf from his pocket and tie it over his mouth; the cold was turning into agony.

He got to the corner and leaned against the side of the building. He held up his wrist and slowly brought his watch into focus. He had made it. He *thought* he had made it. Was it three before the hour when he left? Or eight?

He looked around. Nobody on any of the four streetcorners. A cab parked a few feet west on Fiftieth. Harland saw from backlighting further down the street that it was driverless, accumulating snow. No moving traffic either direction on Fiftieth, almost none on Fifth. A police car went by. Harland touched a button on his wristwatch. *Two minutes. Then I go back to the office.*

When he looked up, the headlights on the cab were blinking at him, in the same rhythm as emergency flashers.

He shielded his eyes as he approached it and saw that it still appeared to be empty. He looked through the driver's-side window and saw that there was a piece of paper taped to the steering wheel. Harland looked around, still saw no one. The door was unlocked; keys dangled in the ignition.

"Eighth Avenue Port Authority bus terminal," read the message typed on the paper. "Take the next Carey airport bus to Newark. It leaves in eleven minutes. Wait in front of the Eastern ticketing counter. Pull red wires to disconnect the blinker. Drive carefully. This is stolen."

Harland yanked at the wires, which brushed at his knees. The lights burned steadily.

He drove carefully the first few blocks, less cautiously the next several. As the timer on his watch blinked past nine minutes, he began driving through red lights.

He nosed the cab to the curb in front of the Eighth Avenue entrance in front of a cab that was inching up from the head of the cab line to pick up a fare. He turned off the motor, left the keys, and ran inside the terminal to a barrage of obscenities.

Had he not ridden the Carey Newark bus enough times to know where in the terminal to go, he would not have made it. The driver had shut the door and had put the bus in gear to back it out of the bay when Harland pushed through the terminal door, waving his arms. He stood, panting, and watched the driver sigh, conspicuously, and open the door.

On the bus, Harland figured the percentages on whether or not Sam Painter still had him in sight. Assuming that they had begun watching for him before he was sent out of the building, the chances were reasonably good. He was one of five people on the Carey bus, and it was unlikely that any of them was one of Painter's people. But if Copper Creek had him through the terminal, they had him getting on the bus, and the bus was going to Newark. While he waited for the plane—he *assumed* he was going there to wait for a plane—there was a little pad for Copper Creek to catch up.

But he was being paged as he walked in the door: ". . . arriving passenger Harland, please answer the white courtesy telephone, Eastern Airlines." *Nobody can time it that tight. They have somebody in the terminal, at one of the phones, watching for the bus.*

"I have a message," he said into the white courtesy phone. "My name is Harland."

"Just a moment, Mr. Harland," said the Eastern operator. A couple of clicks, then she said: "Go ahead, please."

"Mr. Harland, in the men's room just behind you. Under the second sink from the entrance. Very quickly, Mr. Harland. The bus was late."

A man walked into the john just ahead of Harland. He said

"Shit," quietly, at the possibility of having to wait the man out before he could reach under the sink for whatever he was supposed to find. But the man walked right to the free stall and shut the door behind him. Harland waited until he saw his shoes turn outward and heard the clink of beltbuckle on tile. Then he dropped to one knee and peered under the sink.

An envelope, taped to the cast iron. He pulled it off, opened it. A United Air Lines boarding pass and a flight coupon. One way to Kansas City. Leaving from gate twenty-four in . . . *Jesus. Three minutes.*

He ran out of the men's room. *I can make it. But I have to do everything right the first time.*

Back out in the ticketing area, he looked for the signs. Gates 12–32 that way. Motion at the side of his vision, and a wash of cold air. Someone coming in through the front doors. Someone from Copper Creek, catching up with him? What if they haven't yet?

Leave breadcrumbs. He thought of leaving a message with Eastern, have Painter paged and given the United flight number. But there was no time. And he was probably being watched.

He ran down the concourse, was blessed by encountering three people who didn't even have to be asked to let him through the security-station magnetometer ahead of them. He got to the gate as the attendant was about to walk down the jetway to move it back from the plane. He walked through the door, and the attendant swung it to for the stewardess to secure.

Harland leaned against the lavatory door and kneaded a stitch in his side.

"You almost didn't make it," said the stewardess.

"Tell me about it," said Harland.

The clump of the gear going down and locking woke Harland up. There was light on his face. When he opened his eyes he saw the wing, and that the plane was about to descend through a layer of clouds turned lemon-colored by the ascending sun. The side of his face was chilled from the cold penetrating the window and the thin airline pillow against which Harland had rested his head. He ached, a little from running, mostly from tension.

The seatbelt sign was on, and he brought his chairback to the upright and locked position before the steward got to his row to prompt him.

Kansas City, Kansas City . . . Harland had fallen asleep almost the moment his adrenaline rush had permitted him, and hadn't thought about why it was Kansas City on the ticket. Sundown. The place where the terrorists had sabotaged the coal train. That was in Kansas. Harland entertained, briefly, a surreal image: interviewing an unknown number of terrorist leaders on the porch of a Norman Rockwell farmhouse, the wheat in the background being waved by the wind. Nice irony, but inapplicable. The wheat's stubble now, and the stubble's covered by snow.

He again revalued the chances of his still being in Copper Creek's sight; poorer than before, but still not too bad. The Newark terminal was all but empty when he was there; people would probably remember him, if questions were asked when memories were still fresh.

The plane had touched down. As it began working its way along the taxiways to the terminal, a stewardess began her memorized announcements: "Welcome to Louisville . . ."

Louisville?

"For those of you going on with us to Kansas City, our approximate ground time here will be fifteen minutes . . ."

Harland then vaguely remembered an earlier announcement, just as he was drifting off to sleep, of an intermediate stop. He fluffed up the niggardly pillow. If he was lucky, he could sleep through it.

He was halfway asleep, diminishingly conscious of the last Louisville passengers shuffling up the aisle past him, when he heard words very close to his ear, spoken from behind through the space between the seats: "Mr. Harland, we would like you to wait until the last passenger has left, then stand up and walk to the front of the plane. Do not look behind you."

Harland felt his stomach churn. *I'm getting off in Louisville.* He waited, not looking back, until fifteen or twenty seconds passed with no one walking up the aisle. Then he stood up. Walked toward the front of the plane. As he got into first class, the soft voice again, just behind him. "Step into the galley and ask the steward for aspirin and a glass of water. Stay in the galley to take them."

Has Copper Creek covered this?

The steward was disposing of used plastic glasses. He put them aside to deal with Harland's request.

Yes. They would have realized that just because I was ticketed through to Kansas City . . .

"Excuse me. Sir?"

Harland felt cold on his neck. He moved a little to make room for a workman loading breakfast trays from a caterer's cart.

"Pardon me . . ." The voice said from behind. "I can't seem to get this overhead compartment open."

"Let me see what I can do," said the steward, moving back past Harland.

Harland jiggled the aspirin in his hand, not daring to look back. *They'll cover it. Copper Creek will be inside at the gate, and they'll see me when I get off, and follow me out of the terminal and—*

"Sir," said the caterer's man, "if you could just give me a little room here . . ."

"Sorry," said Harland, and half-turned. He felt two hands on the front of his coat, jerking him sideways. He grunted, stumbled. He was pulled inside the caterer's truck and pushed against the flat wall, in a niche between two racks of food trays. It was dim. He saw, inside the parka hood, only the bottom half of a face, one of the caterer's men. "Very quiet, Mr. Harland. Very still."

The inside smelled of bacon even after the other workman had finished offloading the last of the trays. Harland heard the man and the steward exchange banalities as the steward signed receipts. "Stay warm," said the steward.

Assume that Copper Creek is outside at the gate. They don't see me get off. They'll think I've gone on to Kansas City. I don't get off at Kansas City. They assume I didn't get on in Newark.

Harland knew that if he did not that moment walk off the truck and back into the plane, his status would change to captive.

A thump felt through his feet made any decision moot. The cargo bed of the truck, hoisted to the level of the plane's galley door, now began sinking like a slow elevator. At ground level, the caterer's man got out and shut the door behind him.

Harland shivered. His coat was still in the overhead compartment of the plane, and the residual heat from the preheated breakfast trays was dissipating. An insulated parka with the caterer's logo embroidered on it was hanging from a hook. He put it on just as the truck started.

He held on to a rack as the truck passed through the whine of a series of idling jet engines. The airport noises softened; but they were still audible when the truck stopped, somewhere near the airport's periphery.

The back gate opened. The truck had been parked beside an anonymous building, near an anonymous door. "Step outside, please, Mr. Harland," said the caterer's man. "Are you wearing the parka? Yes," he said as Harland stepped out from behind the rack. "I imagined that you would be. Inside here, please." They waited outside the door for a moment, then it was opened from the inside.

Harland imagined that the place had something to do with aircraft maintenance. There were charts on the walls listing airplane parts. A couple of battered chairs, a battered desk. Sitting at the desk and in two of the chairs were three unexceptional-looking men, ages late twenties to early forties.

The man at the desk smiled. "Just as easy as that, Mr. Harland. Aren't you glad now we practiced? Have a seat."

Harland remained standing and looking around him. "Is this it? Am I there?"

"Close but not quite, I'm afraid," said the man at the desk. The men were dressed routinely: Clean work clothes—denims, flannel shirts. Two of them had beards. "Now that we're reasonably confident you're traveling alone, you'll go directly to our people on our transportation. I'm sure you'll be relieved there'll be no more running to catch buses and planes."

"It was getting a little old."

"There's just one more step. However, we are stopping here to explain it to you because you may find it a little . . . well, unsettling. Being a rather intelligent man, I'm sure you have realized this by now: Equally as important to us as your not knowing where you're going . . . is your not knowing where you've been." His hand came out of his pocket with a small bottle—a vial.

"This is Katamine," he said pleasantly. "It's a superb sedative. Really. It's not one of those sledgehammer things where you wake up feeling like you've been dead. I wouldn't wish that on anybody. With this stuff you wake up like after a natural sleep. My man over there in the red coat is an RN. Used to be an Army corpsman. He'll travel with you. You'll wake up rested. And you'll be there."

"Shit. This is totally out of hand," said Harland.

"I've been told that if it spooks you for any reason, if this prejudices you against us . . . please, call it off. This is not a kidnapping." He tipped the bottle back and forth on the desk with a fingertip. "There is a problem, though. If you do call it off, we're going to need some lead time, in case you want to call the cops . . ." He smiled and shrugged.

"So I've bought the zinger either way," said Harland.

"Yeah."

"I hate needles."

"Boy, I do too. Sorry 'bout that."

The three men looked at him.

Harland looked at the dirty venetian blinds covering the window. Let out a puff of breath. "I'm tired of this shit," he said. "Just get me there." He stood and took off his coat.

"Aw-riight," said the man at the desk enthusiastically. "Let's get cookin'. My man there is going to need a vein or two . . ." Harland was rolling up his sleeve.

"Have a needle phobia, Mr. Harland?" said the corpsman, still behind him. "I'm your man. When I was at Brooke General —at Fort Sam Houston?—I used to work the children's wards. I don't think one kid in fifty ever cried on me." Harland was still rolling his sleeve when he felt a small pressure and a quick sting just below his elbow.

He turned to see the corpsman grinning and holding up what seemed to have a distant relationship to a water pistol. "Air syringe. The trick is not to let people see you're coming. You wanna lie down now? Stuff's a bear."

There was nothing in the room to lie down upon.

"Floor will do, Mr. Harland," said the man behind the desk.

Harland sat down, feeling foolish. Then lay down, feeling cottony. He looked at the acoustic-tile ceiling and heard a jet take off. "So," said the man behind the desk. "Cold enough for you?"

Harland opened his mouth in anticipation of forming a reply. But he realized there was no point in beginning the sentence, since he knew he wouldn't be awake to finish it.

18

HARLAND OPENED HIS EYES AND SAW A WHITE WALL. HIS EYES traveled over the field of his vision while areas of his brain plugged themselves back in. He first thought *I don't know where I am.* Then he thought: *Because you aren't supposed to know where you are.* Recollection started coalescing around that seed. He remembered the catering truck, a grimy office, three men, the injection. As advertised, he remembered nothing after that and felt rested and alert. As the inventory continued down his body, he realized he had to urinate, desperately. He rolled over, sat up on the edge of the bed.

The corpsman was sitting on a chair, waiting for him. "My man," he said.

"I gotta take a leak."

"Right over there."

Harland was in a windowless hospital room. At the end of the corpsman's gesture he saw an open door and a toilet. He closed the door and pissed for what seemed like five minutes.

When he came back out, the corpsman was hanging up the phone. "How do you feel? If you don't feel together, I'm gonna be real guilty about it."

"I feel fine. I don't suppose you can tell me where I am."

"Hey. Looks like a hospital room to me."

"Thanks."

"Okay, okay, that was cute. If you don't want me getting cute on you, don't make me have to be cute. Hey, I was just talking with some people, and something's gonna pop real soon now. Are you cool here?"

"Thirsty."

"You've been asleep awhile. Orange juice in that pitcher."

"How long?"

"Hey, I'll have to be cute again." He was at the door. "You saw the shower in there, didn't you? And there's clothes in that closet. And . . . well, I guess that's it. Hey. Later. The door's gonna be locked, incidentally."

He left. Harland saw fifteen feet of an unfeatured corridor, then the door closed. He poured some orange juice and sat sipping it. What sort of terrorist safe-house would come equipped with a hospital room?

He showered, found soap and a razor, and used them. The clothes were denims and flannel shirts, the kinds of fabrics chosen by the men in the office at the Louisville airport.

As he stepped back into the room, walked to the bed to put on his shoes, the door opened. A large man with a bland expression came in and sat down in a chair against the wall opposite the bed. He said nothing. Another man came in and said, "Mr. Harland, you look better. I'm sure you feel better. Lunch in just a little while." He stood at the foot of the bed, waiting. The door had been left open. Harland heard footsteps in the corridor.

Martin Vandellen came into the room, smiling, and held out his hand for Harland to shake. Harland sat down upon the bed. He was still holding his shoes. He stared up at Vandellen.

"John, you're at Sandstone. I wanted to come by as soon as you woke up. I tried to put myself in your place at this moment, and I realized how confused, and perhaps a little frightened, you must be. We're going to talk, and I'll answer all your questions, but over in my quarters. I'll join you there, after I finish an errand. On the way over, maybe you'll have time to collect your thoughts." He smiled. "The weather is perfect today. Everything is going to go very well. I feel it." He moved to the door. "This is Danny, and over there sitting down is Bob."

Danny waved and Bob said, "How ya doin'?"

"They sort of look after me. Have for years. They'll take you to my quarters, and . . . for a while, at least, they'll look after you. We need to hurry. You have some very big decisions to make." He said to Bob, "He'll need a coat," and left.

Harland continued to look at the space in the doorway where Vandellen had last been. Bob got up and walked over to the bed. He reached down and gently nudged the shoes Harland still held and said: "You'll wanna put these on."

Danny and Bob had left Harland on the sofa in the room in Vandellen's quarters where he and Harland had once had breakfast. Then they stood against the glass wall that looked out upon the mountains.

Harland had realized, walking between Danny and Bob through the rock galleries of Sandstone, that he had no thoughts to collect, because there was no basis of reason around which to organize comprehension.

Vandellen entered the room and Harland suddenly pointed.

"I know what's wrong with the picture."

"What picture, John?" said Vandellen, and sat down in a leather chair across a low table from Harland.

"I've spent days looking at you on the screen of that god-damn KEM table. You were sitting in this room, and I knew there was something changed. And now I know what it is. Your art collection, it's gone."

"Yes."

"Just some of it was gone when we shot here the second time, so it wasn't obvious. But now it's all gone."

"Yes."

"That's a relief, to figure that out. It was about to drive me crazy." Harland looked back out toward the mountains. Vandellen glanced at Bob and Danny, made a small gesture toward the door. The two slipped out quietly.

Vandellen sat up in his chair, rubbed his palms on his knees, took a breath. "John? What would you like to know first? How about logistics? You were put in an ambulance and flown here in a jet ambulance. Perhaps the anesthetic wasn't strictly necessary, since you would know your destination, but we reasoned it would be better for you to wake up here rested and feeling immediately secure rather than . . ."

"These photo-opportunity people . . . they work for you."

"Yes, John."

"The planes . . . you were responsible for the train in Kansas . . ."

"Well, first understand it's not a 'me.' It's a 'we': Sandstone. It is part of the work in progress here."

"The work in progress . . ."

"You must understand that—"

"The *work* is *killing people?*"

"Please be patient. That issue will, I promise you, come into focus, and you'll be able to make a judgment about it from a better perspective. What I want to do immediately is to assure you that the extraordinary means we have gone through to get you here do not even begin to reflect your importance to us at this moment. So much thought has been given to you, so much depends upon you. In all but present fact, you are part of that work."

"What in the shit are you talking—"

"Sandstone was conceived as a contingency. Had Sandstone never fulfilled more than its ostensible purpose, its creators would have been grateful beyond words. But the worst possible scenario has happened. The contingency is here."

"Contingency for what?"

"Sandstone . . . John, pick your simile: The emergency brake. The lifeboat."

"For what?"

"For the whole country. The system has stopped working.

It breathes and there's a pulse. But the vital signs are missing."

Vandellen looked at Harland as if Harland had been prompted. And Harland suddenly understood, whispering in the enormity of the room: "This isn't about defying the feds. This isn't about monopoly. You're trying to take the government."

"We're just going to do the simple kindness of pulling the plug."

Harland struggled—at first for breath, then for vocabulary. "You can't do it. I don't . . . Jesus, I can't think. Just putting aside the issue, you *morally* can't do it. *Practically* you can't do it. It's berserk. The United States government is not some fucking Fourth World clown-act junta. Have you got an army somewhere I don't know about?"

Vandellen smiled and looked at his hands, folded in his lap. He said patiently: "Sandstone is an understanding among more than two hundred of the largest corporations on earth—within the United States and having interest in the United States. The association controls forty-three percent of the gross national product. An army would be . . ." He laughed. "Redundant."

Nurturing the image of a comedy-sketch banana-republic coup had comforted Harland, but he saw it evaporate. Still, he tried sneering, hoping to hold the chill of plausibility at a distance. "So what do you do first? Commandeer the networks and—"

"It will not be necessary to commandeer, since—"

Harland sobered. "You mean the networks are part . . ."

"Two of them are. The videotape of me won't originate from the networks, anyway. Security considerations. The networks do not control the interstate transmission facilities. The networks will send out their nine o'clock programs, but the stations will be receiving me. That was a copy of it that you were sent through the mail. A practice tape, actually, so it could be evaluated. A Sandstone employee too sentimental for his own good. We found out about it too late to intercept it.

"The tape will be broadcast continuously for the next three hours, for those who miss it the first time. I will argue essentially what I said to you. Then I will announce that as of that moment all restrictions on the use of energy have been removed."

The commercials. Happy people being warm in their toasty houses. The ad campaigns suddenly ending February fourteenth . . .

"We picked February fifteenth because it is statistically the coldest day of the year in the Northeast. There have been a few days colder so far this year, but we're pleased enough with the temperatures today.

"I will announce that convenience and comfort, and even excess, will reappear. Big cars with big, powerful engines. Beer in cans you can throw away. Small electric appliances the regulators have banished as frivolous. We will give license, John. To frustrated and frightened people, who have heard their government say nothing but 'No, you can't,' we will say 'Yes, you can.' And I will announce that as of that moment none of these goods or services, and no form of nonrenewable energy, may be purchased with the present U.S. currency . . ."

In a mine in Arizona. Thousands of packages wrapped in brown paper . . .

Vandellen read the expression on Harland's face. "You must have seen some of them. We've had some breaches of security. No harm in that one, fortunately. There are thirty-three distribution points around the country for the kilowatt-hour bills. By noon tomorrow, the present currency may be exchanged, one dollar for thirty kilowatt-hour certificates. Our studies indicate that use of the present currency will be abandoned within three to four weeks. Ninety percent of government is making rules about the distribution of the currency. If it is our currency the people choose to use, we get to make the rules." Vandellen smiled. "As I said, we need no guns."

Harland squeezed his eyes shut. "It won't work. You'll scare everybody shitless for about twelve hours, then they'll come and get you. You're going to end up standing in front of a wall."

"John, look in the Declaration of Independence. This is

totally within its spirit. Government by consent of the governed. Consent means nothing unless there's a choice. All the choice the people have now is which incompetent will be elected to try to keep the fantasy of the system's viability alive. There is no choice of *system*. So you see, it will work. They will march to banks and take out their money and choose us. Because we can keep them comfortable."

"At rates of unlimited energy consumption? For about twenty *minutes*." Harland crossed his arms, trying to act calm.

"The stockpiled fuels will last just long enough. Long enough to get *used* to, and long enough so Americans won't want to go without again. Long enough so we can get the knowledge we've been developing at Sandstone on stream. The technology has been waiting, *begging* to be used for more than twenty years. We're standing on a twenty-foot seam of coal. Half of the United States is bursting with it, and now it will come out, now that the country can escape the reactionaries who in the holy name of sentiment prefer the land to lie fallow. Besides, we will have two thousand nuclear generating plants on line within eighteen months, now that we're no longer dominated by the handful of hysterics who think nucleonics is a black art."

A sudden hardness came to Vandellen's face. "That's at an end—the hearings and the regulators, the commissions and professional obstructionists. Regressive self-interests will never be allowed to stop this country from achieving its potential and its full growth. We can't afford any longer to live with an obsession for individual liberties—not when they're in clear conflict with overwhelming evidence of common good. The society has simply become too complex. The present government reveres the individual citizen at the obscene cost of mismanaging him collectively. The country needs managing. Now it's in the hands of good managers. These men already run organizations the size of other countries. They'll do a superb job with ours."

"And you're chairman of the board."

"More like the CEO."

Harland slowly shook his head in amazement. "You want this much to be president."

Vandellen stood and walked toward the windows. "This is exasperating. Can't you understand that if they have their warm house and their television and their convenience food, if they have a front yard they can mow and cars they can drive wherever they want, do you think they'll really care who prints their money?"

"Ah Martin. You poor— Don't you listen? They've told you twice. They don't want you."

Vandellen sighed. "I wish it were as simple as one man's ego." He walked over to the door and opened it. "Bob, Danny." The two came into the room and stood by the door.

"John, Sandstone has been monitoring you for two years. We've seen the public come to like you, then prefer you, and by now trust you to a degree that amazes us and I'm sure would gratify you. You are one of the most respected persons on television, and yet our studies show that you do not have a strong identification with the existing system. We need someone people trust, who appears to be neutral, to go on television and tell everybody that everything is going to be all right. We want it to be you. We think we can trust you. At the very center of all our plans is the use of the country's communications system. We want you to run it."

"Hey, congratulations," said Danny, beaming like a boy scout. Vandellen looked at his watch. "I'm afraid we're absolutely out of time. You're going to have to think while we walk."

Bob held the door open and they went out into the hall. Danny led the way, Bob trailed, Vandellen walked abreast of Harland.

"The process has started; it will succeed. That's not even at issue. I suspect that you may be deciding that for yourself right now. The studies we've done on you suggest that although you suppress them, you have pragmatic instincts. I anticipated quicker acceptance from you of this reality. A new reality, but reality nevertheless. I still anticipate it. But it's another measure of your importance to Sandstone that I'm willing to wait on you."

They turned another corner. "I don't want you cooperating through fear. You know things now, I suppose. But at this point in time, what you know is harmless to us, so the only consequence to your refusing us is that you go home. I can give you a little time to think, but not long. And not here. Danny, he'll go in the second van."

They walked through the central reception gallery of Sandstone. A woman passing brushed at Vandellen's arm, her face flushed.

"Hello," said Vandellen, and smiled at her over his shoulder, not breaking stride. "I hope you believe that I get no pleasure from assuming this responsibility, nor for the operations our studies said were necessary. I regret seeing blameless people die. The studies said that the illusion of terrorist activities was critical. There needed to be a feeling created that the present government was losing control."

He waved cheerfully at another person passing in the corridor. "I regret more what must happen now. The . . . studies suggest that there is a percentage of possibility, an unacceptably large percentage of possibility, that Sandstone might not be accepted and obeyed on faith alone. The studies say there must be . . . a degree of fear. And so this has already been put into work. It is irreversible. The core at Green Falls will be allowed to melt down. In about two hours the containment vessel will rupture, and radioactive steam . . ."

Harland stopped and said, "Oh Jesus Christ."

Bob took his arm and urged him back in stride. ". . . will reach Denver in about forty minutes," said Vandellen. "Denver is downwind this time of year. The radioactivity is contained in water vapor, and it will be odorless and tasteless and colorless, and since there will be no warning . . ."

He sent away his art. Sandstone is between Green Falls and Denver. Harland looked around, expecting to see chaos, but saw none. It took him an instant to realize it. He stopped and looked at Vandellen.

"Those who need to," said Vandellen very quietly, "have already left, or will leave with you. To expedite our rationality we must perform an act of irrationality. If it is known that we did this to our own people, then it will be known we have the strength of will to exert whatever general discipline is necessary."

"And if there was ever going to be an opposition," said Harland, "it would start with these people, here at Sandstone."

"Almost certainly."

"And this stops it before it starts. You build the best and brightest an irresistible sandbox, and when you're through using them, you bury them in it."

"Something like that," Vandellen said.

Harland gestured at the complex and the tranquil surroundings visible through the side entrance. "The better mousetrap."

Vandellen looked wistful. He walked to the glass doors and looked out toward the mountains. "This place. I love it more than anywhere I've ever lived, and I can never come back here in my lifetime. Nor can anyone." His breath fogged the glass. "There is pain enough in this place for everyone."

He pushed through the doors and they stepped down onto the pavement under the portico, where four white vans were lined up. Harland saw someone slide the side door of the first van closed, and it pulled away. Bob and Danny got into the second van and waited until Harland got into the seat in front of them.

Vandellen stood on the pavement beside the van. "I won't see you again until tonight . . ." For the first time, Harland saw signs that Vandellen finally might be about to lose his stomach. He was looking at the ground. "If you were to become as intimate in the management of Sandstone as we hope you will, you are certain, eventually, to learn this. I want you to deal with it now. Decide how it makes you feel, and how you feel about me, and see if you can get it behind you before tonight.

"Of all my regrets . . ." He looked at Harland. "Through the most extraordinary set of appalling circumstances, and because I had absolutely no other choice, I had to have Molly Rice killed."

The side door to the van was slid shut.

The van headed north, up altitude. As soon as it got out of sight of Sandstone, Harland saw the men in front of him take automatic rifles from under their seats. He could tell from the metal sounds behind him that Bob and Danny had them as well. "Who's Molly Rice?" said Bob.

"His old lady," said Danny. "Give me some of those rounds."

"And she got wasted?"

"Yeah. Ballsy lady."

Bob made a clucking sound. "That's a bitch, Johnny. Real bitch."

"Where's Vandellen?" said Harland.

"Behind us," said Danny. "Third or fourth van."

"I thought you looked out for him." Harland felt a gun barrel rub against his neck.

"We do," said Danny. "Right now, looking out for you is looking out for him." Bob snorted.

So I will join them, Harland thought. *I will do as they ask, for as long as it takes for him to believe that I am with him. I could kill him sooner. But with Danny and Bob around, I would have to move so quickly. I would have only seconds before they'd kill me. To make sure he'd die, I'd have to do something that would kill him immediately. I couldn't stand that. I want time with him. Time.*

As they approached and passed the timberline, the topography abruptly changed. There had been a perversity to the weather patterns that winter; in Colorado it was manifested by the dumping of monstrous snows at lower elevations and aridity higher up, punishing the resort operators already suffering from skiers' being unable to travel to the slopes because of fuel restrictions. Rocks showed through the thin cover of snow.

The caravan rounded a switchback. Harland saw the ridge thinning ahead, knew that they were coming to a pass.

"What's that?" said Bob.

"What's what?" said Danny.

"That high-pitched whine."

Harland heard nothing. Neither did Danny: "You and your high-pitched whines. Are you sure you're not a German shepherd?"

But then Harland heard it—a pulsing whine. It immediately took on bass harmonics, and in an instant became overpowering. The snow at the margins of the road began dancing. "It's a fucking chopper," yelled Danny.

The snow rose to white out the windows. The van caromed into the banks of snow at the inside of the road. "You stupid fuck, stop!" Danny screamed at the driver. "You'll run off the side of—"

The van ran into the rear of the one ahead of it. Harland saw it a millisecond ahead of anyone else in the van and was better braced. He took most of the impact with his shoulder, against the back of the seat in front of him. He rebounded onto the floor between the seats.

The whiteness outside invaded the inside of the van; the sliding side door had popped open. Harland rolled out of the van and staggered away into the blur, leaning into the diminishing downwash of the prop. He only hoped it was the side away from the dropoff.

Vision improved as the snow fell back to earth. He had thrashed about a hundred feet through the drifts when he heard the first automatic rifle fire. He saw something at his feet that could be a depression, filled with snow, large enough to offer him cover. He rolled into it, burrowing until he felt rock against his cheek. The propwash stopped and Harland heard the descending whine of the turbine as it decelerated. *Chinook. Never forget it.* He very slowly turned his head and saw it, just below the ridge line. It was tilted to an impractical angle, and thick smoke was coming from its exhausts.

As the whine thinned, he could discriminate among the noises. Gunfire was originating from positions near where the vans had collided and from points higher on the ridge, near the Chinook. He could hear shouts, screams, sounds of confusion from the vans. He heard nothing from the helicopter but shots.

Rounds of automatic fire hit so near to him that ice stung his face. Harland tried to burrow himself further into the snow. He had been pinned once like this in Iran, just once, when from his own carelessness he had been separated from a party of correspondents. During a firefight he had lain in a ditch. When he got back to safety, CBS had called him back to New York. CBS would have let him stay if he'd asked. But he thought about lying in that ditch, and he decided to go home.

The firing became more widely spaced. Behind him snow was being compacted. There was a grunt, then a weight rolled across his legs, into the depression with him. He heard panting—scrambling in the snow. Danny. With the back of his hand, Danny was wiping blood from his eyes. Half of his left ear had been blown away, but he was smiling.

"Hell of a note, huh, Johnny?" said Danny. "Those sumbitches are *mean*. They 'bout killed everybody who came out of one of those vans with a weapon. Poor Bobby took a round right in the chest. Knocked him over the side of the mountain." He wiped more blood from his eyes, then settled the muzzle of the pistol into the hollow just below Harland's larnyx. "Johnny, you got a problem here. The boss told Bob and me that if something happens to him and it didn't look like an accident, we were supposed to waste you. I seen the boss come out of that third van just after the shit hit the fan. But Johnny, I ain't seen him since. Now, I'm going to give the boss another minute or so to show he's all right, and if he don't I'm gonna have to put you away, because I caught me a round in the stomach, and I'm gonna start passing out pretty soon."

Harland closed his eyes and turned his face into the snow. After a few moments, he heard Danny moan and felt the pistol slide a few inches away from its nest.

But Danny caught it and moved it back into place. After a few more moments, he said: "Johnny, it looks like . . ."

Harland heard a thumping noise. The pistol dug painfully

into his larnyx, then slid down off his neck. Harland waited a few moments, then very slowly turned his face back out of the snow. Eight inches away he saw an exit wound in Danny's forehead about the size of a half dollar. It steamed.

He flinched as he became aware of a field of intense color at the corner of his vision. He cut his eyes toward it. Incandescent orange. A pair of pants legs. More crunch of snow, then another pair of pants legs arriving to stand beside the first. Harland rolled over on his back. Sam Painter was looking down at him.

"Hello, John," said Painter.

"Is Vandellen dead?" Harland realized he hadn't been able to apply enough volume to be heard, so he said it again.

"Not the last I saw," said Painter. "He's hurt a little. Doesn't look bad." Painter sat on his haunches next to where Harland still lay on his back. "I'm hoping you can tell me what . . . what's going to happen next."

"Oh, Jesus," said Harland. He laid his arm over his eyes.

"John, quickly. What do I need to know first?"

"The nuclear plant at Green Falls. It's going to melt down. Explode. And then—"

"The Chinook?" said Painter to Lanark.

"Totaled."

Painter spoke into his boom microphone. "Carmi. Find how far it is overland to the Green Falls nuclear plant."

"Working," said the miniature voice in Painter's earphone.

Painter stood and held out his hand. "John, can you get up?"

Harland passed bodies as he walked back to the vans. He stopped counting after nine. There were perhaps a dozen survivors, scientist types who, unlike the Sandstone security men, had not come out of the vans with weapons. They sat in the road behind the last van, hands on top of their heads, while one of the orange parkas held an automatic rifle on them.

Martin Vandellen sat on the middle seat of the third van, leaning forward, holding his left arm to his side at the elbow. His chin was tucked into his chest from pain. "Probably caught a spent round in the wrist," said Sutton, who held a sidearm on Vandellen as Harland and Painter approached. "Bleeding's just about stopped. Bone might be broken. He's hurting, but he's not dying."

Vandellen looked at Harland with a sad smile, his eyes lidded by pain and an analgesic Sutton had given him. "You told them, and they followed you," he said. He shook his head. "I can't begin to tell you what a sad mistake you made."

"How much time do you figure we've got before the reactor goes?" Painter asked Vandellen.

Vandellen continued to shake his head. "And it will change nothing."

"Okay, we'll find out when we get there. You're coming with us."

Carmi came up with a map and pointed out a route to Green Falls. It was twelve to fifteen miles; half an hour if the roads were clear.

The first van had had two of its tires shot out. There was no room for the other vans to pass it. Harland helped push it off the side of the mountain.

Sam Painter's men distributed themselves and their gear from the disabled Chinook among the three operable vans and moved off. The last one of them leaned out and held his weapon on the survivors, still sitting in the road, until they were out of sight.

Harland sat beside Painter in the lead van.

"Did you lose any men back there?" Harland said.

"No," said Painter.

"They were clowns," said Lanark, sitting behind them. "Total clowns. Couldn't shoot, and really disorganized."

Harland tied the drawstring of the hood of his parka. The side windows of the van had been shot out.

"Apparently you didn't lose me," Harland said.

"No," said Painter.

"You had me from the beginning, when I walked out of the CBS building?"

Painter looked ahead at the road, but he smiled. "John, we had you earlier than that."

"You've had me followed since before I told you about the meeting?"

"Yes."

"Since when?"

"Since the first night you called me. Does that make you mad at me?"

"I imagine that later I'll be indignant. Right now I feel pretty good about it."

Carmi—navigating for Ramsey—said: "Hang a right up here."

"You waited a while to get me out of this," said Harland.

Painter looked at him and smiled. "If I had moved any sooner, you wouldn't have heard all the exposition."

Ramsey turned off the road that the Sandstone caravan had been following.

"Sam, he's trying to pull off a coup. Vandellen and the Fortune Five Hundred want to foreclose on the government."

"I'm not surprised."

"You knew?"

"No. I'm not surprised."

19

THEY CAME UPON THE POWER-TRANSMISSION LINES AND FOL-
lowed them until they rounded a bend. Green Falls was there,
in a valley. Harland recognized the familiar dome of a nuclear
power plant containment building at the center of several
ancillary buildings. The whole complex was surrounded by an
outer fence and a concentric inner rectangle of barbed-wire
fence. He remembered going on location when the first electric
fencing went up at the first power plant, to do a story on the
creation of the Federal Security Forces and its job of guarding
fissionable materials against theft by terrorists.

There was a remote checkpoint on the road, half a mile from
the outer fence. Harland could see that it was empty; still,
Painter asked Ramsey to stop the van. The other two vans
slowed and stopped behind them. "Bring up Vandellen," said
Painter into his microphone.

Carmi was surveying the plant and its fortifications with
binoculars. "This is not regs," said Carmi. "There should be a
guard at this station twenty-four hours a day. And there's not
one in the station by the main gate either."

"Would you stick to regs if you knew the core was melting?" said Ramsey.

"They don't know," said Harland. "Vandellen didn't even tell but a handful of his people at Sandstone. Maybe some of the technical types inside the place know. Maybe they killed the others, set timers, and left the security men to guard the fort."

Vandellen was led up then, still clutching his wrist.

"Is the FSF still there?" Painter asked him. "Is there anyone left in the containment building?"

"This is totally pointless," said Vandellen. "I'll say it again: The process is irreversible. The core cannot be prevented from melting down. Unless you're determined to be martyrs, I suggest you get back to the highway and continue north, upwind."

"They're there," said Carmi, still looking through his binoculars. "I made somebody running into one of the emplacements."

"Let's get on the horn and ID ourselves and get the hell in there," said Lanark.

"They won't answer," said Painter. "I'll bet they've been told terrorists are on the way, and they think we're it. Right?" Vandellen said nothing. "I don't think we can talk our way into this one. And even if we could, I don't think we have time to wait for FSF to calm them down enough to let us in."

"Yeah," said Carmi. "They've circled the wagons and they're very nervous. I'm surprised they haven't started shooting already."

"But let's put it in motion. Lanark, raise our contact at FSF and tell them to get back to these people here and tell them we're friendlies."

"Working," said Lanark. "It might take fifteen-twenty minutes with these turkeys."

"So what are we looking at here?" said Painter.

"All these plants were retrofitted for security," said Carmi, "and they tried to do it for nickels and dimes. Commerce didn't know shit about security. DOD should have handled all this, but civil libertarians wouldn't stand for it. Can't say now that I'm complaining. This is just lick-and-a-promise, colonel. Standard complement at an installation like this is twelve men, and all they've got are automatic rifles and nonlethal chemicals."

Painter looked intently at the plant complex. "What will the tank rockets do to the emplacements?"

"Bad things, colonel."

"Do it. Take out the two positions nearest. It doesn't look as though the ones on the north and west points can defend the main entrance."

"They can't," said Carmi. "Like I said, really dumb."

Painter looked at Vandellen. "Dana, I want him to ride up here with me, on the point. So he can have a good view. Just because he won't speak doesn't mean he won't talk; just watching for when he starts to sweat will say a lot." Dana got into the third van, and Vandellen was shoved into the seat behind Harland.

Sam Painter looked at Harland. He smiled. "John? You want to get out?"

Yes. "No."

In the design of the emplacements there had been little thought given to scenarios in which attacking hostiles would be equipped with state-of-the-art ordnance supplied by the United States Department of Defense. The rockets were laser-guided, the emplacements were stationary. There was no question of missing. Within seconds they were rubble.

The marksmen and their loaders got back into the vans. The three vehicles rolled the rest of the way down into the valley, stopping short of the double gates. From a window Dana tossed a satchel at a point on the fence about fifty feet to the side of the gate. Fifteen seconds later it blew and there was a hole wide enough for the vans to scrape through.

Painter had the vans approach the building over the rocky terrain, in case the road was mined. They drew no fire as they approached. But from where they spilled out of the vans near the main entrance, the men from Copper Creek had no route but across a path open to fire from anywhere in the plant complex.

None came. Painter and his men found the front door open

and no one inside the guard station where employees' badges were verified and visitors given passes before being admitted into the complex. Harland trotted in after them.

"They've cut and run," said Carmi. "The guys FSF hires aren't what you'd call the cream of the crop."

Painter was looking through the double glass doors that led to the rest of the complex. "No, but I think it might be a good idea to assume they're still around. Carmi, how do we get to the containment building?"

"Not where we want to go, colonel. If we're going to be able to do anything, we do it from the control room. It's outside the containment building, usually about thirty feet above grade. Third floor."

"There's a courtyard and a covered walkway to another building. We go across two at a time, reassemble inside the next building. Ramsey brings Vandellen across last. John? Still along?"

Harland nodded.

"Just before Vandellen."

"Colonel . . ." said Carmi.

"Yeah."

"We have to be sort of careful in there. If the core's melted, the uranium has come out of the fuel bundles and collected on the floor of the reactor in globs. Theoretically, if it forms into the right shape, and if it's disturbed, it could go super-critical and cause a steam explosion. It would pop the reactor vessel and the containment building. It's never happened before. But then nobody has ever wanted it to happen before."

"What, we shouldn't sneeze?"

"We shouldn't set off any tank rockets."

Someone found a button at the guard station, which opened the double glass doors. Painter went through first. Then Sandoval and Sutton. No fire. Lanark and Hardin. Dana, Carmi, and Ramsey with Vandellen, Harland trotting among them.

They reassembled in a small receptionist's area. The place was glazed-cinder-block utilitarian. "We didn't pass any cars on the way out and the parking lot is half full," said Painter. "We should see employees."

"They're probably evacuated to a place where terrorists would have no interests," said Carmi. "A mechanical or maintenance building." He nodded down a corridor. "Elevator is probably that way."

"Keep twenty feet between you," said Painter. "Ramsey, bring Vandellen up here on point with me." They moved down the corridor. Fifty feet down, it branched. Right turn to the elevator and the stairwell beside it. Vending machines lined the walls in the area around the elevator.

Most of the men from Copper Creek had turned the corner ahead of Harland. He heard Painter say: "No, no elevator. Two men get up one flight before the next—"

Harland sensed motion behind him. He turned, saw two men with automatic rifles coming from a room off the corridor. He screamed Painter's name and felt himself being pulled and pushed by Dana, through the swinging door of a women's room.

Harland lay on the tile and heard fire both from where he'd seen the men with the guns, and from a point down the perpendicular corridor past the elevators.

Twenty seconds; half a day. Two rounds punched through the door, which was calmly swinging shut on its pneumatic hinge after Harland was shoved through it. Harland crawled under the sinks and huddled.

After several moments of quiet he opened his eyes. The door to the women's room had not completely closed. Harland crawled toward it and, still on his stomach, cracked it. Dana was dead; a tight pattern in the chest. Harland tried to see through the smoke.

"Sam . . . ?"

"John, are you hit?"

"No."

"Can you see down the corridor? Both directions?"

"Yes." Harland rose up high enough to see over Dana and

looked down the corridor. "Two guys in FSF uniforms lying in the hall. They gotta be dead."

"Thank you."

Harland saw a sudden shape in the smoke. Painter came out from between two vending machines and fell to the floor, his weapon ready. A couple of other shapes emerged from the doorways into which they had compressed themselves.

After a moment, Painter rose slowly to his knees. "I think that's it."

Sutton, Lanark, and Hardin were dead. There were six dead FSF; maybe six. Harland walked toward the elevator and saw Carmi trying to get up, discovering that he couldn't. Vandellen was sitting on the floor, back against the wall. He was panting. Harland saw him wrap his arm across his eyes and make a laugh from two sharp intakes of air. "And useless," he said. "Totally useless."

Carmi was hit in the side. He had gathered up his shirt and made a pressure bandage of it. Sandoval took off his pack and came out with a morphine styrette. Carmi waved it away. "Don't give me any of that shit. I won't be able to think."

"He knows nuclear better than any of us," said Painter. "We've got to get him to the control room, and he can't get up the stairs." He pushed the call button for the elevator, then along with Harland helped Carmi half to his feet.

They all flattened themselves against the wall on either side of the elevator door. But when it opened, the car was empty. The five got on. Once the doors closed and the car started to rise, Sandoval dropped to his knees.

"Your tenacity is beginning to look a lot like stupidity, colonel," said Vandellen. "I should have thought you'd realized by now you cannot stop this, and that you should give your men a chance to get out of this alive."

Painter looked at Vandellen. "Yep. He's starting to sweat a little."

Harland felt the elevator car slow and position itself at the control-room level. When the door opened wide enough to allow him, Sandoval shoved the barrel of his weapon through the crack in the door and fanned a burst of bullets in an arc. The precaution had turned out to be unnecessary. The door opened upon an empty corridor and a sign reading SHIFT ENGINEER'S OFFICE, which a bullet had knocked from its fastening.

"Hang a right," said Carmi, dimly. "Through the double doors."

Painter was on point as they moved the ten feet to the set of double doors. Through glass ports he saw a panel choked with dials. He pushed through, then flinched at an explosion. Glass cascaded from a ruined panel of dials near him.

A fat, middle-aged man stood there behind the control consoles with a sawed-off shotgun. Painter saw him tremble, and knew that to miss from that close, with a sawed-off shotgun, the man would have to be very frightened.

"That one was free," said Painter. "If you reload, it's going to cost you." Sandoval and Harland came in, half-dragging Carmi. Ramsey led Vandellen.

"You cocksuckers aren't gonna hurt my reactor," said the middle-aged technician, his face flushing. "I'll kill you if . . ." Harland saw two other technicians squeezing themselves against a wall.

"How long before it goes?" said Painter to the middle-aged technician. The man blinked. His breathing slowed a little.

"What goes?" he said.

Harland had put Carmi in a swivel chair on casters. His face distorted from pain as he pulled himself along by the countertop, looking at the instruments.

Painter leveled his weapon. "Answer my questions instantly."

"Jesus Christ, *what* goes?"

"This reactor has not melted down," said Carmi. Painter kept his eyes on the technician, who said: "Goddamn it, no, it's *not* melting down. Who's saying that it is?"

"It has not melted down, and it is not now melting down," said Carmi. "They've got sixteen feet of water in the vessel, they've got full pressure, they've got condensate—" Carmi kept pulling himself along the consoles. "—the radiation level in the containment building is nominal, temperature in the fuel bundles is nominal. The control rods are almost completely extended and the reactor water is boronated. This reactor is operating normally at about thirty-five percent of capacity."

"What the *shit?*" said Harland.

Painter looked at Vandellen, who smiled. "Scram it anyway." Carmi pushed one of the red buttons marked SCRAM that were dominant on every control panel.

"Aw god*damn*," whined the technician. "It's going to take two goddamn *weeks* to get that thing back up . . ."

Painter lowered his weapon. "Find some place that locks," he said to Sandoval, nodding his head toward the technicians, "and put them in it."

As Sandoval herded them out, Harland grabbed Painter by the arm. "Sam, it's going to happen. I don't care what it looks like, it's going to happen."

"Take a look at the instruments," said Carmi.

"They've committed themselves, Sam."

"Instruments don't lie," said Carmi.

Harland froze. Then he turned around and looked at Vandellen. Then he turned back to Painter. "His do, Sam. He built this place. He lies to everyone. Why shouldn't his fucking instruments lie?"

Painter kept his eyes on Vandellen's face. He walked over to him.

"As I said from the very beginning, colonel. Irreversible."

"How about it, fella?" said Painter and pointed to Vandellen. "Is John Harland right? Have a seat."

"We have very little time, colonel."

"Oh, now he's beginning to sweat a little more. Have a seat, fella." Vandellen sat down in one of the technician's swivel chairs.

"He is right. John is right." Painter went on. "You people have been planning this for quite a while, and this place is part of it."

"Yes, *yes*, colonel," said Vandellen. "Yes, John. Yes. That is very bright of the both of you, and I will confirm it if it makes you feel intelligent. But the knowledge is useless, and we have no . . ." Vandellen looked from Harland to Painter. "Colonel, if any action is taken against any of the men who participated in Sandstone, or their corporations—and by 'act,' colonel, I include any hostility, indictment, or even public accusation of wrongdoing—there are other irreversible processes that can be set into effect. Move against any one of them and radioactive iodine will be pumped into the Alaskan gas fields. Into the North Sea fields. It will be twenty thousand years before anything can be taken out of them. Move against anybody in Sandstone and an outage in the Northeastern power grid will occur. New York will be without power for a minimum of four months. Viruses will be introduced into processed foods . . ."

Painter said nothing. Didn't move. Harland saw Vandellen look again at the control panel. He scrubbed at his chin with the back of his hand. Harland saw him diminish. "There is a microprocessor that was buried in the concrete when the reactor pallet was poured. When it is turned on—and it cannot be turned off, not by me, not by anyone—it will execute a series of commands that will melt down the reactor, and if certain contingencies are met, it will vent radioactive steam."

"And send out normal readings to all the instrumentations while the process is taking place," said Painter.

"I will trade that confirmation, colonel, for your coming to your senses and our leaving this place. We have *no time*."

"We'll make time," said Painter. Sandoval came back through the double doors. Painter pointed at him and Sandoval held his position, his weapon held in front of him.

Painter smiled at Vandellen. "Lookie there, he's sweating a little more."

"He's not the only one," said Harland.

Vandellen was hugging himself. Harland saw his eyes return to a cluster of dials on a panel near him. "You obstinate pinbrain. I can't stop it. Nobody can stop it."

"You know what the contingencies are."

"I do not. Not minutiae like that."

"An anal retentive like you? You delegate nothing."

"Colonel." Ramsey was indicating the television monitor mounted on the wall above the control consoles. The picture came from a security camera mounted high to pan three hundred and sixty degrees through the whole complex and surrounding terrain. A helicopter was landing, and armed men were jumping from it.

"FSF," said Ramsey.

"They must have called for the cavalry before we got here," said Sandoval.

Vandellen put his hands over his face briefly, then grabbed the arms of his chair.

"Where we are, what do you figure we'd get?" said Painter. "A dose of about two thousand rads? Think that's not going to cause that famous white hair to fall out?"

"The contingency," said Harland. He was staring at the control console. "Sam, Sam, it's something to do with the weather. I've seen him looking at those dials, over and over." He read off the labels: "Relative humidity, temperature, wind direction . . ."

"It is irreversible," said Vandellen. "It is irreversible, and even if I am dead, it will happen without me."

Painter sat down and put his feet up on one of the consoles. "Fella, nothing is irreversible."

Vandellen began trembling.

Harland leaned toward Vandellen. "Martin, it *will* happen without you. You poor kid, *that's* your problem. You're not afraid of dying." Harland was only inches from Vandellen's face. "You . . ." he whispered. "You just can't bear the thought of it happening without you there, in control."

Suddenly Vandellen was calm. He looked through Harland, through the control panels. Harland saw his shoulders relax. "No, John. No. I just can't." He smiled then, glad the final truth was said.

He leaned back in the chair. Took a deep breath. "To maximize the kill ratio in Denver, the microprocessor will not release the steam until the wind sustains twelve knots from the northwest for thirty consecutive seconds."

Painter moved to the console, studied the instruments. *Westnorthwest. Six knots—just gusting to ten.* "Where is the microprocessor, Vandellen?"

"In four feet of concrete. I told you, I told you, it is irreversible."

"We'll have to stop the anemometer before it registers twelve knots. Carmi, where . . ." Carmi was unconscious. Painter said to Ramsey and Sandoval: "The meteorology instruments are probably at the highest point of the complex, and that's on top of the containment building." Painter took Carmi's automatic weapon from the floor where it had slid, took off the safety, and cocked it.

"John, I'm going to need both these guys. I don't think these new FSF people will like us crawling around on top of their containment building. Watch him." He nodded at Vandellen and handed the weapon to Harland, who was holding it before he really thought about it.

Painter took a last look at the wind-speed readout. *Northwest. Eight knots sustained. A gust to eleven.* He looked back at Harland as he stood at the door. "We need to talk later."

Harland watched the space where Painter had been, then became conscious of the weight in his hand. He glanced at the dials.

Westnorthwest. Eight knots sustained. Gusts to twelve.

Painter, Ramsey, and Sandoval went through an airlock into the stairwell. One flight up to the decontamination floor, the level where the personnel hatch led into the containment building. Another half flight, another airlock. The sign said they were on the roof. Painter started to shove open the first door. Stopped.

"No. This is wrong. There are three of us, maybe fifteen of them. They'd blow us away. I think I could get to the anemometer if nobody looked up and saw me. You two go down to the first floor, where we came into the building, and fire. Don't hit anybody, and when they get close, surrender."

Ramsey and Sandoval looked at each other. "Colonel," said Ramsey, "you won't make it."

"I am the six-hundred-pound gorilla," said Painter, "and I sit wherever I please. Get the fuck down the stairs."

They went.

From the west. Nine knots sustained.

Vandellen looked from the LED digital readout of the meteorological data back to Harland. "John, so as not to alarm you: At eleven knots sustainèd there's going to be a release of steam from the turbine room."

"Then stop it."

"I can't, John. The steam will not be radioactive. It's just to create some thermals in the area so that when the contaminated steam is released it will be lifted higher and carried further. We still have a little time."

"Let's wait for Sam before we leave."

"Your friend is not going to come back, John."

Harland looked at the instruments again. *Gusts to twelve knots.*

Painter pushed through the second airlock door onto the roof and saw that most of the effort of opening it was caused by an accumulation of banked snow. He went to his knees and crawled across the roof to the edge, wishing for white arctic gear instead of orange, wishing for mittens instead of the thin gloves he had to wear to be able to handle his weapon.

He saw the FSF men trotting from the helicopter toward the main entrance of the complex. He turned and looked back at the dome of the containment building and the railed stairway, which described a spiral as it angled up the side of it.

No kind of cover, he thought. If the FSF men came close enough, the administration building would cut off their view of

Painter's route. Mostly he had to count on Ramsey's and Sandoval's fire to keep them too busy to let their eyes wander. *Let them a little closer, guys. Let them just a little closer before—*

Painter was about to speak into his microphone to order them to hold back when he heard fire from the front of the building, saw the FSF men hit the ground. *Not close enough. Oh well.* He got back on his knees, slung his rifle across his back, and trotted for the stairs in a crouch.

Winds from the northwest. Nine knots sustained. Gusts to thirteen.

Harland heard the firefight as distant popping through the shielded walls of the control room. So did Vandellen.

"After the boiler steam, John, the contaminants will be released within five minutes. If we go right now . . . The FSF men will recognize me. The helicopter . . . but it's landed downwind. Even if the contaminated steam is being released, we could get in one of the vans, and if we head directly northwest . . ."

Painter slipped on the third step of the stair. Almost every tread was plated with ice, and as he grabbed the handrail for balance, he winced from the serrated ice biting through his thin gloves.

Five more steps up, he paused to look back. The firefight was beginning to subside. Against the deliberately ineffective fire from Ramsey and Sandoval, the FSF men should have advanced against the front entrance. They hadn't. *Real bunch of hero types*, Painter thought. With altitude he was losing the obstruction value of the administration building. He was beginning to feel undressed.

Another ten steps and he slipped again. The edge of a stair tread brought agony to his shins; but he was more concerned by the sound his rifle made when it banged against the stair railing.

He felt his back muscles tense against the inevitable. It didn't come, and he moved on. He saw the anemometer began rotating a little faster.

Northwest. Nine knots sustained. Gusts to thirteen. Fourteen.

"Sit down, Martin."

Vandellen looked at Harland to judge his conviction. He remained standing. He nodded at the rifle. "John, I don't think you would dispatch me with that. Your friend could—easily. But I don't think you—"

"Sit down, Martin."

"At any rate, I am now walking toward that door, no matter what the consequences. I am not prepared to die of radiation sickness. It is too appalling to consider."

"Sit *down*, Martin." Harland took the four steps to Vandellen. He had turned the gun sideways and used its length to push Vandellen across the chest. Vandellen's knees hinged against the seat of the swivel chair. He sat back down upon it hard and it rolled a few feet backward.

The firing had stopped. Painter looked back, saw an FSF man running from the chopper to where the others had taken cover behind the white vans, heard segments of shouts as they were blown up over the curve of the containment building: ". . . radio in the chopper . . . they're friendlies, they're friendlies . . ." ". . . fuck friendlies, they're shooting at us . . ." ". . . hold fire, but get back to that radio and reconfirm they're friendlies before . . ."

That would be nice, thought Sam. *If they find out they're not supposed to kill me.* He was a dozen steps from the anemometer.

Northwest. Ten knots sustained.

"John, give *in* to it. You're not a martyr like Molly Rice." Vandellen stood up. "You want to live. You aren't stupid, you aren't—"

Harland was oblivious to the noise and recoil of the automatic rifle in his hands. Vandellen folded in on himself, falling backward and down.

Northwest. Eleven knots sustained.

The venting turbine steam was a sudden and enormous bass rumble from the other side of the containment building. Sandoval reflexively ducked, like everyone else, at its beginning. It made him a millisecond too late to react when he saw the FSF man, who looked up at the spume of steam and saw a patch of orange on the stairs toward the top of the containment building. Sandoval saw the FSF man bring up his weapon as he shouted, over the roar, "Shit, they've got *snipers.*" Sandoval brought up his own weapon; but before he could kill him, the FSF man fired half a clip.

Upon hearing the escaping steam, Painter felt a moment of sick panic. *Easy, easy. That's from the turbine room. It's not contaminated.* He realized that any eyes lifted to see it would be drawn to him. He was turning, reaching back for his weapon, to see if he had already been spotted when he felt the implosion in his side. It sat him down on the stairs, and he bumped a few steps down.

Painter's perception irised down to his most immediate environment. He saw nothing but what his body touched, heard nothing but his heart in his ears. He took inventory. The left side of his body was numb from shoulder to waist. *That won't last long.* He clenched his hands, very slowly, and saw that they still operated with reasonable symmetry. He stood, very slowly, and found that he could still climb the stairs if he tilted left to accommodate for whatever the bullet had done to his ribs.

And so he began to climb again, in utter quiet.

Four steps from the top he fell again; he would have gone off the stairs, but his weapon, still slung across his back, caught one of the posts supporting the guardrail.

One step from the top he had to stop because vision had drained from his eyes. He held on to the handrail and panted.

He felt a breeze freshen on his face.

He leaned on the rail that surrounded the meteorological platform and looked at the anemometer. It sped up.

Now that you're here, Sam, how do you stop it? It must be going a hundred RPM. He thought about sticking his weapon into the blur of the spinning cups. No. It would just knock it out of his hands.

No way. No way.

Then he looked just below the spinning cups. Smiled. *Sure there is, if you've got enough juice left to do it.*

He moved toward the anemometer, ducked under the spinning cups. Just before he reached, he saw the serrated ice glisten on the rotating shaft. He grabbed the shaft and squeezed. The ice cut through his gloves instantly.

He was not too weak to scream.

Harland looked up and saw Ramsey and Sandoval come into the control room. He didn't move from where he had sat on the floor after killing Vandellen. He was expecting one of them to come back, to kill him now that his utilitarian value had diminished, so he said quickly, because he wanted someone to hear him say it: "I haven't even been in a fistfight since I was eleven years old. Not even a fistfight. And I have this guy's brains on my pants legs."

"Sam wants you," said Sandoval, and helped him up.

They had bandaged Painter and put him in an office while they waited for a medevac helicopter. Ramsey and Sandoval indicated Harland was to sit on the sofa beside Painter.

"John, I think we can take out the Sandstone people, but you're going to have to help us, because it's going to take some time."

"How do I help? Shoot myself so you won't have to feel guilty doing it?"

Painter didn't respond to Harland's question.

"If we can do it quietly enough, get them one by one, we can weaken them so that they won't feel threatened as a group.

Maybe they won't take the retaliatory measures." Painter re-adjusted his position. "The media is going to have to participate, John. For the greatest good."

"What if I decide I don't want to participate? Jesus, Sam. Just *do* it now. You're a bastard to make me wait."

"Nothing's going to happen to you, John. You can break this story if you want to. It's up to you. You're the man with the code of ethics."

Sandoval looked out the window. "Chopper's coming, colonel."

Painter looked at Harland and smiled. "You're going to get a laugh out of this. I happen to believe in the First Amendment."

20

IN THE FAMILIAR CHAOS OF THE NEWSROOM JUST BEFORE AIRTIME, John Harland sat in the pool of light at the desk and arranged the script of the newscast in front of him, tamping the sheaf of papers straight.

Not a bad newsday, he thought. Have to use the cold-weather story toward the front of the show, even if the film is dull. But the coal-conversion-breakthrough piece is a grabber, and there was good stuff from the National Transportation Safety Board hearing into the Learjet crash that killed Martin Vandellen.

The voice came over the speakers: "From the CBS newsroom in New York, this is the CBS *Evening News*. Substituting for Walter Cronkite, here is John Harland . . ."

"Good evening," said Harland to the camera. "There are reports from the Dominican Republic that a chartered yacht carrying the chairman of the board of Encon America has apparently been lost at sea . . ."